## "I WISH YOU HADN'T SENT HIM AWAY."

Elizabeth watched Nicky go. "If I'd had just a little more time, I might have discovered what's bothering him."

"Not tonight. Once he figured out I was with you, he dummied right up—I could see him do it clear across the room. The kid didn't like my looks a pound."

Elizabeth glanced up at Quint in surprise. "Why not?"

"He's jealous."

She almost laughed outright. "Jealous! Come on, Quint. The child is barely eleven years old."

Unsmiling, he bent and brushed his lips across the backs of her fingers. "Elizabeth, you have a lot to learn about men."

## LET ARCHER AND CLEARY
## AWAKEN AND CAPTURE YOUR HEART!

**CAPTIVE DESIRE** (2612, $3.75)
by Jane Archer

Victoria Malone fancied herself a great adventuress and student of life, but being kidnapped by handsome Cord Cordova was too much excitement for even her! Convincing her kidnapper that she had been an innocent bystander when the stagecoach was robbed was futile when he was kissing her until she was senseless!

**REBEL SEDUCTION** (3249, $4.25)
by Jane Archer

"Stop that train!" came Lacey Whitmore's terrified warning as she rushed toward the locomotive that carried wounded Confederates and her own beloved father. But no one paid heed, least of all the Union spy Clint McCullough, who pinned her to the ground as the train suddenly exploded into flames.

**DREAM'S DESIRE** (3093, $4.50)
by Gwen Cleary

Desperate to escape an arranged marriage, Antonia Winston y Ortega fled her father's hacienda to the arms of the arrogant Captain Domino. She would spend the night with him and would be free for no gentleman wants a ruined bride. And ruined she would be, for Tonia would never forget his searing kisses!

**VICTORIA'S ECSTASY** (2906, $4.25)
by Gwen Cleary

Proud Victoria Torrington was short of cash to run her shipping empire, so she traveled to America to meet her partner for the first time. Expecting a withered, ancient cowhand, Victoria didn't know what to do when she met virile, muscular Judge Colston and her body budded with desire.

# KAREN RHODES
# Strings Of Fortune

**ZEBRA BOOKS**
**KENSINGTON PUBLISHING CORP.**

ZEBRA BOOKS

are published by

Kensington Publishing Corp.
475 Park Avenue South
New York, NY 10016

First Printing: March, 1993

Printed in the United States of America

*with love to Carlotta, Elizabeth and Kevin*

## Chapter One

A gust of wind blew a whisper of snow against the window as Elizabeth Mason stood wringing her hands. Her tiny studio apartment felt close and overheated. She offered up a silent wish-prayer, hoping it wasn't in bad taste to pray for something valuable.

"Can't you hurry this up, Grant?" She crawled onto the end of her bed to get a better look.

Grant Holbrook was kneeling on the floor, rubbing his square chin as he studied the long wooden crate. It nearly filled the entire walk space between the bed and the glass-topped table at the end of the settee in the adjoining sitting room.

She squinted at the Hungarian shipping label and told herself it looked exotic. In reality, the smudged label was quite ordinary, with her name and Kansas City address spelled out in grease pencil.

"Stop looming over me like a half-starved turkey vulture." Grant smiled at her good-naturedly. "Get me a hammer and your biggest screwdriver."

Elizabeth squeezed by the box and sprinted into the kitchen, where she yanked open her tool drawer. She was back in a flash.

Grant accepted the tools with a wry grin. The screwdriver was bent, and the hammer head wobbled on its age-blackened handle.

"What happened to the nifty tool set I gave you a couple of years ago, Lizzie?"

"I swapped it with Jake for these. They belonged to my great-grandfather."

A dull ache filled her chest at the reference to Jake, her grandfather. She sighed it away and resumed her hand-wringing, eyeing the crate anxiously.

Grant chuckled and shook his head. "Jake always was hell on wheels at a swap meet."

Elizabeth couldn't help noticing that Grant spoke of Jake in the past tense. The ache settled rocklike into her stomach. She tried to ignore it, along with the painful image of her once-strapping grandfather wasting away on a nursing-home bed.

"I'm warning you, Grant. If you don't open that crate in the next sixty seconds, I'll go stark raving buggers."

He laughed again. Grant was a much-respected senior curator at the stodgiest Western culture museum this side of the Mississippi. Even so, she sometimes wondered if he had a serious bone in him.

"What's the rush?" He patted the lid of the crate. "This thing's been down in the basement since Friday."

She sniffed in annoyance. "Only because the

apartment-house manager neglected to tell me about it for two days."

Elizabeth could have pitched a fit when she found out. She wished now that she had.

Grant hammered the point of the screwdriver under the edge of the lid. Nails screeched in old wood as he moved down one side of the crate, carefully prying off the lid.

When he reached the end, he tilted his head to glance once more at the shipping label. "Who's this Uri Skupasky?"

"He's my great-great-uncle. Jake's mother's younger brother, as nearly as I can figure out. At least, he was until he died last month in Hungary. I'd never heard of him until I got the letter from his attorney in Budapest, telling me he was shipping my inheritance."

"Apparently, good old Uncle Uri had heard of you."

"Isn't that something?" The thought still filled her with a sense of wonder. "The attorney says Uncle Uri has had this stuff all boxed up for years, ready to be shipped after he passed on."

Standing, Grant wriggled thick fingers under the slightly raised edge of the lid and grunted as he pulled up on it. "Damn thing's tighter than a tick," he muttered, straining.

The nails gave one last screech, and the lid came free. Grant lifted it off and set it to one side. "Phew!" He waved a hand in front of his face and backed up a step. "Smells like King Tut's tomb."

Elizabeth crossed her fingers behind her back,

her eyes shining. "It's something valuable. I just know it is!"

"You just *hope* it is." As usual, Grant had come much closer to the mark.

A layer of brittle yellowed newspapers filled the top of the crate. She plucked out a piece, studied the incomprehensible language for a moment and tossed it aside impatiently.

Her family had never been what could even remotely be called rich. There was no reason to believe that her European ancestors were any different. Since she had never actually met any of her distant Old World kin, however, Elizabeth clung to the hope that Uncle Uri had left her something of value. Such as the family silver.

Not even Grant had any idea how close she was to being bankrupted by Jake's nursing-home expenses. As of today, she was a week behind on the monthly payment. Every time she visited her grandfather, she expected the director to pounce on her and demand that she cough up funds.

Again Elizabeth felt a dull, grinding ache deep within her. She had suddenly and tragically lost her entire family eighteen months ago — except for Jake. But for all intents and purposes, Jake was lost to her, as well.

Grant cautiously lifted away layer after layer of wadded newspapers as if he were unwrapping a fragile museum artifact. It was all Elizabeth could do to keep from diving headfirst into the crate and slinging paper like a madwoman.

"You should get rid of this old newspaper as

soon as possible," he said. "It's a fire hazard."

"At the moment, so am I." Elizabeth fanned herself with a corner of the bedspread. She suddenly caught sight of something beneath the paper and froze.

"What's that?" She pointed.

"Looks like a foot."

Grant removed the last layer of packing, and they both peered down at Elizabeth's anxiously awaited inheritance.

"Why, they're string puppets." Grant sounded intrigued.

"Marionettes," Elizabeth said dully.

The musty smell filled the room. For a moment, it even seemed to cloud her vision. As her initial disappointment bottomed out, however, Elizabeth began to feel something quite different. She leaned forward, watching Grant stir around in the crate.

"I count seven — all different kinds," he said. "They look very, very old." He looked at Elizabeth quizzically as he noted her stillness, the odd change in her demeanor. "You helped pay your way through college by giving puppet performances, Lizzie." He gently lifted out one of the wooden puppets. "This has to be quite a thrill for you."

Elizabeth's vision blurred again. Wiping at her eyes, she suddenly realized why Grant continued to study her questioningly. Her cheeks were wet with tears. She bit back the startling glut of emotion that had welled up inside her at the sight of the puppets.

On the one hand, she was disappointed that they weren't likely to help her out of her financial difficulties. But on the other, they filled her with feelings of longing, remembrances of her past. For marionettes were part of her family heritage. When she was a small child, Jake had begun teaching her the intricate art of manipulating string puppets, as his grandfather had taught him. She had spent endless hours in his basement workshop, watching him make marionettes and stitch intricate little costumes.

That part of her life collapsed, however, on that day eighteen months ago. She hadn't had the time or energy even to think about puppetry since.

As she gazed down into the crate, she felt a familiar sense of connection with the heaps of carved wood and wrinkled fabric. Still, she couldn't imagine why a great-great uncle she'd never met had chosen to send the little wooden people to her.

Grant put aside the puppet and selected another one, examining it closely, too. The elaborate hand-stitched costumes on some of them were fragile with age. He fingered the dusty velvet and faded silk almost reverently. Elizabeth couldn't bring herself to touch them—they reminded her too much of what she had lost.

"I guess Jake's nursing-home expenses have eaten up the insurance your folks left," Grant said quietly, without looking at her.

*Bingo,* Elizabeth thought. Grant always had possessed an uncanny ability to strike to the heart of what was on her mind. Especially when something was troubling her. She answered him with silence.

After a while, he sat back on the newspaper-strewn carpet, rested both forearms on his raised knees, and pursed his lips. "What about Jake's house? Have you had any offers?"

Elizabeth winced and shook her head. "Just a couple of lookers. The housing market is in the pits this winter."

Going to court to get power-of-attorney so she could list Jake's modest frame house for sale was one of the hardest things she'd ever done. For a while she'd been able to convince herself that soon her grandfather would be well enough to go home. Putting his house on the market made her feel as if she'd slammed the door on hope. But in order to make sure Jake continued to receive decent nursing care, she had to come up with a sizable lump of cash. Selling the old homestead was the only way.

Grant hissed sympathetically through his teeth. "Look, I have some money put away—"

"No!" The word came out too sharply. Elizabeth cleared her throat. "Thank you, Grant. Really. But we aren't engaged anymore."

He grinned crookedly and rubbed at his prematurely receding hairline with a thumb. "I'm sure Mandy will be glad to hear that."

Elizabeth grinned back, in spite of her dismal mood. "When do I get to meet your lady love?"

"Soon. But, don't change the subject, Lizzie. You're in a financial bind, aren't you?"

"Getting there. Fast."

"And you won't take a helping hand."

At this point, Elizabeth was desperate enough to beg, borrow, or grovel for almost any help that was offered. But she wouldn't have felt right about accepting money from Grant, not knowing how or when — or, even if — she would ever be able to repay him.

Besides, she knew Grant well enough to realize he couldn't afford the kind of bucks she needed. Making the nursing-home payment this month was a drop in the bucket compared to the cost of long-term care for someone in Jake's condition. No matter how scary the situation was getting for her, Elizabeth couldn't bring herself to let Grant throw his meager savings into what was rapidly turning into a catastrophe. The past year and a half had been one long horrendous battle, and she wondered grimly if it would ever end.

Grant tapped a thumb against his jaw, thinking. "So maybe you need a better-paying job, Lizzie. Hotel catering manager isn't the only kind of work the world has to offer."

"It's all I know."

"Oh, I doubt that." Grant flapped a hand in a gesture of dismissal. "But assuming it's true, didn't you tell me the catering director was being transferred to the West Coast this spring? Why don't you go after her position? It would mean better pay, and the hours couldn't be any worse."

Elizabeth laughed humorlessly. "Marge Holt would never recommend me to fill her shoes."

That was an understatement. Where her job was concerned, Elizabeth sometimes felt like a reluctant bungee jumper teetering on the edge of a towering cliff. Marge Holt stood two paces back, just waiting for the right moment to shove her over the rim. And Elizabeth had a sick feeling the ropes tied around her ankles were rotten.

The telephone on the nightstand warbled. In no mood for a social chat, she considered letting the answering machine take the call. But that always made her feel guilty when she was at home. Her conscience finally got the better of her. On the next to last ring, she scurried over to snatch up the receiver.

And immediately regretted it.

Elizabeth listened to Marge Holt's clipped voice, nodding at the wall from time to time as if she were looking at her boss, instead of a small stain on the wallpaper. When Marge finally let her get a word in edgeways, Elizabeth told her she was on her way. Marge hung up without saying goodbye.

"Let me guess." Grant pressed his fingertips to his temples, pretending to concentrate. "Horrible Holt."

Elizabeth nodded disconsolately. "She wants to discuss the greeting-card-company banquet that I managed last night. She didn't sound pleased."

"Does she ever?" Grant began gathering up wads of newspaper. "Can't she wait until tomorrow? This is Sunday, for crying out loud."

Elizabeth hunched her shoulders and made a feline growling sound in her throat. There were times when she would dearly love to pounce on Marge Holt and send the woman's bottle-black hair flying in clumps. No matter how hard Elizabeth worked or

15

how good a job she did, Marge always managed to find something to fault.

Marge Holt was the sort who would walk all over you if she thought she could get away with it. In Elizabeth's case, the catering director got plenty of exercise. When it came to the crunch, Elizabeth never quite had the nerve to stand up to the woman. Thanks to Jake's skyrocketing bills, she couldn't afford the luxury. She needed her job too desperately to risk being fired.

The dreadful fear that Marge might be writing up her walking papers at that very moment tied a hard knot in Elizabeth's stomach. She ducked into the walk-in closet, emerging seconds later wrapped in a nondescript gray wool coat with her purse slung over one shoulder.

"I'll hang around for a while and clean up this mess, Lizzie."

Grant spoke too late. She was already out the door.

Minutes later, the frigid January air burned her lungs as Elizabeth hurried through the picturesque Country Club Plaza shopping district, a stunning replica of old Seville, Spain. She barely noticed the bronze statues scattered along her route, or the colorful ceramic-tile murals that adorned the walls of the buildings. She was too busy worrying about the future—and the fact that she didn't appear to have one. When the carillon bells on nearby Giralda Tower rang out the hour, the sound seemed to come from a different universe.

On the far side of the plaza, she dashed across

busy Ward Parkway and skirted the broad parking apron fronting the Parkway Arms Hotel. Tiny needles of sleet stung her flushed cheeks. She raised the collar of her coat around her ears as she approached a gleaming white stretch limousine idling beneath the blue-and-gold hotel canopy.

Limousines were a common sight around the stately luxury hotel. The Parkway Arms even leased a couple of its own to coddle the well-heeled clientele. Spotting a hotel decal in the darkly tinted rear window, she barely gave the vehicle a second glance.

A powerful gust of wind caught her just as she rounded the back of the limo, filling her coat like a spinnaker sail. She threw out both arms, windmilling wildly to keep herself from being thrown off balance. The rear passenger door swung open in a blur. Elizabeth staggered sideways and smacked hard into what felt like a lightly padded hickory tree.

"Got you!" a deep voice rumbled.

A pair of arms clamped securely around her shoulders, anchoring Elizabeth to a wide chest divided by a bright paisley tie. She tilted back her head and looked up into flashing black eyes and a smile that made her toes curl.

"Quinton Lawrence, at your service." He smiled affably. "But *you* may call me Quint."

Elizabeth found herself suddenly speechless. Never in this world would she have recognized Quinton Lawrence. He looked so much different from the studious, boardroom cover photo on his bestselling book, *Time to Be.* For one thing, he wasn't wearing glasses. *Contacts,* she thought disjointedly.

17

Without glasses, his gaze seemed naked, almost invasive.

The wind tousled thick brown hair across his broad forehead. Pressed close against him, she couldn't help but feel the athletic strength of his tall muscular body inside the tailor-made suit. He wore a black leather trench coat casually draped over his shoulders like a cape. Elizabeth was almost paralyzed by his rugged good looks.

"Elizabeth Mason," she finally managed, her voice sounding slightly strangled.

"My pleasure, Elizabeth." The corners of his eyes pinched slightly and his smile tilted rakishly. "Are you just checking in?"

She shook her head. "I work here."

"Ah. How convenient."

What did he mean by that? His hold tightened when she attempted to pull away. She felt a blush coming on.

"I just moved my human-resources consulting business to Kansas City from New York." He nodded to the east, as if New York were just down the block. "One week from tomorrow, I'm starting a six-week seminar in your hotel."

"I know."

*Everyone* knew. The Parkway Arms switchboard was taking fifty or more calls a day for Quinton Lawrence, and since he had an apartment in the city, he wasn't even a guest at the hotel. He was the hottest ticket in the country right now, having recently appeared on all the top television talk shows. Rumor had it that he would grace the cover of next week's *Time* magazine.

And he had his arms around her.

"What kind of work do you do here, Elizabeth?"

"Catering manager."

Quint arched a perfect eyebrow. "Interesting. I'll be conducting daily motivational luncheons—catered—along with the seminars."

"I know." Elizabeth couldn't seem to get her responses beyond two or three words.

He looked amused. "Since you seem to know so much about me, Elizabeth, perhaps you would be so kind as to take me to your leader."

"The hotel manager?"

"The hotel owner."

She swallowed dryly. George Keen didn't spend a lot of time at the Kansas City Parkway Arms Hotel—possibly because he owned four more just like it, widely spaced around the globe. He had been in town all this week, however, his presence indicated by a bright blue-and-gold pennant fluttering atop the hotel.

Quint gave the limousine a sidelong glance. "He insisted on providing the transportation. Claimed I'd be a public menace until I got in some driving practice."

Elizabeth's eyes widened.

He grinned. "I just got my driver's license last week. Never needed one in New York."

The idea of a man of Quint's stature being a novice behind the wheel seemed bizarre. Elizabeth had been driving since she got her learner's permit at fifteen and a half.

He beat a quick little tattoo between her shoulder blades with his fingertips. Even through the thickness of her heavy coat, it sent a ripple of gooseflesh down her spine. "How about it, Elizabeth? George Keen is expecting me."

*And Marge is expecting me,* Elizabeth thought, knowing how much her immediate boss hated to be kept waiting. But George Keen was *the* boss, and that gave him top priority. Especially when it came to the care and keeping of a client as important and high profile as Quinton Lawrence.

"Of course." She hoped her reply didn't seem too belated.

Quint still made no move to release her. He just smiled down at her with a gentle confidence unblemished by arrogance. He seemed totally relaxed, as if it was perfectly natural to be standing on a sidewalk with his arms wrapped around a virtual stranger. For her part, Elizabeth had enough pure adrenaline pumping through her system to supply a herd of stampeding buffalo.

"Perhaps we should go on inside . . . Quint. It's freezing out here."

"Oh? So it is. I hadn't noticed."

He dropped his arms. The fringed end of her wool scarf blew up into his face as Elizabeth stepped back. He caught it, holding it like a leash as they moved up the sloping entrance walk to the smoked-glass lobby doors.

"I'm told your seminars have been sold out for

two months." Looking impressed, George Keen tugged down the pin-striped vest over his generous midsection.

Quint nodded and smiled. He counted Keen as a personal friend, from way back. The hotel magnate was one of the few people who had expressed genuine faith in Quint's future, back in those dark days in the hospital when it appeared he didn't have one. But Quint was determined to keep their current relationship on a strictly-business footing.

They stood next to a large tubbed ficus tree in the lobby near the door to a hallway servicing the hotel's staff offices. Quint had politely resisted going up to Keen's penthouse office. He preferred to get his first impressions of a business by keeping close to its heartbeat—and in a hotel, that was always the lobby.

At the moment, the spacious Parkway Arms lobby was crowded with guests and luggage. Quint observed that the three harried clerks manning the front desk didn't seem to be making much headway with the steadily growing check-in line. There wasn't a doubt in his mind that he could improve on their efficiency quotient overnight, if given half a chance.

First one, then several of the guests began looking his way. Quint had grown accustomed to being gaped at in public. But he couldn't help noticing how the curious gazes initially fixed on him, then, as if magnetized, slid inexorably toward Elizabeth Mason, who stood at his side. Quint glanced over at her. He couldn't blame them.

Elizabeth had unbuttoned her calf-length wool coat. Underneath the bulky garment, she had on a colorful flowered jersey mini-dress that showed an intriguing expanse of shapely leg. It was like glimpsing a brilliant butterfly inside a drab cocoon.

He had a feeling that Elizabeth Mason was full of such interesting surprises. Easing back discreetly to get a better view of her left hand, he was relieved to find she wasn't wearing a ring.

Quint forcibly returned his attention to Keen. "Have you had a chance to look at the proposal I sent last month?"

"Yes." Keen surveyed the lobby down the length of his patrician nose. "Yes, indeed."

The owner of the Parkway Arms was almost bald. A thin fringe of graying hair gave him an appearance of rotund nobility—an image he apparently took pains to cultivate. In spite of Keen's streak of vanity, Quint liked him, even admired him. Keen was the kind of straight-up businessman with whom he enjoyed dealing.

Quint rocked onto his toes, at least symbolically rising to the challenge. He badly wanted the Parkway Arms account; it would be a stepping stone toward gaining contracts with other luxury hotel chains. But he wasn't being entirely self-serving about it. From the looks of the front desk, he figured Keen could use his wide-ranging efficiency expertise. But he could also tell from Keen's body language that the hotel owner was prepared to play hard to get.

He sensed rather than saw Elizabeth stir at his

side. When he looked at her, he noticed that she seemed to have spotted someone across the lobby. With an apologetic glance at Quint, she edged away into the crowd. He watched her cut a beeline toward a thickset stately-looking woman with salt-and-pepper hair and a boy of about ten.

Keen reclaimed Quint's attention. "I must say, I found parts of your proposal tempting."

"Which parts?"

"Your guarantee that you can raise the performance level of any employee on my staff, for one." Keen eyed him doubtfully. "That struck me as a pretty bold statement."

"It's true." Quint kept his tone matter-of-fact, careful not to indicate how pleased he was that Keen had taken the bait. "If you care to choose an employee I can use as a guinea pig, I'll be happy to prove my point."

The door to the administrative corridor behind them opened. Quint stepped aside as a tall, raven-haired woman in her early forties strode purposefully into the lobby. With one look at her steely eyes as she scanned the lobby, he made a snap evaluation: the woman was smart, calculating, and coldly ambitious; if she was in a supervisory position — which was likely, judging from her imperious air — she could be the devil to work under.

"Marge Holt!" Keen broke into a broad smile and reached for her arm. "Come here and meet Quint Lawrence."

Her expression changed as if someone had thrown a switch. The hard line of her lips softened

23

into a smile as she extended a welcoming hand to Quint. He took it, unmoved by the dramatic alteration in her demeanor. Beneath her sudden cordiality, he still detected a flinty hardness.

"Marge is my top catering director," Keen said.

*So,* Quint thought, *the lovely Elizabeth has the misfortune to work under a two-faced superior.*

Marge stretched her neck and looked Quint squarely in the eye. "I've read your book, Mr. Lawrence. Fascinating."

Quint murmured his thanks as he continued studying her. He couldn't help wondering if the woman had found herself in the section of his book that described various management personalities. He might be dead wrong about the woman, but he had a hunch she fit perfectly under the heading "Career Cannibals."

"I'm transferring Marge to the San Francisco Parkway Arms this spring." Keen made the announcement under his breath, as if it were a state secret.

"Is that so?" Quint went on point. "I suppose you already have her replacement in mind?"

Keen chuckled. "I'm afraid not. As a matter of fact, we're having trouble filling Marge's shoes."

Quint spotted an opening and made a mental dash for it. "Choose a candidate from among your staff, George. Let me use him or her as my guinea pig."

Keen peered at him with the suddenly alert eye of a craps shooter. "You wouldn't be interested in a little sporting wager, would you, son?"

"Name it."

"If you can fill Marge's position with someone already on the staff within the next six weeks, I'll give you a contract for the entire Parkway Arms chain."

Quint took a slow, deep breath. "And if I can't?"

Keen laughed heartily. "I didn't think 'can't' was in your vocabulary. But if you fail—and Marge herself will be the judge—you will conduct your two-week time-management seminar for this hotel's senior staff for free."

"Deal."

Quint could see that the deck was stacked heavily against him, with Marge as the judge. She wasn't likely to vote against her employer if it turned out to be a close call. But it was worth taking that risk.

"Good!" Keen turned toward the catering director. "Would you care to select a candidate, Marge? Now, don't make it easy for him."

Marge's smile stiffened. She seemed to consider for a moment, then turned to slowly scan the lobby again. Her gaze fell on Elizabeth Mason, who stood near the bank of brass elevator doors talking with the woman and boy.

The catering director nodded almost imperceptibly to herself. "Elizabeth Mason." She sounded like a judge pronouncing a death sentence.

"Now, Marge!" Keen chuckled. "I didn't say you should make it *impossible* for the man."

Quint looked from Marge to Keen and then across to Elizabeth. He was delighted by the choice—and puzzled. Their apparently low opinion of Elizabeth's prospects contrasted sharply with what his own instincts told him about her.

Keen seemed to sense his confusion. "Please, don't misunderstand, Quint. Miss Mason is an able, conscientious, and valued catering manager. She's a tremendous public-relations asset — clients and guests adore her. But Marge and I have already eliminated her as possible supervisory material. She simply isn't assertive enough to manage a staff."

"My theory is that leaders are made, not born." Quint carefully concealed his excitement at the prospect of working one-on-one with Elizabeth. "She'll do just fine."

Keen thrust out a hand. Quint took it, and they exchanged iron grips to seal the bet.

"I think it best we keep this little wager under our hats." Keen looked pointedly at Marge Holt, who nodded.

"Fair enough." Quint smiled, thinking, *All's fair in love and war.*

He frowned at the thought, even as he warmed at the recollection of holding Elizabeth in his arms in the biting wind just a short while ago.

The elevator door opened. Elizabeth watched Nicky Elledge step into the plush, crystal-chandeliered cubical with his aunt Nadine. As usual, her heart went out to the boy. With his big pale eyes and flaxen mop of hair, he seemed far too shy and sensitive to have developed such an unfortunate reputation at the tender age of eleven. Nicky wanly returned her smile just before the brass door glided shut between them.

With a sigh, Elizabeth turned back toward where she had left Mr. Keen talking with Quint Lawrence. She wasn't sure that she should have stolen away from Quint and her boss the way she had, but the Elledges were important clients, too. And like most of the other people who frequented the Parkway Arms, they expected—and received—velvet-glove treatment.

As she made her way back across the crowded lobby, Elizabeth experienced a rush of pleasure when she spotted Quint Lawrence. He stood with his arms crossed over his broad chest, pulling at his chin and watching her approach. A soft, oddly speculative smile played at his lips. It was flattering to be looked at that way by someone as celebrated as Quint. At least, it was until she stopped to consider that he probably was used to women hanging on him like Christmas-tree ornaments.

Then she noticed that Marge Holt was standing between Quint and Mr. Keen—and that all three were watching her. Elizabeth's pleasure shriveled. She had an uneasy feeling that the trio had been talking about her, and she knew with absolute certainty that anything Marge had to say about her was bound to be unfavorable. Marge was not a generous person, especially when it came to her subordinates.

Quint held out his hand as Elizabeth rejoined them. Her breath hitched slightly when she slid her fingers onto his broad palm. She smiled up at him, hoping he hadn't noticed her embarrassing physical response to his touch. He didn't shake her hand, but simply held it cradled in his as his gaze locked onto hers. He leaned forward slightly, and for one astounding moment, she thought he was actually going to touch his lips to the backs of her fingers.

Instead, he winked playfully. "I'm looking forward to getting to know you better, Elizabeth."

Since coming to work for the hotel, Elizabeth had gained plenty of experience in the delicate art of *politely* fending off mashers. After all, guests would be guests; there was something about being away from home that seemed to supercharge the male libido. But Quint's blatant advance had a distinctly different undercurrent, one she couldn't decipher.

She glanced at Mr. Keen and found him watching Quint with a self-satisfied smirk. By contrast, Marge eyed her with an odd blend of indulgence and contempt, as if Elizabeth were a bit of leftover goose-liver paté smeared on a broken cracker.

*What's going on, here?* Elizabeth's smile grew uneasy.

Before she had a chance to sort out the signals, Quint released her fingers, leaving them feeling cold and rejected. He shook hands first with Mr. Keen, then with Marge. With a parting nod and another wink at Elizabeth, he strode off across the lobby.

Elizabeth stared after him, bewildered. He had the loose confident gait of a big cat. Without seeming to be the least bit aloof, he appeared totally oblivious to the way people stared at him as he passed through the crowd.

In spite of his wealth, fame, and spectacular success, there was something reassuringly ordinary about Quint. The man had depth, substance. *And charisma that won't quit,* she thought, not quite certain that charisma and sex appeal were two separate qualities.

"A remarkable man." Keen, too, was watching Quint move across the lobby. "You know, he had quite a football career going for himself years ago, before he blew it."

Elizabeth blinked, vaguely remembering the brief biographical sketch on the dust jacket of Quint's book. It said that he had played for the Kansas City Chiefs more than a dozen years ago, when she was still in high school. She had little interest in professional sports and so had never even heard of him back then.

Now she found herself curious about how Quint might have blown his football career. He didn't seem capable of failure. But before she could ask, Mr. Keen had already turned and disappeared through the doorway leading to the staff offices.

Marge Holt made a testy noise. "Jocks are all the same." Her thin tight lips barely moved, the statement hardly more than a whisper. "Big bodies, small brains."

Elizabeth took one last look at Quint before he moved out of sight down the banquet-wing corridor on the far side of the lobby, just beyond the elevators. As far as she could tell, the catering director's biting assessment of Quint Lawrence flew in the face of all evidence to the contrary. She clamped her jaw shut, resisting a powerful temptation to point out the obvious to Marge: that Quint's current notoriety was in no way based on his past gridiron exploits.

*Neither is your attraction to him.* Elizabeth swallowed down a fluttery sensation that rose from her stomach at the recollection of his penetrating gaze and surprisingly gentle touch.

Marge, on the other hand, appeared remarkably unimpressed by Quint on any level. Nor was she in the habit of wasting pleasantries on anyone who wasn't in a position to further her own relentless ambitions. The industrial-strength congeniality she had worn like a social camouflage suit while in the company of Quint and Mr. Keen had vanished almost instantaneously. Carmine lipstick made the hard line of her lips look like a fresh knife wound.

Among the hotel staff, Elizabeth would not be alone in breathing a huge sigh of relief when Marge transferred to the West Coast that spring. She only hoped she was still around to bid Marge farewell.

"About that banquet last night . . ." Marge raked her gaze over Elizabeth. Then, without another word, the catering director turned and marched off toward the catering-service offices, clearly expecting to be followed.

Elizabeth was certain she'd done a good job with the catering of last night's banquet. Afterward, the chairman of the board of the greeting-card company had personally expressed his appreciation to her. She was equally certain, however, that Marge had managed to find fault somewhere in her performance.

She glanced back across the lobby toward the

banquet-wing corridor, hoping for one last glimpse of Quint's broad shoulders. He was long gone, of course. Still, Elizabeth experienced a ripple of disappointment. Compared to Marge's chameleon style, he was a breath of no-nonsense fresh air.

Or was he?

*Be honest with yourself, kiddo.*

Quint had said he looked forward to getting to know her better, but that didn't mean he intended it as anything personal. After all, she was just a hotel employee — a service person. Catering to people was part of her job. Even so, his parting remark lingered pleasantly at the back of her mind, along with the almost palpable memory of his touch. But as she trailed along in Marge's turbulent wake, Elizabeth had an itchy premonition of difficult times ahead.

## Chapter Two

The Royal Ballroom would do just fine, Quint thought with satisfaction. He stood on the low portable stage, peering out across the richly appointed room where he would conduct his six weeks of seminars.

Four enormous crystal chandeliers hung from the high ornate ceiling. Paneled oak wainscoting covered the lower quarter of the walls, with champagne-colored silk wall covering above. Polished brass hardware shone warmly on the series of tall double doors that nearly filled the wall to his left.

"You're standing in tall cotton, boy," he said, his voice carrying across the empty room.

There were times when he still had trouble believing he had come so far from his ramshackle boyhood home across the river. At other times, he thought he still had a long way to go. He couldn't say exactly *where* he was going, other than that it was somewhere up ahead. Always forward.

"The grand guru of get-up-and-go," Quint murmured, then laughed sardonically.

Next week, the burnished hardwood floor of the ballroom would be filled with chairs. The chairs would be occupied by men and women—corporate types, one and all. And they would be looking eagerly to him, Quinton Lawrence, to help them change the course and quality of their lives.

He felt a shudder in his gut. He smiled, acknowledging the mild forewarning of the gripping spasm of stage fright he always experienced just before bounding out in front of a crowd. Oddly enough, he enjoyed the fear.

No—that wasn't precisely true. What he enjoyed was the challenge of confronting and overcoming his own fear, the heady exhilaration of *beating* it. Quint hoped he had captured the essence of that in his new book, *Risky Business,* due on the stands late next month.

He reached back and massaged the muscles at the back of both shoulders. They always tensed when his neck kicked up. And his old neck injury had been giving him hell ever since he'd returned to Kansas City. Somehow Quint had known it would. But his former stomping ground was a veritable gold mine of major corporate headquarters, and he couldn't bring himself to pass it up.

He stepped down off the stage, suspecting he may have gone too far in betting George Keen that he could turn Elizabeth Mason into catering-director material within six short weeks. He grinned nevertheless, not regretting the rash wager one bit. It was just the sort of risk he continually urged people to take.

Besides, Elizabeth had struck him as bright and intelligent. The fact that she also happened to be extraordinarily attractive was simply icing on the cake. In addition, she had a natural graciousness that couldn't be taught. Quint genuinely wanted her to succeed. And she would, he told himself, if she could only learn to commit herself to taking risks.

Quint took a deep breath and let it out slowly through pursed lips. He had to admit that Marge Holt worried him. If he read the signs correctly, the woman intimidated the hell out of Elizabeth. Worse, he had gotten the distinct impression that Marge would as soon pull the plug on Elizabeth as look at her. Convincing Marge that Elizabeth deserved to be named her successor wouldn't be easy.

He whisper-whistled a marching tune through his teeth. Quint had wagered that Elizabeth had it in her to beat the odds, but he didn't consider himself a gambler. He preferred to think of his championing of Elizabeth as a goal. He was determined to bring out her hidden courage and turn her into a lioness among women.

The idea of Elizabeth Mason in full possession of her destiny gave him pause. Quint had always been attracted to spirited women. In this case, however, it wouldn't do for him to become emotionally involved with his pupil. He couldn't afford to lose sight of what was at stake. Quint didn't like losing bets.

He frowned. Wagering with other people's lives — Elizabeth's, in particular — didn't set well with him, either. But if he won, Elizabeth had as much to gain as he did. Perhaps, more.

A door opened soundlessly at the far end of the banquet hall. The same thickset woman and young boy he'd seen Elizabeth talking to earlier entered. He noted that the woman was well turned out in a smart mauve designer suit with matching pumps and a purse the size of a small suitcase, and guessed her to be on the far side of fifty, probably too old to be the boy's mother.

The woman glanced around at the room, seemingly unaware of Quint's presence as she took in the lavish decor. He watched her meander in his general direction, turning her head this way and that as if she were in a museum and didn't want to miss anything. When she was less than ten feet away, Quint's curiosity got the better of him. "Are you looking for someone?"

She gave a little start, as if he had suddenly materialized out of nowhere. Quint was familiar with the ploy. Strangers often used it just before they asked for his autograph.

"I'm sorry, Mr. Lawrence." She shifted the purse to her left arm — another familiar move that indicated her intent to shake his hand. "I didn't want to disturb you. I just stopped by to inspect the room."

Quint wasn't surprised that she already knew his name. His life-size mug was plastered on a color poster just outside the ballroom door. "You have me at a disadvantage, Mrs. . . ."

"Miss." She offered a narrow, heavily veined hand. "I'm Nadine Elledge. And this is my nephew, Nicky."

Quint took her hand briefly, then extended his to the boy. Nicky's surprisingly firm handshake told Quint that the kid spent a lot of time around adults.

"My dear brother's widow, Vivian, has reserved this room for her prenuptial party, next month." Nadine paused, and seemed to count the chandeliers. "We three are staying here at the Parkway Arms until Vivian marries Byron Thompson, the famous documentary film producer."

"I thought Thompson lived in California." Quint had met the producer at a fund-raiser some time ago, the same year Thompson received an Oscar nomination for a film on Civil War robber barons.

"Yes, in Carmel." Nadine nodded. "And *we* are from Boston, don't you know. Since Byron and Vivian both have family in Kansas City, they decided to have the ceremony here."

Her tone left little doubt in Quint's mind that Nadine Elledge disapproved of that decision. He had a pretty good idea that she would have much preferred the ceremony to take place amid the glitz and glitter of Beverly Hills. From what Quint recalled of Byron Thompson, however, the producer avoided the Hollywood scene like the plague.

"It's all very tiring, having to be here an entire month before the wedding." She let her purse sag on her arm. "All those cousins and in-laws insisting on throwing their own tacky bachelor parties and showers and, well, you know."

Quint didn't know, nor did he much care. He was too busy noticing that the woman hadn't once so much as glanced at the boy. He touched the kid on th shoulder. "Nick, I guess you're pretty excited about all this."

Nicky nodded disinterestedly. He drew his left arm from behind his back, revealing a worn, but obviously expensive, hand puppet with a clown face. He stood there plucking at its garish features.

Nadine scowled. "Child, I told you to leave that awful thing in your room." She stared at the boy for a moment, her gaze softening as she smoothed a lock of hair off his forehead. Then she bit her lip, drew herself up, and turned back to Quint. "I don't know what I'm going to do with that boy. He seems determined to be a troublemaker. Why, he single-handedly ruined poor Vivian's previous engagement, don't you know. If he has half a chance, he'll probably try to do the same to this one."

Quint was appalled to hear her talk about the

boy as if he weren't there. Nicky's pale face colored slightly along the jawline. But he continued fiddling with the puppet, giving no other indication that he was aware his aunt had even mentioned him.

At first, Quint had thought Nicky looked too old to be playing with a hand puppet. Curiously, however, the longer he watched the kid handle the thing, the less it looked like a toy. Quint made another effort to draw him into the conversation. "Do you go to school, Nick?"

Nadine didn't give the boy a chance to answer. "Of course he does. Nicky attends an exclusive private academy in Boston, but I'm tutoring him while we're in Kansas City. I'm a retired schoolteacher, don't you know."

She glanced around and lowered her voice. "Vivian is determined not to let history repeat itself, Mr. Lawrence. She thought it would be worthwhile to take Nicky out of boarding school so he could be with her this month, in hopes that he will form a relationship with his future stepfather." Nadine rolled her eyes toward the ceiling, as if to say the tactic had fallen on its face.

Quint gave up trying to get a word out of Nicky. His aunt seemed bound and determined to do all his talking for him. He felt sorry for the boy. For some reason, Quint had always been drawn to shy people, especially kids. From the way Nicky's attention was riveted on that hand puppet, Quint guessed that he used it for escape. Quint could sympathize with that; at the moment, he'd jump at a chance to remove himself from Nadine Elledge's presence.

As if in answer to his silent wish, a door opened and Elizabeth Mason strode in. She had jettisoned her gray wool coat. Quint didn't know which he found more entrancing: the way her reddish-brown hair tumbled over her slender shoulders or those incredible legs.

"Nadine!" She smiled broadly. "Vivian is looking for you."

Nadine shifted her oversize purse to the opposite hip, excused herself from Quint, and turned to leave. "Come along, Nicky. You and that stupid puppet."

As aunt and nephew passed her, Elizabeth reached out and shook hands with the puppet. The boy's face broke into a fleeting smile that was gone before he cleared the door. By the time Quint wandered the length of the room to join her, Elizabeth's smile was history, too, replaced by a worried frown.

"Nice kid." He pointedly neglected to mention Nadine.

She nodded, then shook her head. He wasn't sure what that meant.

"Nicky can be a real pill, according to his aunt," she said. "But I'm very concerned that he's being lost in the shuffle of his mother's wedding plans. No one except Nadine seems to have time for him."

"And Nadine is worse than no one at all?"

Elizabeth looked up at him, her hazel eyes tactfully devoid of all expression. A puddle of warmth spread through Quint's chest.

"I didn't mean to imply that, Quint."

He shrugged, as if to say he might be wrong, although he thought he was probably right as rain. At the same time, he gave her points for diplomacy. His interest shifted swiftly from Nicky to Elizabeth. Her sincere concern for the boy had already made a deep impression on him. For her own sake, he was more determined than ever that Elizabeth come out a winner in his wager with George Keen.

When she started to turn toward the door, Quint put a hand on her arm. She was as soft as a rose petal. It was all he could do to keep his fingers from caressing the delicate skin in the crook of her elbow. She looked up at him, and his thoughts snarled hopelessly.

"Do you have time to go somewhere quiet to talk, Elizabeth?"

She sucked her full, inviting lips between her teeth, then released them slowly. Quint waited for her hesitation to play itself out, hoping she would decide in his favor.

Finally she nodded. "I suppose we should."

*Amen!* Quint let out a breath he hadn't realized he was holding. He followed her from the banquet room and down the broad, wool-carpeted corridor. Elizabeth stopped at a door inset with beveled glass etched with an elaborate Victorian pattern, and peeked inside to make sure the room wasn't occupied.

"This should be free for another hour." She led the way inside.

The small dining room had already been prepared for a private dinner party. The white damask-covered tables were set with gleaming bone china bearing the gold Parkway Arms crest. Elizabeth motioned him toward an antique mahogany drop-leaf table in one corner. As Quint settled onto a French Provincial chair, she disappeared through a nearby doorway.

She returned moments later carrying a pair of Spode cups and saucers on a silver tray. Quint would have preferred buying her a drink in a quiet lounge. But he settled for the coffee—and knew he would have settled for a good deal less just to be in Elizabeth's company.

"You work on Sundays, do you?" he asked.

Elizabeth shook her head. "I just came in to discuss a matter with Marge Holt."

She took a long sip from her cup. Judging from the painfully introspective look in her eyes, Quint figured that Marge had done a good deal more cussing than discussing. And Elizabeth had soaked it up like a sponge, according to his next educated guess. That was one pattern he fully intended to change.

Suddenly shifting gears, Elizabeth looked

straight into his eyes. "By the way, what made you decide to leave football?"

The question blindsided Quint. He paused for two beats before his old reliable stock answer kicked in. He grinned crookedly. "I was strapped to a backboard. The stretcher-bearers sort of made the decision for me."

Before she could dig deeper into that rusty can of worms, he resolutely shifted a few gears of his own. Putting down his cup and crossing his lanky legs, he said, "To tell you the truth, Elizabeth, I don't think much about those years anymore. I'm more interested in the present than the past."

A pensive frown line appeared between Elizabeth's eyes. She trailed a finger lightly around the delicate rim of her cup. "You don't believe in learning from the past?"

"By all means." Quint raised an index finger for emphasis. "Learn from it. Just don't live in it." He planted his elbows on his knees, choosing his words carefully. "You see, Elizabeth, it's important to keep moving steadily toward tomorrow. The moment you stand still, you start backsliding. In life, there's no such thing as marching in place."

Quint straightened suddenly, grimacing at the pompous tone he'd used. "Sorry. I didn't mean to climb onto a soapbox."

"But isn't that your job?" The hint of a smile twitched at her lips.

Quint shook his head emphatically. "Preaching

at people is like trying to push a wet string—it just doesn't work. On the other hand, lighting fires under them . . ." He raised a finger again.

"Motivating them."

"Exactly. Showing them their options and how they can recharge their own batteries. Making sure they're doing the type of work that's best suited to their temperament. A lot of people, maybe even most, aren't."

"You make it sound pretty cut-and-dried."

"It was for me."

She glanced at his expensive London-tailored suit and handmade Italian shoes. As she took another slow sip of coffee, Quint had a feeling she was balancing his success against his philosophy. He was amazed at how important it was to him that he measure up in her eyes.

"I would count it as a personal favor if you'd sit in on my seminars, Elizabeth."

Her eyes widened. She seemed taken aback that he had put his invitation on a personal footing. In all honesty, Quint had high hopes of her being more than just a face in the crowd before he was finished. But he had to start somewhere.

"Well," she said, "I suppose that would be a good idea, considering."

"Considering what?"

"I've been put in charge of catering arrangements for your motivational luncheons." The cup rattled faintly in its saucer as she placed both on the table.

"Terrific!" Quint reached impulsively across the corner of the table and took her hand. He gave it a squeeze, then had to force himself to let go. "Welcome aboard."

"It would help if I got to know your style a little better." She looked distractedly at the hand he had grasped. "And I'll need a list of the topics for your luncheon speeches."

"Anything you need, just ask." Quint jammed both hands into his pockets to quell the crazy desire to touch her again. "Tell me, how do you feel about the assignment?"

Elizabeth gave it some thought, then laughed nervously. Quint smiled to himself. That nervous laugh wouldn't last long, he thought. Its demise would be one of the first indications that he was making progress toward winning his wager.

"Catering your luncheons will be quite an opportunity." Her smile twisted ruefully. "It'll also be a curse."

Quint's smile fizzled like a burned-out light bulb. "I've been called a lot of things before, but never a curse."

Her hand flew to her mouth. "Oh, no! I didn't mean *you*, Quint."

"What *did* you mean?"

She drew herself up in her chair, and he could tell she was regretting the choice of words that had left her marooned on such treacherous ground. Quint watched her carefully, his teeth clenched, wanting desperately to help her out. But this was as good a time as any for him to find out how Elizabeth handled herself in a pinch.

"I'm anxious to do a good job with your luncheons, Quint. But if I drop the ball, it'll make the hotel look bad."

He gave her major points for not voicing a concern that had just now struck him—that if she muffed the luncheons, Marge Holt would have her pretty head on a platter. That prospect bothered him a lot, partly because it hadn't occurred to him before that if he lost his wager with George Keen, Elizabeth might lose, as well. He would have to give that unforeseen wrinkle some serious thought later.

"Elizabeth, I learned a lot of important lessons playing football. One is that the quickest way to get someone to drop the ball is to tell them not to." He paused to let that soak in. "You'll do just fine with the luncheons. I promise."

"You promise?" Elizabeth tilted her head and looked at him quizzically. "How can you be so sure of my performance?"

"Simple." He measured his smile carefully. "I'm going to take it upon myself to *make* sure."

Elizabeth tapped a slender, manicured fingernail pensively on the polished tabletop. Quint locked his gaze with hers. He could sense her temper heating up behind the pleasant veneer of her expression. He was tantalized by this evidence that she had spirit. She held it tightly in check, but it was there, like a plump bud just waiting for the sun. Quint felt an answering rush of excitement. He had been right about Elizabeth—the lady had real promise.

"Mr. Lawrence." She raised her chin. "Why do I get the feeling you're trying to manipulate me?"

Quint laughed outright, giving her another solid point for simply reverting to his last name, instead of calling him an arrogant bastard. She couldn't quite conceal her consternation that he seemed to be taking her so lightly. Quint wished he could tell her that, at the moment, she topped the list of things he took very seriously.

He stretched his hand across the table, palm up, and waited. Elizabeth looked suspicious. He hoped that wouldn't last. He was through testing her mental reflexes. What he needed now was her trust.

She finally gave in and placed her hand in his. Quint curled his fingers around her palm, one finger extending up her narrow wrist. The feel of her pulse beating steadily against his fingertip awakened a deeper excitement within him. He had to force his concentration back on track. Being distracted by Elizabeth's obvious physical charms was the last thing he needed right now.

"I'm in the business of helping people reach their full potential, Elizabeth. I swear, I have no intention of manipulating you. That isn't my style."

He could say that with total honesty. If she did end up in Marge Holt's job, it would be because

46

of her own efforts. All he could do was give her the tools with which to work — and only if she wanted to accept them.

Elizabeth started to relax. Her gaze drifted down to their hands, then on to the gold Rolex turned to the inside of his wrist. The watch seemed to snag her attention — she tilted her head to peer at the face. Suddenly she gasped and jerked her hand free.

"Good Lord, I forgot all about Grant!" She jumped up and hurriedly gathered their cups back onto the silver serving tray.

"Grant?"

"He's been cooling his heels in my apartment with all that mess. I had no idea I'd be gone this long."

*What mess?* Quint scowled. *And who the devil is this Grant character?*

She disappeared with the tray, returning a long minute later carrying her gray coat. Quint helped her into it as they left the dining room. She barely came up to his shoulder. Even so, he had to stretch his long stride to keep up as she all but ran down the corridor toward the lobby.

He recalled that Elizabeth had arrived at the hotel on foot. "Say, George Keen insisted on putting one of the hotel limousines at my service this week." He was fumbling. Quint cleared his throat and got to the point. "Could I give you a lift?"

"Thanks, but I live just across the plaza."

Quint stopped before they reached the lobby.

47

When she realized he was no longer at her side, Elizabeth halted and came back.

"Sorry to run off this way, Quint. Do you suppose we could get together tomorrow and hash out details for your luncheons? Guest numbers, speech topics, that sort of thing."

"I'll be at meetings all day tomorrow. But I'll fax all that information over here to the hotel tonight."

Elizabeth laughed and splayed both hands. "What would we do without our wonderful machines?"

She had a delightful laugh, Quint thought. Warm and seductively husky for such a lithe wisp of a woman. He raised two fingers to his forehead in a casual farewell salute and watched her rush off across the lobby, her captivating body encased in the shapeless gray cocoon of her coat.

"Grant, you're a lucky son of a gun," he murmured, "whoever the hell you are."

## Chapter Three

The low clouds broke momentarily. A bright shaft of late-afternoon sunlight angled through the window into the sitting room of Elizabeth's apartment. Grant slouched on the settee, his feet propped up on the glass-topped coffee table. He sipped absently on a can of beer as he watched a dense swarm of dust motes floating in the sunbeam.

He was grinning like a fool.

After Elizabeth left for the hotel. Grant had taken off his sport coat and rolled up his sleeves before getting serious about the puppets. After two solid hours of examining Elizabeth's inheritance, his lungs and nostrils were thoroughly coated with the dust of the ages. He felt as if he had been breathing starch, but barely noticed the discomfort. He was too busy gloating over his discovery.

He hadn't said anything to Elizabeth immediately after they'd opened the crate; he hadn't wanted to get her hopes up, in case his hunch turned out to be wrong. Even before consulting his reference materials back at the museum, however, Grant was now certain that good old Great-great-uncle Uri had come through for Elizabeth — big time.

Puppets were outside his area of expertise, but Grant knew enough about antiques in general to realize he was looking at objects of tremendous value — and he was notoriously conservative when making that sort of judgment. To make darn sure Elizabeth understood the situation, he had tacked a large paper sign to the lid of the crate:

Elizabeth: —

DO NOT, under any circumstances, let your janitor touch this. DO NOT relegate any of this to the basement. If you do anything with these puppets before first calling me, I'll never speak to you again for the rest of your life — which will be about ten seconds.

Love, Grant

Dropping his feet off the coffee table, he leaned over and toasted the seven puppets lined up on the floor next to the shipping crate. They leered back at him with comical, surrealistic faces.

The first two in the row were rod puppets, worked from below a stage by means of slender wooden rods inserted in their soft torsos and arms. Judging by the style of their clothes and carved wooden heads, Grant thought they were probably from seventeenth-century Spain. A pair of hand puppets lolled next to them, their costumes covered with intricate geometric beadwork patterns. He wouldn't venture even a guess as to their age or place of origin, but they likely were at least as valuable as the rod puppets.

Two tall, heavy string-puppet knights towered over the others. Clad in chain mail, with tarnished brass breastplates, each held a narrow-blade sword in his clenched wooden fist.

"Hail, Camelot!" Grant toasted the knights. "If you're half what I think you are, you're worth a king's ransom."

His gaze lingered on them. As a museum curator, Grant was used to ancient artifacts. So he was more than a little surprised to find himself so impressed by these two puppets in particular. They clearly belonged in a museum — under glass.

Grant chuckled softly as his attention was drawn to the last puppet at the end. Setting his beer can on the coffee table, he reached down and hoisted the dusty string puppet onto his lap.

"Kasper, my man!" He tweaked the bulbous nose. "I have a feeling Lizzie is going to fall in love with you."

The puppet's head lolled to one side on a sprung neck. The face, with its bulbous nose, smirked rakishly from beneath a jaunty pointed hat on which the name Kasperl was stitched in dull gold thread. The white lace ruffles at its neck

51

and wrists were gray with age, and one leather ear had dried and loosened. As with the others, however, all the parts were there.

"You're old enough to be somebody's great-great-uncle yourself." Grant admired the puppet's red woolen coat, which was remarkably free of moth holes. He returned Kasper to his place at the end of the row and settled back once again to finish his beer. He couldn't stop grinning.

Uncle Uri obviously hadn't been simply a puppet enthusiast. He had been a collector. All seven of the remarkable little people lined up on the floor were of museum quality. All they needed was a thorough and careful cleaning.

"This makes my day." Grant sighed happily.

If anyone deserved a windfall, it was Elizabeth. She'd had a tough row to hoe, this past year and a half. Although she tried to put a good face on it around Grant, he knew that Jake's nursing-home expenses had her backed against the wall. This box from out of the blue would give her more than just much-needed breathing space. He was pretty sure it would buy her any dream she cared to name.

He sighed again, wistfully. He still hadn't figured out how he and Elizabeth had gone from being engaged to being just friends several years ago. The transformation had been gradual and virtually painless. He hadn't been left with any lingering regrets. At least, not since he had met the enchanting Mandy Wade. Mandy was special—the absolute and fated love of his life. But that didn't stop him from observing that Elizabeth was one remarkable woman.

There was something unique buried deep down in Elizabeth, a spark he had never been able to ignite. Like her puppets, she was a hidden treasure. Grant sincerely hoped that someone would come along someday and take her heart out of storage.

He drained the last of the beer and checked his watch. It was time to go pick up Mandy for dinner. Elizabeth had apparently gotten tied up at the hotel. He couldn't wait around for her any longer.

Grant shoved himself up off the settee and took the beer can into the kitchen to deposit in the plastic recyclables bin. He washed his hands at the sink, swatted the dust from his pants with a dish towel, and rolled down his sleeves as he went back to the sitting room for his coat.

"Be seeing you, gentlemen." Grant bowed to the puppets as he shrugged into his coat. He noticed the brocade skirt on the rod puppet at the far end, and added, "Madam."

Kasper stared up at him with a frozen smirk, as if they shared some outrageous secret. Perhaps they did, Grant thought, recalling Elizabeth's disappointment when they'd opened the crate a couple of hours ago.

Grant chuckled.

On his way to the door, he suddenly threw back his head and laughed outright.

* * *

The frigid north wind whipped icy fingers under Elizabeth's coat as she hurried across the busy parkway in front of the hotel. Her teeth chattered. By the time she reached the opposite curb, she already regretted that she hadn't accepted Quint's offer of a lift home. She could see her apartment house at the top of an incline behind the Country Club Plaza. With her face to the lacerating wind, it seemed miles away.

A car braked sharply behind her and its horn blatted, nearly frightening her out of her shoes. She whirled around and spotted Quint loping toward her through heavy traffic. His open leather trench coat was kited out behind him, and he was grimacing from the cold. He waved at her, dodged a taxi with a graceful stutter-step that reminded Elizabeth he was a former pro running back, and sprinted the last few yards to the curb.

Elizabeth held her coat collar up around her ears and kept her back to the wind while waiting for Quint to catch his breath. He stood with his shoulders hunched, gasping arctic air into his lungs.

"You're supposed to wait for a break in the traffic, Quint. It has something to do with a law of physics. A movable mass meeting a squashable one."

Quint laughed and stomped his feet, his face reddening from the cold. Protective tears glistened in his eyes, turning his pupils to polished obsidian.

"I was afraid I'd lose sight of you," he said. "I don't know where you live."

"Up there." She pointed over his shoulder.

Quint glanced behind him at her apartment house and nodded. "Handy."

He started buttoning his coat. When she noticed that he wasn't wearing gloves, she gave him a helping hand, tugging the ends of the belt around to corral the wind-whipped leather.

"This is *raw*, Elizabeth. I forgot how blasted cold it gets here in the winter."

"It isn't the temperature. It's the wind."

"Sure." He fumbled with the last button. "Down in New Orleans, they say it isn't the heat, it's the humidity. That doesn't make it any less miserable."

"Then why did you move back here?"

Quint turned up his collar, secured the collar tab, and jammed both hands into his pockets. "Good old-fashioned greed. Come on. We'll freeze our tails off if we don't keep moving."

They started across the plaza toward her apartment house. Elizabeth tried to walk close behind him, willing to risk looking like a subjugated wife if it would preserve her windbreak. But Quint hooked his arm through hers and brought her up alongside him.

"I forgot to mention." He raised his voice to keep his words from being whipped away on the wind. "It might be a good idea if you came to an orientation dinner at my place. It would give you a chance to get acquainted with my seminar programs."

"When?"

"Sometime later in the week."

A sudden gust of wind shoved Elizabeth rudely into Quint. It felt like being thrown into a telephone pole. Without breaking stride, he clamped an arm around her shoulders and anchored her securely against his side.

Elizabeth walked along in silence for half a block, vividly aware of his size and strength. She wondered what it would be like to walk this close to him if she weren't in the process of freezing to death. Her imagination accepted that concept without a struggle, and a quiver passed through her body that had absolutely nothing to do with the cold.

"How about it?" Quint trotted her smartly across an intersection on an amber light.

She glanced up at him. He kept his head ducked into the wind. His hair blew frenetically across his broad forehead and feathered softly around his ears. His teeth were clenched, making the muscles in his jaw stand out. He looked rugged and weathered and incredibly alluring.

Elizabeth felt the quiver again. This time, it centered around a growing pool of warmth deep inside her. She cleared her throat and took a big gulp of icy air in an attempt to quell the rising heat. For a moment there, she hadn't felt the least bit cold.

Eyes front again, Elizabeth tried to approach Quint's suggestion from a practical standpoint. She desperately needed her job. Further, if she hoped to continue providing Jake with the care he required, she needed *Marge's* job. And if she was perfectly honest with herself, Elizabeth knew she might not have the courage to seek her full potential if she wasn't forced into it.

She made up her mind. With so much at stake, she could use Quint as her human-resource consultant. After all, he'd made a spectacularly successful career of lighting fires under people.

*And inside them,* she thought with another quiver.

"I suppose I could make it, if I don't have a catered dinner booked at the hotel." Several years as a hotel catering manager had turned Elizabeth into a compulsive nose-counter. "How many people will be there?"

After crossing the last intersection, they began climbing the steep hill toward her building. Thinking Quint hadn't caught her last question, Elizabeth was about to repeat it when he finally answered.

"Oh, as many as necessary for the occasion."

That was the sort of response that drove caterers up the wall. It could mean ten people, or a hundred and ten. But having enough beans for everyone's plate would be Quint's problem, Elizabeth thought. For once, all she had to do was show up.

They rounded the corner, and Quint walked her right up to the glass door of the apartment house. Elizabeth hesitated there, debating whether or not to invite him up to her place to thaw out. Remembering the crate and mess she'd left in the middle of the floor—not to mention the musty smell that had probably permeated the apartment by now—she decided against it.

"Maybe we should call a cab to take you back to the hotel, Quint."

He hauled open the heavy glass door for her. "I'd rather walk."

Elizabeth glanced up at him, surprised to see he didn't look nearly as cold as when they'd started out. His cheeks were still reddened by the wind, but his shoulders were no longer hunched, and he had actually unfastened the collar tab of his trench coat. And now his coal-black eyes were focused on hers. Elizabeth felt a throbbing resurgence of warmth deep inside her.

She swallowed and took a step back into the heated vestibule, as if she were moving away from a greater source of heat. Quint blinked. His chest swelled with a deep intake of breath, then he, too, took a step back. He said goodbye with an odd awkwardness. Elizabeth felt none too smooth with her goodbye, either. She watched him stride back down the sidewalk and disappear around the corner.

She stood in the quiet vestibule for several minutes, staring out at the winter-denuded trees lining the street. Gradually the warmth inside her faded, replaced by an all-too-familiar ache.

As unremitting worry pressed down on her, she closed her eyes in fatigue. She had no business letting herself get all stirred up by a man, not while disaster still stared her in the face. The prospect of her grandfather being booted out of the nursing home onto the street made her groan aloud.

"Blast it, I *have* to have Marge's job!"

Even with the better salary, covering Jake's rapidly mounting expenses would be a tight squeeze. But at least there'd be hope of keeping their heads above water. If Elizabeth failed, however, there'd be no hope. No hope at all.

Suddenly she felt an overwhelming need to be with Jake. She phoned up to her apartment from the lobby, and when no one answered, she knew Grant must have given up on her and gone home. So, without going up to her apartment first, she went to the parking area, jumped in her car and drove to the nursing home.

From the balcony window of his twelfth-floor condo in The Tower, Quint could see everything. Straight ahead was the sprawling skyline of Kansas City, basking in the soft wintery glow of the setting sun. Over to the west, State Line Road, the boundary between Kansas and Missouri, slicing through the south part of the city almost to the junction of the Kansas and Missouri Rivers.

About a mile away and just barely visible was the place where Elizabeth Mason ate, slept, and probably took long, leisurely bubble baths.

Reluctantly tearing his gaze from the off-white stucco apartment house, Quint pulled a blue T-shirt down over his broad chest. His sneakers whispered softly over the plush carpeting as he turned toward his workout room with tight-lipped determination.

He'd already warned himself to not get involved with Elizabeth, however attractive he found her. Not with a grueling month and a half of seminars and luncheon speeches staring him in the face. He certainly shouldn't have walked her home that afternoon. Considering her effect on him while he had her tucked under his arm, Quint hadn't been surprised to find his shirt drenched with sweat by the time he got home.

He switched on the lights and the stereo as he entered the workout room, choosing an upbeat Scott Joplin CD. As was his custom, he paused before a box display frame on the back wall before moving on to the array of high-tech exercise equipment.

Quint stared at the brass whistle mounted on red velvet behind the glass. His breathing grew shallow. A distant, habitual cousin of the old hurt made a cold fist in his chest. He visualized the whistle hanging around the neck of his coach, the man he had trusted above all others as a youth. The man who had betrayed him.

There was a kind of irony, Quint thought, in the way he had turned the whistle into an icon. His high-school football coach had sold him down the river, yet Quint had ended up owing the man a bizarre debt of gratitude. Quint's success was almost a vendetta against the wreckage of his past.

As always when he looked at the whistle, his body had tensed. He made himself relax before turning away. By the time he swung onto the computerized bicycle and flipped on the viewing screen, he had already shifted his thoughts eagerly toward the new horizons challenging him in Kansas City.

After switching on the digital speed and pulse-rate indicators on the low-slung handlebars, Quint focused his gaze on the animated road scene playing on the screen in front of him. Peaceful country vistas rolled past for several minutes. Then the pedal tension on the bike increased automatically against his powerful leg strokes as he started into a simulated hill climb. Three miles along the twenty-mile course, he was sweating heavily. He leaned into a sharp curve, then picked up the pace again on a long, flat straightaway.

Quint had been over this course many times. He didn't need to concentrate. His mind wandered to the upcoming seminars. The wager with George Keen had added unexpected spice to the next six weeks. If Quint won, Keen would give him a contract as human-resources consultant for the entire Parkway Arms Hotel chain.

"What do you mean, *if* you win?" Quint chuckled, his teeth bared in an eager grimace as he pumped up another hill.

With the prestigious Parkway Arms in his pocket, Quint would be in an ideal position to win similar contracts from other major hotel chains around the world. As far as he was concerned, winning was the only game in town.

Winning—and Elizabeth. For the time being, the two went hand in hand.

Was that what had grabbed his attention about her so quickly? He didn't think so. He'd been attracted to Elizabeth Mason from the moment she careened into his arms as he stepped from the limousine in front of the hotel. Linking her with George Keen's wager had come later.

Thanks to Elizabeth's singular lack of wind resistance, Quint had been blessed with an opportunity to hold her snugly against his body twice that day. The first time, when they met, was definitely a pleasurable experience. The second, during their frigid walk across Country Club Plaza, had turned into a kind of ecstatic torture.

When they finally reached her apartment house, he had hoped Elizabeth would invite him up to her place. And she'd seemed to consider that possibility. But in the end, she hadn't, and Quint put that down to the old three's-a-crowd rule. Grant What's-his-face was already up there.

Quint's taut lips twitched, then relaxed into a faint smile as the intent expression in his eyes became distant. Some time later, he shook his head as if to rouse himself from a trance—and realized that he had come to a dead stop.

A utility cart with a bad wheel rattled down the tiled corridor outside the door. Elizabeth didn't notice. Nor did she register the too-sweet scent of industrial air freshener that filled the nursing home like an invisible fog.

She slouched in a vinyl easy chair, watching Jake sleep. When she arrived an hour ago, the tray containing his supper was still on the bedside table, the food untouched beneath the stainless steel covers. Obviously, nobody had bothered to rouse Jake to feed him.

Elizabeth hadn't had the heart to awaken her grandfather just to poke cold mashed potatoes at him. Swallowing her anger, she had marched off to the kitchen and returned with a cup of warm soup.

It had taken at least half an hour to get the soup down Jake, coaxing it past his flaccid lips one patient spoonful at a time. He had stared disinterestedly at the ceiling the entire time, as unconscious of her nurturing presence as one of the wooden-headed puppets her uncle Uri had sent.

A tear stole silently down Elizabeth's cheek. She and Jake had been incredibly close since she was old enough to stare up into the infinite warmth of his hazel eyes. Eyes just like hers, people said.

That special connection had been broken one fine summer day eighteen months ago. Elizabeth had stood on the porch of Jake's house by the river and watched it happen.

The doctors called it a stroke, possibly brought on by the news of her parents' tragic deaths in a four-car pileup out on the interstate.

Elizabeth called it a broken heart.

Her heart also had broken, although she had been too anesthetized by shock to realize it at the time. The bleak days surrounding the funeral were a merciful blur now. Through the lonely weeks and months that followed, Elizabeth had somehow managed to hold herself together with the spit and glue of hope. Hope that Jake would come back to her. Hope that grew dimmer with each passing day.

The terrible truth was that Jake hadn't spoken a coherent word since he fell to the painted plank floor of the porch that fine summer day. And he didn't seem to know Elizabeth from the burly male nurse who shaved him twice a week.

Suddenly choking on a sob, she doubled over in the chair, hugging her stomach with both arms. Tears streamed hotly down her face to drip from her chin. Elizabeth clenched her fists, furious with her weakness. Tears sure as heck wouldn't help Jake get better, any more than they would help pay his mounting bills.

Grabbing a handful of tissues from the box on the nightstand, Elizabeth resolutely dried her face.

After the emotional torment of these past eighteen months, she was surprised she had any tears left.

"No more." She went to stand next to the bed.

The nursing-home attendants kept the side rail up on Jake's bed, although Elizabeth had never seen him stir. In the beginning, his body had made a large mound beneath the waffle-weave hospital blanket. The mound had gradually shrunk, however, until he was a fragile shadow of his former self.

His beard stubble prickled as she touched his sunken cheek with the backs of her fingers. Tomorrow was his shaving day, she thought, reminded of all the times she had watched Jake scrape his lantern jaw with his old bone-handled straight razor. She would perch on the edge of the claw-footed bathtub, and he would tell her stories — endless stories.

He liked best to talk about the forty-three years he'd spent with his sweet Lydia, Elizabeth's paternal grandmother. His love stories about him and Lydia had filled Elizabeth with dreams of someday finding her own perfect soulmate, with whom she could make tender and joyous memories.

For some reason, an image of Quint Lawrence seeped into the picture. His crooked smile, and the way the corners of his dark eyes crinkled. Elizabeth blinked away that vision, dutifully and lovingly returning her full attention to the figure on the bed.

She had almost forgotten what a special gift

Jake had for acting out a story. Seemingly without effort, he could have the child Elizabeth rolling on the floor with laughter or blubbering over some fanciful character's sad fate. When he really got rolling, Jake was apt to run to his closet and haul out Juniper, a gangly old string puppet he'd owned since he was a boy. Together, Jake and Juniper would spin out a tale that kept Elizabeth enraptured for hours.

"It's funny, Jake." She traced the pale shell of his ear with a fingertip. "I don't seem to dream at all anymore."

Whatever happened to Juniper? she wondered. She hadn't set eyes on the dear old marionette in years. The thought reminded her of the crate of dusty puppets she had left back at her apartment. She hoped Grant had cleaned up the mess a little. Knowing him, he probably had.

After Quint left her at the door to the building, she had phoned up to her apartment from the lobby. When Grant didn't answer, she knew he had given up on her and gone home. So she hadn't bothered to take the elevator up. She had jumped in her car and driven over to the nursing home, needing to be with someone.

Needing Jake.

*But Jake isn't here.* She stroked his frail, liver-spotted hand. *Jake is somewhere far away, out of my reach.*

Jake was gone. Her parents were gone. The insurance money her father had left was gone. The only things Elizabeth had now were this shadow of a man she still cherished so dearly—and bills, bills, bills.

"I'm lonely, Grandpa." The whisper curdled in her throat. "I'm so lonely, sometimes it's hard to breathe at night."

Jake didn't move. He didn't so much as twitch. After a while, Elizabeth leaned over, touched her lips to his silvered brow, and left.

## Chapter Four

The band swung into a bouncy version of one of Jake's favorite old tunes, "Little Brown Jug." The Wednesday-evening party crowd that packed the dance floor in the Crystal Ballroom seemed to hesitate, as if unsure what to do with the "ancient oldie."

Standing near the doorway, Elizabeth worried that she might have reached back too far by choosing a big-band theme for the realtors' convention bash. Couple by couple, however, the mixed-age group showed a distinct talent for improvisation, matching the rhythm to everything from the fox-trot to jive, to the mashed potato and the twist.

Elizabeth smiled, relieved, swaying slightly to the lively beat. It seemed to be a perfect blend of the old and the new.

*Like my old puppets and new fortune.*

The thought stretched her smile into a grin. She was finally beginning to shake off the daze in which she'd existed for the past three days.

She was rich! The antique puppets that Uncle Uri had willed to her were worth a king's ransom, according to Grant. He had already found museum buyers for the two knights. She hated to part with them. But her grandfather's welfare was at stake, leaving her no choice.

Elizabeth had finally given in and accepted a loan from Grant to tide her over until she received payment for the pair of string puppets. Then she had gone straight to the phone and taken her grandfather's house off the market, although she had postponed indefinitely making a decision about what to do with his stored personal possessions.

With her anxiety over Jake's nursing-home care alleviated at last, she felt as free as a butterfly. Along with the sense of liberation, she was deeply grateful for her great-great-uncle's generosity. And although Elizabeth had no idea what he'd looked like, she had come to think of him as having a bulbous nose, a rakish grin, and one loose leather ear.

A bubble of laughter spilled from her. Elizabeth glanced around to make sure no one had noticed.

The band changed pace, drawing still more of the conventioneers away from the banquet tables and onto the dance floor. She watched a moment longer to make sure everything was running smoothly. Then, intent on paying yet another quick visit to Uncle Uri's alter ego, she slipped out into the corridor.

A row of exclusive boutiques and gift shops lined a quiet concourse off the far side of the hotel lobby. Elizabeth had almost reached the jewelry store near the end when she spotted Nadine Elledge strolling toward her with Nicky in tow. As their paths converged in front of the jewelry store's display window, Nadine took in Elizabeth's jade silk cocktail dress with an openly appraising eye. Elizabeth couldn't tell what the older woman thought of her new dress—and she wasn't sure she cared.

Elizabeth's attention was drawn to the hand puppet crammed into Nicky's jacket pocket. "It seems we have something in common, Nicky."

The boy gave her a look of shy curiosity. She indicated the jewelry-store window. "I'd like you to meet my friend, Kasper."

The string puppet grinned at them from his perch on an antique child-size wicker rocking chair. Across his lap lay a delicate gold chain with a stunning brooch set with intricate diamond florets. A matching bracelet was draped over his thick-toed left shoe.

Nicky stared at the puppet, wide-eyed. "It's yours?"

Elizabeth nodded, pleased the marionette had so easily aroused the boy's interest. "My great-great-uncle Uri left him to me. His real name is Kasperl, and he's come all the way from Budapest, Hungary."

Her gaze lingered on Kasper for a moment. She was still amazed that the string puppet bore such a striking resemblance to Jake's old puppet, Juniper. The thought that she had grown up playing with a puppet that might well have been as valuable as Kasper boggled her mind.

Of all the puppets in Uncle Uri's treasure trove, this was the one she considered totally priceless. The moment she set eyes on Kasper, she'd known that nothing in the world could ever persuade her to sell him. She would sacrifice the remaining four, if she had to. But never old Juniper's double.

"Wow." Nicky stepped closer to the glass. "It looks so *old.*"

"I'm told he goes back over a hundred years."

"What's it doing in the window?"

Elizabeth was suddenly uncomfortably aware that while Nicky had used "it" to refer to Kasper, she had been saying "he." She looked at Nicky. "The jewelry store leased Kasper for a month. The idea is to show two completely different objects of equal value."

Nicky blinked. "You mean, Kasper is worth as much as *diamonds?*"

She smiled proudly and nodded.

Nadine gasped.

Nicky eyed Kasper with reverence as he absently fingered the hand puppet crammed in his pocket. Watching him, Elizabeth began to have doubts about his bratty reputation. Other things about him bothered her, as well. His pale eyes looked too old for his age. She realized she had never heard him laugh.

The boy's globe-hopping travels with his jet-set mother and aunt seemed romantic and glamorous. But moving in an almost exclusively adult world — when he wasn't being farmed out to a boarding school — must be an incredibly lonely life for a

71

child. Elizabeth resisted an urge to lean over and hug him. Instead, she reached out to him in another way.

"Nicky, would you like me to give you puppetry lessons sometime?"

His head snapped around. Elizabeth felt an unexpected thrill at the excitement in his eyes.

Nicky glanced back at Kasper. "With a real marionette?"

Elizabeth nodded, pleased that he used the proper name for a string puppet. As she had suspected when she noticed him carrying around the frayed hand puppet, Nicky had more than a passing interest in puppets that were worked with strings or rods — varieties collectively known as *fantoccini*.

"Maybe even with Kasper." She recalled the hours she had spent with Juniper, under Jake's patient guidance. "I have a feeling you're a natural puppeteer."

Nicky looked overwhelmed. "When?"

"Not this evening." Nadine planted a firm hand on the boy's shoulder. "You haven't finished your math assignment, young man."

A knot of anger settled in Elizabeth's stomach as the light died in Nicky's eyes. She could have throttled Nadine for dampening the first sign of enthusiasm she'd seen in the boy since he arrived at the hotel. With one last longing glance at Kasper, he turned and scuffed dejectedly toward the bank of elevators.

"That boy." Nadine said the words as if they were a guilty verdict. "It's been so difficult, ever since the heart attack took his father." She turned and strode after her nephew.

Elizabeth watched them go, shaking her head.

"She keeps the kid on a pretty short leash, doesn't she?"

Elizabeth whirled toward the quiet voice that had so accurately stated her own thoughts. Quint Lawrence stood close behind her, resplendent in a hand-tailored tux. In place of the customary stiff formal shirt, he wore a soft dress shirt. He looked comfortable, almost casual, as if he wore a tuxedo every day.

She hadn't seen him since he walked her home from the hotel Sunday afternoon. A sudden rush of warmth reminded her vividly of how it had felt to be bundled close to his side.

He slid a thin, foil-wrapped gift box into his inside coat pocket. He must have been in the jewelry store while she was in the doorway with the Elledges, Elizabeth thought.

She had to force her mind back into gear. That seemed to be a common condition for her when she was around Quint. "Nadine does seem to run a tight ship."

He pried his gaze off her and watched the brass elevator door close behind the Elledge duo. "Well, I'm sure glad I'm not sailing on it."

Elizabeth realized she was coming perilously close to openly criticizing an important client. Backpedaling fast, she said, "I'm afraid I have to run, Quint."

"Work?"

"Yes. A convention gala in the Crystal Ballroom."

"I'm off to a dinner party myself." Quint patted the gift packet through his coat.

Elizabeth wondered what he had bought for his date. *And who she was.* The thought roused a startling little twinge of jealousy. She quickly squelched it by bidding Quint a doubly gracious good-evening before heading back across the lobby.

The band shifted smoothly into the opening bars of "Stardust" as Elizabeth entered the ballroom. She was making her way between crowded banquet tables toward the service door to find out how the wine supply was holding up when a strong arm slid around her waist and propelled her onto the dance floor.

"Quint!"

He held her gently against his tall lean frame as if he were cradling an armload of eggs. Elizabeth danced in silence for a moment, acutely aware of how well their bodies moved in rhythm with the music and each other. Finally she cleared her throat.

"Quint, staff members are forbidden to socialize with guests and clients. It's hotel policy."

"Then I seem to be committing a grave social error." He did not sound overly concerned.

Imagining how Marge would react if she happened to spot Elizabeth dipping and twirling with Quint, she tried a different tack. "You're going to be late for your dinner party."

He removed his right hand from her waist and tapped his chest over the jewelry-store packet. "I'm prepared to buy my way back into Eleanor Keen's good graces, if necessary."

Elizabeth couldn't decide which amazed her more—her willingness to risk Marge's wrath in order to finish this dance, or the absurdly intense surge of relief at learning that the gift was for the hotel owner's wife.

His right hand settled onto her back just below the diamond-shaped cutout of fabric between her shoulder blades. As his thumb stroked her bare skin, a tremor raced through her body, and she became acutely aware of the musky scent of his cologne.

"Quite a shindig you've put together here, Elizabeth."

She shrugged, murmuring her thanks. She was dancing too close to see Quint's face, but she thought she sensed a sudden frown.

"I couldn't help but overhear the last bit of your conversation with Nicky Elledge, Elizabeth. You were talking about puppetry, and I noticed how animated you were. You should have that much enthusiasm for your work."

She kept her voice low, inaudible to anyone but the two of them. "It's hard to be gung-ho when you work for someone like Marge Holt." Elizabeth regretted the words as soon as they were spoken. "Please forget I said that, Quint."

To her surprise, he chuckled softly. "Never regret the truth, Elizabeth, even when it hurts. And consider this—you wouldn't have to work for the Marges of this world if you were top dog." Quint twirled her dizzily, as if to punctuate his statement.

"Or if I had enough money." Elizabeth thought of her Uncle Uri's bequest and sighed happily.

"Stardust" played on, a hauntingly romantic melody out of time. Quint began humming along, the sound of his soft baritone oddly hypnotic. She closed her eyes, drifting, until the humming stopped in midnote.

"You realize, don't you, Elizabeth, that there are only four basic ways to get rich. Of course, you can steal a fortune."

"Or inherit it." She smiled.

"Or win it. But I've always firmly believed that the only honorable way is to earn it."

Her eyes popped open. It was Elizabeth's turn to frown, annoyed by his implication that her inheritance from Uncle Uri was somehow dishonorable. She reminded herself that Quint knew nothing of her windfall. But that only seemed to drive the backhanded insult deeper.

His thumb feathered across the bare skin between her shoulder blades. Disturbed by the rush of warmth generated by his touch and realizing they had been dancing entirely too closely, she took a half step back. An invisible wall of cool air rushed in to fill the narrow gap between them.

"I'm of the opinion that good luck is honorable, regardless of what form it takes." She had to struggle to keep her tone even.

They stopped moving. The other dancers whirled past in their peripheral vision, barely noticed. Quint stared at her for a long moment, his face expressionless, then he broke into a disarmingly crooked smile.

"I like a woman who takes a stand, Elizabeth. Even when I don't agree with it. Frankly, I find your spirit quite—" his gaze deepened, flowing into her like a hot river "—something."

Her irritation with him suddenly collided with the stunning realization that Quint Lawrence wanted to kiss her right there on the crowded dance floor of the Crystal Ballroom. She could see it in the infinite, molten depths of his black eyes.

His smile gradually transformed itself into a slightly bemused expression. He dragged a hand across his mouth, then glanced around at several nearby dancers whose attention they'd apparently attracted.

"I, uh, guess I'd better be going." He took a step back.

Elizabeth nodded, trying to hide her own emotional disarray. "I certainly would if I were invited to the Keens."

Quint touched her arm, leaning close to murmur something she didn't quite catch over the sound of the music. Then he turned and strode off through the crowd, leaving her lost in the faint lingering aroma of his subtle cologne.

Her mind dazedly wandered down unfamiliar paths as she watched him wend his way toward the door. Before her windfall, before Jake's stroke, Elizabeth had dreamed of owning a catering service of her own. Now, as her gaze clung to Quint's broad, immaculately tailored shoulders, she had a sudden compulsion to carry the dream one step further.

She could specialize in intimate little dinners for two. Candlelight and roses. Soft music. A table small enough for holding hands.

Quint disappeared through the doorway, and the dreamy image burst — but not the basic idea. It captivated her. She could do it. Selling Kasper would provide all the funding she would need.

Then, reality horned into the equation. No amount of money could buy the single most important element that would give the new enterprise a fighting chance at success: experience.

Elizabeth wandered off the dance floor, smiling automatically at couples gliding past on the last, fading notes of "Stardust." Her mind busily examined her options as a new kind of determination took root inside her. She wasn't about to let reality pull the plug on a perfectly good dream.

The path she needed to follow seemed clear. Right now, she had a shot at what she needed most — Marge Holt's job as catering director. A year of ramrodding the Parkway Arms catering service would prepare Elizabeth for anything. But she wasn't blind. She knew very well that Marge wouldn't leap at the chance to recommend her for the job. Elizabeth would have to fight for it tooth and nail, and hope for the best.

*Earn it.* Quint's words taunted her. Elizabeth lifted her chin, threw back her shoulders, and marched on toward the service door in search of the wine steward.

* * *

A shaft of pallid winter sunlight lay across the carpet a few feet away. Elizabeth sat cross-legged on the floor at her coffee table, sorting and rearranging stacks of menus. She had been hard at work since dawn, plowing through the endless details of Vivian Elledge's lavish prenuptial bash and Quint's thirty motivational luncheons. She didn't mind the hard work. Far from it. For the first time, she felt she had a powerful, driving purpose in life.

She reached absently for her teacup. It was empty. With a groan, she stretched mightily and boosted herself stiffly to her feet. Her head felt as if it were stuffed with cotton, and her eyes ached from staring at numbers all morning. Elizabeth bent at the waist and touched her toes with her palms a few times. It didn't help much.

Padding across the carpet, she opened the French doors to the tiny balcony. A blast of frigid air made her flinch. She stepped out onto the balcony anyway, hugging herself against the cold as she peered down at the Saturday-morning traffic in Country Club Plaza.

A bank of clouds rolled in to blot out the feeble sun. The gusty north wind carried the sharply metallic smell of snow as it whipped around the apartment building to tug at her new, richly embroidered caftan. It was funny, Elizabeth thought, the way she had come to associate cold wind with a particular man.

She leaned against the railing, taking deep breaths to clear her head. She wondered what Quint was doing. Was he having one last fling before tackling the demanding six-week seminar schedule on Monday? As a celebrity with well-above-average looks, Quint surely had all the offers he could handle. All kinds of offers. Business *and* pleasure.

When she caught herself wondering if Quint preferred blondes, brunettes, or redheads, she abruptly retreated from the balcony. "Back to the salt mines."

Elizabeth took her teacup to the kitchen for a refill. Already she was mentally skipping down the list of Quint's luncheon speeches, trying to match them with menus and table decorations that would complement each day's topic. She had all kinds of themes in mind.

Her newfound wealth had produced the unexpected side effect of unchaining her spirit. Her entire attitude toward her work had undergone a sea change. She had even come to view Marge as a challenge, instead of a blockade. Best of all, her creativity had taken flight — along with the courage to use it. She had some real surprises in store for Quint.

She stopped dipping the bag of black-currant tea into her cup of steaming water, baffled by the depth of her eagerness to strut her stuff for Quint. On second thought, she decided it was only natural to feel such energy when she was around him. After all, he made a living by motivating people.

"Hah! He's made an absolute *killing* at it," she said to the walls.

Elizabeth scuffed back to the sitting area with her tea and a leftover puff pastry rescued from the hotel kitchen's discard tray. The snack reminded her that Quint had made no further mention of the orientation dinner. His apparent oversight was probably for the best—she was buried in work. Still, as she settled back down next to the coffee table, she couldn't help feeling a tug of disappointment.

Her gaze drifted to the enameled parson's table next to the balcony door. The two hand puppets from Uncle Uri's shipment leered back at her. Elizabeth took a moment to admire the intricate beadwork on their costumes. She hadn't forgotten Nicky Elledge these past few days. In fact, the idea of sharing puppetry with him filled her with anticipation.

Jake had been proud of her when she'd gotten the job at the Parkway Arms. But way down deep, Elizabeth had a feeling he would be just as happy to see her helping another generation tap into the family puppet heritage. She sighed, then dragged her attention back to her menus and catering schedules.

The country road curved gently, then headed up a long steep hill that seemed to go on forever. Quint stared at the image on the screen, gritting his teeth as the pedal tension on the bike increased. Instead of gearing down, he pumped harder, straining up the wicked incline. He deserved the punishment after the dumb stunt he had pulled Wednesday evening.

Quint hadn't found out until this morning that Elizabeth had inherited a bundle from some great-great-uncle she'd never even known. By then, of course, it was eons too late to get his foot out of his mouth.

How the devil was he to have known she'd been struck rich by a bolt from the blue? Quint never dreamed that sort of thing really happened to people. Even with the lottery, you had to buy a ticket.

Obviously Elizabeth's newfound wealth had dealt a crippling blow to his wager with George Keen. Quint had no idea yet how he would go about overcoming that setback. But he had to, as much for Elizabeth's sake as for his own. Because he knew something she might not find out for years—there was a lot more to wealth than just money. In a sense, her entire life was at stake here.

For just a moment, the soothing notes of "Stardust" played through his mind. Then came an incredibly real recollection of Elizabeth Mason in that knockout jade dress floating in his arms. He shook his head and focused his concentration back onto the screen.

The hill climb steepened near the top. He bore down on the pedals, straining to maintain his speed. Perspiration beaded his forehead and soaked his sweat suit.

"Stick to business, chump." He growled the words through clenched teeth, standing up on the pedals to make the crest of the hill. The image on the screen suddenly leveled off, then sloped down the far side as the pedal tension slackened.

Quint settled back onto the seat, coasting. He was burning up, but not entirely from physical exertion.

Ten miles later, he was still intermittently thinking about the damnable jade dress and the satiny feel of that diamond-shaped patch at Elizabeth's back. He took one more steep hill at full tilt, thinking, *Business, business, business,* on each downbeat of the pedals. Then he finally gave up and went to take a cold shower.

"It's going to snow, Viv." Byron Thompson uncrossed his legs and leaned forward to check the label on the cashmere suit his fiancée was modeling.

Vivian Elledge glanced past him to the frosted windows at the front of the dress shop. Clouds had shouldered across Country Club Plaza while she was in the changing room, turning the sunny winter morning gunmetal gray.

She moaned in protest. "Not again!"

"Keep the faith, my precious. By this time next month, we'll be sipping margaritas on a private beach in Cozumel. And I sincerely hope you'll be wearing that lace-trimmed black bikini I brought you from Paris last year."

"You never tire of it, do you?" Vivian smiled, patting his cheek.

"Never." Byron kissed the palm of her hand. "I have to confess, the only reason I'm marrying you is for the way you look in that bikini."

She laughed, and he joined in. Vivian loved his irreverent sense of humor. In fact, she adored everything about Byron.

"Why don't we forget about all the elaborate and demanding expectations of our friends and families, and elope right now?" She lowered her voice so the clerk hovering nearby couldn't hear. "I could be wearing that bikini tomorrow."

Byron's expression grew somber. "I can't tell you how much you tempt me, Viv. But we still have a couple of wrinkles to iron out."

"Such as?"

"Nicky. And Nadine."

Vivian nodded slowly, stroking Byron's wavy dark hair off his forehead. "I know, sweet. And I'm so sorry about that."

He shrugged. "It isn't your fault that Nicky hasn't warmed up to me."

"Well, it certainly isn't yours. You've tried so hard. I just don't understand why Nicky seems so cool toward you."

"We'll work it out." Byron sounded more determined than optimistic. "Nadine, too."

*Yes,* Vivian thought, her spirits taking a nosedive. *Nadine, too.*

Byron tried to be patient and understanding about her indomitable former sister-in-law. But she could tell he was seriously worried about Nadine's status in their future home. So was Vivian.

She was grateful to Nadine for all her help with Nicky since Todd died three years ago. But the woman had some truly maddening habits, such as mentioning Todd whenever she was around Byron. It was about time Nadine got a life of her own, whether or not she wanted one.

The door opened at the front of the shop. Vivian tensed as Nicky entered.

It was dreadful to find herself feeling so edgy

every time her son joined her and Byron. She loved him so. But the closer she and Byron came to tying the knot, the more fearful Vivian became that Nicky would spoil it for them. It had happened before, with her previous engagement.

"What do you think of my new outfit, Nicky?" She pirouetted, then pulled him close for a hug. She couldn't let him guess what was on her mind.

"Nice." Nicky hugged her back. Then he moved off to one side, just out of Byron's reach, and stood staring at the floor.

"Where should we take your mom to lunch, Nick?"

The boy shrugged mutely and dug at the carpet with his toe. Watching the two most important males in her life, Vivian could almost see history repeating itself. First came Nicky's withdrawal. Then . . . the incidents.

## Chapter Five

After more than twelve straight hours of shuffling papers, Elizabeth was practically seeing double. She had moved from the coffee table to the dining-room table to the foot of her bed, trying to vary her position as the long day wore on. Even so, every muscle in her back and neck ached with fatigue.

Yawning, she shoved aside a preliminary menu for one of Quint Lawrence's motivational luncheons and crawled off the mattress. If she splashed cool water in her face, she might be able to squeeze in one more hour of work before calling it quits for the evening.

The sun had gone down some time ago; she hadn't noticed exactly when. Beyond the balcony, the lights of Country Club Plaza glowed softly. Ignoring the view, Elizabeth trudged wearily toward the bathroom. Halfway there, she was halted abruptly by a rap on the apartment door.

"Who the devil?" She glanced into the kitchen at

the wall clock over the sink. Then she padded over to the door and squinted through the peephole, wondering who would be paying her an unannounced visit at a quarter past eight.

Quint paced the corridor outside. Elizabeth sucked in her breath, one hand fumbling blindly with the dead bolt as she watched him pivot on one heel and look expectantly at the door.

She swung the door open wide.

Quint took one giant step onto her doorsill and stood with his hands clasped behind his back. He eyed her caftan, the fuzzy wool socks peeking out below, the wild tangle of reddish-brown curls tumbling over her shoulders, in that order. "Am I interrupting something?"

"Yes . . . no!" Muddled with surprise, she motioned him inside. "I was just working."

He came on in, his hands still clasped behind him, reminding Elizabeth of a handsome prince touring a factory. A bombed-out paper factory, she thought, as he surveyed her tiny studio apartment. She hesitated, then closed the door, somewhat mortified that he was seeing her usually immaculate abode in such condition. Not to mention herself. She madly finger-combed her hair while his back was turned.

"Industrious." Sounding impressed, he turned and smiled at her. "Have you been hard at it all day?"

Elizabeth nodded. "Did you need something?"

He gave her a long searching look. She thought she caught a quick glint in his dark eyes, and her skin prickled warmly beneath the caftan. He cleared his throat.

"I've come to take you away from all this for a little while, Elizabeth. We need to get you squared away before the seminar madness begins on Monday."

The orientation dinner. Elizabeth could have screamed. Quint hadn't dropped so much as a hint all week that it was to be tonight.

As if reading her mind, he added, "I know this is outrageously short notice, but I just remembered it myself. And you do look as if you could use a break."

Elizabeth waffled. She was put out that he hadn't given her fair notice. But she wanted the catering-director job, and her success or failure in planning Quint's luncheons had a direct bearing on her prospects. "Give me a few minutes to change, okay?"

"Take all the time you need. Make it something comfortable — and warm. It's as cold as a well digger's — Um, it was snowing earlier. But it's cleared off and turned into a beautiful night."

She glanced at his hooded parka, chukka boots, and corduroy slacks. Thinking casual, she headed for the walk-in closet off the bed alcove.

Quint had anticipated at least a half-hour wait while Elizabeth changed clothes and indulged in all those mysterious rituals of female sorcery required to transform a woman into a goddess. She had taken precisely six minutes and twenty-seven seconds.

The shapeless caftan had been replaced with a soft mauve sweater nipped in at the waist by a matching leather belt, and sleek stirrup pants that hugged every luscious curve of her hips and thighs before disappearing into glove-leather ankle boots. She had gathered her hair into a loose knot at the crown of her head, added pale lip gloss and a hint of blusher, and applied just enough exotic perfume to whet Quint's appetite.

*Wow,* Quint thought. If she could make herself look that good in so short a time, imagine what she'd do given a leisurely hour or so. She'd be capable of stopping his heart. She was, he decided, simply the most stunningly beautiful creature he had ever met.

Down in the parking lot, he helped her into the passenger seat of an obviously new low-slung sports car, then went around to slide behind the steering wheel. She had gotten rid of her dowdy gray coat, he was happy to see. She wore a belted black designer cape with a wide collar that turned up to frame her face.

"I hope you'll be warm enough." Quint turned the key in the ignition and backed out of the slot.

Elizabeth brushed a hand down the cape. "This is nice and cozy."

It also looked brand-new, along with everything else she had on. Quint was a little disturbed that she had apparently used her newly enhanced bank account as an excuse to rush out on a shopping spree, although he supposed that was to be expected. It was a good sign, on the other hand, that she had been working her tail off at home all day Saturday.

He clung to the hope that Elizabeth might not buy herself out of the program before he had a chance to win his bet with George Keen.

But as he pulled out of the parking lot and drove down the hill into Country Club Plaza, Quint had a far more immediate concern. How in the world was he going to stay on a business footing with Elizabeth when even just the thought of her made his blood surge through his veins?

The compact interior of the sports car felt close, almost intimate. Elizabeth sat very still in the low bucket seat, acutely conscious of the large amount of space Quint filled. He somehow seemed to occupy the very air she breathed.

His arm brushed hers as he shifted gears. She tried to tell herself that the resulting shock wave was just static electricity. But she knew it was something far more complex and ethereal. He shot a glance at her, and she was sure he had felt it, too. It hung there between them, building like some kind of magnetic energy field.

Quint had already turned left before Elizabeth realized he wasn't continuing south on Broadway toward Ward Parkway, which would lead to his condo. Instead, they were traveling east in the direction of Giralda Tower. He took Wornall Road past the Abercrombie & Fitch store, cut right at the corner, and whipped into a parking lot just a block from her apartment house.

Surprised, Elizabeth gathered her shoulder bag onto her lap. "I thought the orientation meeting was to be at your place."

He paused with his door open. "What orientation meeting?"

Without waiting for an answer, he got out and came around to open her door. She slid out and waited while he locked up the car.

"I guess we could have walked from your place." He steered her toward the parking-lot entrance. "But I thought it would be better to have transportation close at hand, just in case."

"In case of what?"

Quint grinned and took her gloved hand in his. "In case I want to make a quick getaway with a beautiful woman."

They dashed across J.C. Nichols Parkway and into the bright lights and festive crowd jamming Mill Creek Park. Elizabeth realized dizzily that they weren't on their way to a business meeting. They were on a date!

She had forgotten that the first annual Mid-Winter Carnival opened tonight. Forgotten, because she didn't have a date and so hadn't planned to go. Plaza merchants had organized the event as a fundraiser, with proceeds going to the homeless. Colorful tents and food booths lined the jogging paths, with dazzling ice sculptures to complement the bronze and marble sculptures that graced nearby Plaza streets.

Clowns, jugglers, and magicians in top hats moved through the crowds, trailed by teenagers with red fire buckets collecting donations. Quint had come prepared with a roll of bills. By the time they worked their way through assorted game tents and ran a gauntlet of fire buckets, the roll was almost gone, and Elizabeth was toting a fuzzy chartreuse monkey with purple plastic eyes. She had won her prize in a ring-tossing game. And she was having the time of her life.

As they approached the spectacular lighted fountain at the south end of the park, with its four bronze horsemen on rampant steeds, Quint suddenly went on point. *"Eureka!"*

He grabbed Elizabeth's hand and dragged her toward a red-and-white-striped tent near the fountain. From its center pole, a dark brown pennant fluttered gently in the crisp evening breeze.

"It's just the chocolate booth, Quint."

"Just?" He threw her a look of mock disgust as they joined the end of a lengthy line. "Bite your tongue, woman!"

Bemused, Elizabeth watched him fidget like an impatient six-year-old as they inched toward the ticket booth. When they finally got there, Quint bought two deluxe punch tickets that allowed five samples each, and handed one to her.

"Quint, please! Not after the cinnamon funnel cakes and strawberry Newburg."

"I'm sorry—that was poor planning. But I didn't know this was here."

He prodded her toward a long table covered with a white cloth. Chefs from nearly all the major hotels in the city had outdone themselves, contributing their richest, most elaborate chocolate concoctions. A fudge castle occupied the head of the table, followed by a chocolate Egyptian pyramid and a mousse lily pond.

Elizabeth reluctantly accepted a thin slice of chocolate-cherry torte out of loyalty to the chef at the Parkway Arms. Quint made it all the way to the Dutch Chocolate Alps before his punch ticket ran out.

"You aren't trying, Elizabeth." He compared his paper plate to hers.

"Henri makes the richest chocolate-cherry torte on the face of the planet, Quint. This is all I can handle."

He glanced at her ticket. She rolled her eyes and handed it over. Quint resumed his stalking of the sample table. By the time they found space on a bench outside, his plate looked like a snowless replica of Mount Everest. He closed his eyes when he took the first bite.

"Quint?"

"Mm-hmm?"

"You're what's called a chocoholic, aren't you?"

He grinned happily, totally at peace with his addiction. Within seconds, he had transformed Mount Everest into Mount St. Helens. Elizabeth was getting sick just on the rich aroma. When he scraped the last crumbs from his paper plate, she offered him her barely touched torte. Quint looked surprised, but took it.

She considered his trim, hard, athletic body and sighed. "Speaking for dieters everywhere, you do realize, don't you, that your capacity for sweets verges on being obnoxious?"

He nodded. "I don't often go off the deep end this way. But I haven't run onto a glory hole like that—" he tilted his head toward the tent "—since I went on a pilgrimage to Hershey, Pennsylvania."

Quint took his time with the torte, savoring this last sample. Elizabeth watched four gangly teenagers amble past, all wearing Kansas City Chiefs stadium jackets. She glanced at Quint, seated close beside her on the crowded bench.

"Did you mind having to leave football?" she asked.

He stopped chewing. His dark eyes took on a five-mile stare that made her instantly regret her question. After a moment, he slowly folded the paper plate over the unfinished torte and tossed it into a nearby trash bin. Relinquishing their bench space to other chocolate fanciers, they made their way out of the mob surrounding the chocolate tent.

Quint jammed both hands into the deep pockets of his parka as they strolled at a leisurely pace up the east side of the park. He had suddenly clammed up. Walking alongside him in silence, Elizabeth plucked at the chartreuse monkey, feeling she had somehow spoiled Quint's evening—and hers. Several minutes later, however, she realized he didn't intend to ignore her question.

"I was forced to leave football because of a neck injury." Quint reached up and rubbed the back of his neck. "But I guess I'd had a falling-out with the game long before that. So . . . no, it didn't break my heart when I had to pack it in."

Elizabeth sensed a strong undercurrent of emotion. Not anger, not bitterness. It might have been pain. Before she could pin it down, he tucked her hand into the crook of his arm and changed the subject.

"I heard about your inheritance, Elizabeth. I suppose you'll be quitting your job at the hotel now."

He didn't look at her as he waited for her answer, but she felt his arm tense inside the sleeve of his parka. Did he really care whether she stayed or left? Or was she reading too much into his body language?

She had to assume she was misreading the signals. After all, how much did she really know about what made Quint Lawrence tick? Until tonight, she certainly wouldn't have taken him for a chocolate fiend.

Elizabeth shook her head. "I'm going after Marge Holt's job."

"Oh?"

She explained her dream of having her own catering business, leaving out the part about specializing in intimate dinners for two. "I'm not so naive as to think money can buy success, Quint. I need the experience of directing a first-class catering operation before trying to launch one of my own."

"Sounds sensible."

His tone was casual, but the spring returned to his stride. The crowd grew more dense as they walked along. He seemed to use that as an excuse to drape an arm around her shoulders and ease her closer against him. Elizabeth felt a burst of exhilaration at their nearness.

After a while, Quint cleared his throat. "George Keen told me someone left you a crate of old puppets."

"Yes. My great-great-uncle Uri. There are seven puppets altogether, none of them less than a hundred years old. A couple go back almost to the Dark Ages."

"No kidding?" Quint sounded intrigued. "I didn't realize puppets had been around that long."

"Oh, yes. Some priceless museum specimens date all the way back to the heyday of the Roman Empire."

He smiled. "You don't sound like a novice on the subject."

"It's part of my family heritage. My grandfather Jake began teaching me puppetry when I was practically still a toddler. I helped put myself through college giving puppet shows at children's parties."

"Interesting."

"I've always felt I owed a debt to puppetry." That was even more the case now, she thought, for puppets had made her rich.

"How's your grandfather taking all this?"

Elizabeth sighed heavily. "He doesn't know."

"I'm sorry—he's no longer living?"

"Not exactly." She told him about Jake's collapse following her parents' fatal accident. "The doctors claim it wasn't a severe stroke, but Jake's been just . . . *gone* ever since."

Quint squeezed her shoulder. "You love him a lot, don't you?"

"He's all I have in the world, Quint. I'd do anything for him. Now I can, thanks to Uncle Uri's puppets. Grant says selling six of them should bring enough to insure that Jake gets the best nursing care for the rest of his days, even if he lives to be a hundred." The seventh, Kasper, would buy her dream of opening her own catering business.

Quint stopped walking. "I admire your loyalty to your grandfather, Elizabeth." He hesitated. "Um, who is Grant, exactly?"

"Just a friend." Standing there with Quint, she didn't want to get into explaining Grant's status as her former fiancé. "Grant is a museum curator. He has all kinds of contacts with collectors."

Was it Elizabeth's imagination, or did Quint look relieved? Finding the thought strangely unnerving, she searched for an escape hatch.

"I'm going to hang on to Kasper for a while." She glanced across the park in the general direction of the Parkway Arms Hotel. "He's the marionette on display in the jewelry-store window. I'm hoping Kasper can help to draw Nicky Elledge out of his shell."

Quint grinned suddenly. "I have an idea. Let's take a bottle of champagne back to the hotel and toast Kasper—and your future."

Translating her startled expression as a vote of approval he herded her into the nearest tent and bought a strip of tickets to keep her busy throwing tennis balls in his absence. By the time Quint returned with a bottle of Dom Perignon tucked under his arm, Elizabeth had won a lavender elephant to go with her chartreuse monkey.

"I'm impressed." He tweaked the elephant's

trunk. "So far this evening, I've batted zero."

Elizabeth strongly disagreed but kept that to herself. Instead, she smiled and shrugged. "Puppetry works wonders for one's dexterity."

"Well, come along. I have a cab waiting."

She wondered why Quint had bothered hiring a cab when his car was parked nearby. They could even walk the half-dozen blocks to the hotel.

On the north edge of the park, Elizabeth laughed with delight as he escorted her to a horse-drawn hansom—one of three working the carnival. The driver tipped his hat to them as Quint helped her up into the seat. Quint flipped a heavy wool rug over their legs, and the matched grays set off at a high-stepping trot.

"I've always wanted to ride in one of these, Quint!"

He looked pleased. The streamer-bedecked cab rattled swiftly down a marked-off lane on J.C. Nichols Parkway. Elizabeth snuggled close to him as cold night air rushed through the open carriage. Quint curled an arm around her and snugged her collar around her neck.

At Giralda Tower, the hansom turned into the plaza, and the grays slowed to a sedate walk as they wound through picturesque streets lined with shops. Ignoring the electric lights, Elizabeth concentrated on the lively clop of hooves and the steam rising from the horses' nostrils, imagining that they were driving through old Seville.

Too soon, the hansom crossed Ward Parkway, and the grays pranced smartly across the parking lot to the entrance of the Parkway Arms Hotel. The uniformed night doorman strode out to meet them. Recognizing Elizabeth, he offered his hand, straight-faced, and assisted her to the sidewalk. Quint tipped him generously and ushered her inside.

The lobby was almost deserted. They crossed beneath its graceful chandeliers to the corridor of boutiques and gift shops, most of which were closed at that hour. Quint tucked the bottle of Dom Perignon under one arm and tugged two plastic champagne glasses from the pocket of his parka. He peeled the foil from the cork on the bottle as they approached the jewelry-store display window.

Elizabeth suddenly gasped, halting in her tracks. "Kasper!"

Quint froze, looking at her. "What is it?"

"Kasper's gone!"

He looked at the display window. The wood-and-metal door at the back of the case stood slightly ajar. The wicker rocking chair in which Kasper had sat was turned sideways, tilted slightly off its raised platform. One of Kasper's shoes lay on the floor of the case next to the diamond necklace and bracelet.

"Don't panic, Elizabeth. Maybe the jeweler just took him out of the window for the night."

"And not the diamonds?" She was having trouble breathing. "Look at that — they left one of his shoes. Kasper's running around with one bare foot."

Quint looked at her askance. Placing the bottle and glasses on the floor near the wall, he settled both hands firmly on her shoulders. "Get hold

99

of yourself, Elizabeth. Dummies don't run—anywhere."

"Kasper isn't a dummy! He's a marionette. And he's *gone!*"

Tears stung her eyes. She was having trouble thinking. An avalanche of emotions seemed to be short-circuiting her brain. First the anger, followed closely by a crippling sense of loss. And finally a spasm of grief so real it was all she could do to keep from collapsing on the spot.

Quint pulled her into his arms and stood stroking her hair. "Just take it easy. The thing was insured, wasn't it?"

Elizabeth clamped her eyes shut and shook her head miserably. She had promised Grant she would get the puppets insured right away, but it had slipped her mind. How could she have been so stupid? Besides, insurance only meant monetary reimbursement; it didn't mean she'd get Kasper back.

He cursed softly under his breath and eased her to the wall. "Look, you stay right here. I'll go call hotel security. Maybe this isn't as bad as it looks."

It was.

An hour later, Elizabeth sat hunkered in a corner of the settee in her apartment. Quint had offered to stay awhile when he brought her home, but she told him she needed to be alone. Not until he had gone did she realize that solitude was the last thing she needed.

Grant emerged from the kitchen carrying two mugs of coffee. He handed one to Elizabeth, then sat down next to her and crossed his legs. "I'm glad you called, Lizzie."

"I shouldn't have gotten you out of bed."

"No problem." He patted her foot comfortingly. "How do you feel?"

"As if my soul has been ripped out by the roots."

"That sounds pretty drastic."

"Kidnapping does that to you." She took a sip of coffee and burned her tongue.

"Kidnapping." Grant nodded, watching her closely. "Then you're expecting a ransom demand?"

"Why not?" Elizabeth slammed a fist into the cushioned back of the settee. Kidnapping was the only thing that made sense to her. The fact that the thief had left two valuable pieces of diamond jewelry behind certainly didn't. "It isn't fair, Grant!"

He reached out and covered her fist with his hand. "Lizzie, you can't be thinking of selling the other puppets to ransom Kasper."

She looked at him sharply. That he would even suggest she could do such a thing hurt. "You know me better than that, Grant. I'd never consider sacrificing Grandpa Jake's security. Not for Kasper. Not for anything."

Grant picked up her hand and pressed it between both of his. "Stop beating your head against the wall over this, Lizzie. Give the police a chance. Maybe they'll find Kasper, and you'll get him back safe and sound without having to shell out a dime."

"Fat chance. The jewelry-store manager doesn't even know when the window display was broken into."

"It had to have been just before closing. You said the locked display window is accessed from the stockroom inside the store. Nobody could have gotten at it after the store closed without triggering the night alarm."

Elizabeth stared morosely into her coffee. "I have to get Kasper back, Grant. This sounds crazy, but I'm not sure it has anything to do with his monetary value. I don't know why, but I just have to have him."

He smiled sadly. "Jake could tell you why."

A lump filled her throat. "What's that supposed to mean?"

"Puppets are in your blood, Lizzie. I had an idea you'd feel that way about Kasper the moment I set eyes on him."

She smiled wanly through tears. "You called Kasper 'him.' "

Grant dropped his chin onto his chest like an unstrung marionette. "You always did have a way of messing up a man's mind, Lizzie."

"Sorry."

"Don't be. It's a good feeling. Everyone ought to get out of step with the universe now and then."

Elizabeth punched him gently on the arm. Grant was good company in times of crisis, she thought. It was a shame she'd never fallen in love with him.

He stayed until the coffeepot was empty, giving her time to come to terms with the evening's disaster. By the time she bade him good-night, took a hot shower, and crawled into bed, she was exhausted.

But she didn't sleep.

She lay staring at the shadowed ceiling—and thinking of Quint. Wondering what he would do in her place. It didn't take a lot of imagination to figure it out.

The pragmatic Mr. Lawrence would never ransom a "dummy," if it came to that. He would sell the other six puppets, invest the money, and never look back. That thought somehow made the loss of Kasper even more unbearable.

# Chapter Six

"Cheer up, Lizzie! I have good news."

Elizabeth straightened at her desk with a jerk, nearly dropping the telephone. "Grant—you have word about Kasper?"

There was a short pause. When Grant spoke again, his tone was less buoyant. "No, Lizzie. I didn't mean to get your hopes up. I just wanted to let you know I've found a buyer for one of the rod puppets."

She slumped in her chair, glad he couldn't see her. "That *is* good news." Her enthusiasm sounded forced, even to her own ears.

"The buyer is hooked, but I'm still negotiating the price." Grant paused again, this time for effect. "I think you're going to be pleasantly surprised at what the puppet brings."

Elizabeth pumped up her voice and managed to convey to Grant how genuinely pleased she was by his efforts in her behalf. When she finally hung up, however, she felt oddly distraught. She was still puzzling over that when Marge Holt ducked her raven head through the office doorway.

Elizabeth manufactured a smile for her. The kidnapping—theft, she corrected herself—of Kasper had taken the wind out of Elizabeth's sails. Having not yet given up on her catering-business dream, however, she continued to view Marge as a challenge.

"Elizabeth, Mr. Keen mentioned at this morning's staff meeting that your dummy was stolen from the jewelry store over the weekend."

"He's a marionette."

"Yes, well, the story made the morning paper. That isn't the sort of publicity a hotel likes."

Elizabeth frowned. Marge seemed to be implying that the theft had somehow been Elizabeth's fault.

"Be that as it may, Elizabeth, I do hope the police make a speedy recovery of your property—for everyone's sake."

Elizabeth let the catering director's bogus concern pass without comment. If all seven of the puppets had been stolen, she decided grimly, Marge would probably be standing there at the head of a lynching party.

"I want to review your plans for the Elledge-Thompson prenup if you have time." Marge's tone strongly suggested that Elizabeth had better *make* time. "It's a very important account."

Marge turned and marched off toward her own office. Her spike heels made sharp little clicks on the tiled floor of the hallway. Elizabeth stared after her for a moment, aware she no longer felt intimidated by her boss. Wanting a job and needing a job, she realized, were two entirely different ball games.

Elizabeth was far more anxious over what Quint would think of her work. Marge had given her a free hand on his luncheons—to sink or swim. She had a sneaking suspicion that, deep in her heart of hearts, Marge wanted her to sink like a rock. Yet Elizabeth didn't take that personally.

Perhaps, she thought, Uncle Uri had given her the gift of insight, along with the treasure trove of puppets. She was beginning to see Marge for what she was—a calculating, ambitious woman who was so riddled with insecurities that she measured her own success by other people's failures. For that, Elizabeth could feel only pity.

She hauled the big accordion file containing the working plans for the Elledge-Thompson prenuptial party from the shelf behind her desk. An image of Nicky Elledge wriggled into her thoughts as she headed for Marge's office. With a twinge, Elizabeth recalled his look of awed excitement when she had offered to give him puppetry lessons.

Just three evenings later—before she'd had time to make good on her promise—Kasper had been stolen. Elizabeth slowed suddenly, frowning uneasily.

Shortly after one o'clock, Elizabeth rushed into her office clutching a cold croissant wrapped in a cloth napkin. She had been so busy overseeing the catering of Quint's first motivational luncheon that she hadn't had time to eat. Sliding into her desk chair, she spread the napkin in front of her computer keyboard before glancing at her appointment calendar. She had five minutes to scarf down the roll before she was due to meet a new client up by the enclosed rooftop swimming pool.

"Elizabeth, you — are — a — genius!"

Quint strode into her office carrying an eighteen-inch tall bonsai mahogany tree in a white porcelain pot. He placed it triumphantly on the corner of her desk. Pulling a French Provincial chair from against the wall, he spun it around, straddled the seat, and folded his arms across the backrest.

"The bonsais have to go back to the shop in the plaza," she said. "They were just on loan."

"Not this one." Quint fingered the twisted trunk. "I bought it for you as a souvenir."

Elizabeth blinked. Unlike the smaller bonsai specimens that had been placed on the luncheon tables as theme centerpieces, the mahogany tree was more than thirty years old. Quint had removed the price tag that had been tucked into the sphagnum moss at the base. But she wasn't likely to forget a figure that high.

"Quint, I couldn't possibly . . . You didn't . . . You shouldn't . . ."

He smiled. "I could, I should, and I did. You deserve it. Linking the rain-forest-conservation theme of your menu with my time-conservation topic of the day was brilliant. I improvised a tad, and used the cashew nuts as an analogy during my speech."

She sat dumbstruck by his enthusiastic reaction to the first of thirty luncheons she was catering for him. He was obviously still pumped up from his motivational speech, his legs jiggling slightly as if he were mentally sprinting in place.

"I noticed that you sat in briefly on my morning seminar session," he said.

"Yes. I thought it would help me develop suitable luncheon themes if I got a feel for your style." Intent on maximizing her experience, Elizabeth hoped to sit in on as many of his seminar sessions as possible. Considering the pressure Marge was putting on her, however, she didn't expect that to be many. "I didn't think you would notice."

"Oh, I noticed." He grinned. "In fact, every time I glanced in your direction, I lost my place. Is that a new outfit?"

Her hand flew to the butterfly collar of her drop-waist dress. She suppressed a nervous laugh, but there wasn't much she could do about the quick flush of pleasure she felt rising into her cheeks.

"By the way." He held up a hand before she could speak, "have you had any word from the police about your stolen puppet?"

The color drained from her face. "Not a peep."

Quint grimaced sympathetically. "It's too bad you didn't have the thing insured."

Elizabeth nodded, dismally aware that he viewed her loss from a purely monetary standpoint. But Kasper was a family heirloom — a part of her heritage. And more. Now that Kasper was gone, she had come to think of him almost as a missing part of herself. Aching somewhere way down deep, she wished Quint would hold her the way he had when they first discovered Kasper had been stolen.

He glanced at his watch and shot up out of the chair. "Gotta run. My afternoon seminar session starts in two minutes. How about letting me buy you a drink this evening?"

Quint reached across the desk to squeeze her hand. She couldn't say no. Looking up into his shining eyes, she couldn't say anything at all. So she just nodded.

When he'd gone, Elizabeth sat staring at her warmly tingling hand. Her gaze shifted to the mahogany bonsai. She felt as if a whirlwind had torn through her emotions, scattering them in hopeless disarray. Methodically, dreamily, she scooped her papers together and headed up to the rooftop swimming pool, leaving the cold croissant untouched.

At five o'clock, Elizabeth found Quint finishing a cup of coffee with several of his seminar students in one corner of the Royal Ballroom. She stood back watching them for a moment. The students all looked like young bankers, in their pin-striped suits and power ties. Even the two women among them bore the familiar stamp of corporate ladder climbers, in their shoulder-padded jackets and slim skirts.

Quint seemed to stand alone in the middle of the group. He had doffed his coat, rolled up his sleeves and hauled his striped tie down to half-mast. His hair was tousled. He appeared worn-out and keyed-up at the same time. And *alive* with a kind of animal magnetism.

When he noticed Elizabeth standing by the door, he broke out a grin that sent a warm rush through her. He quickly disengaged himself from the group and came striding toward her.

"You look as if you've been digging ditches — without the dirt," Elizabeth said, indicating his drooping tie and partially-untucked shirt.

"I do get pretty involved in my work." With a chuckle, Quint began brushing and tucking. "Are you ready for that drink?"

"Uh . . . I'm afraid I can't take you up on that, after all." Her expression of regret was genuine. Elizabeth had been looking forward to spending a few quiet moments with him.

Quint looked as disappointed as she was. "Something's come up?"

"I'm afraid so. The nursing home just phoned. I have to go straighten out some problem involving my grandfather."

He pursed his lips, frowning. "You know, nursing homes are paid to take care of patients. I'd think you'd be able to work with them to handle glitches more efficiently. Making unscheduled trips back and forth isn't time-efficient or economical."

Elizabeth stiffened as if he had doused her with ice water. "There is more involved here than time and money, Quint. I love Jake. I don't consider looking after his needs an imposition."

Just to set the record straight, she started to add that the same held true for Kasper — he represented far more to her than money. But Quint was already backing off.

110

"Look, I didn't mean to ruffle your feathers, Elizabeth. I'm just trying to help."

They stood there for a moment, trying to find a way past the awkwardness. Quint made the first move. "Why don't I drive you to the nursing home?"

Elizabeth wavered. "So you can give the place an efficiency rating?"

"Low blow."

She sighed. He was right. He *was* trying to help, and she wasn't giving him a chance. Besides, her trips to see Jake were always such lonely affairs. "I guess I could use some company."

"You guess?"

Her jaw slid stubbornly to one side. He arched one eyebrow. She smiled. He smiled, and went to get his coat.

The nursing home corridors hummed with the usual commotion that surrounded the evening meal. The food cart hadn't made it to Jake's room when Elizabeth pushed open the door. Quint followed her. She really was glad of his company.

As always, Jake lay perfectly still, eyes closed, the bed covers pulled up under his arms. His liver-spotted hands looked like dried leaves on the pale blue blanket. Elizabeth moved to the head of the bed and bent to kiss his withered cheek. As usual, he didn't so much as twitch.

"I brought someone with me, Grandpa Jake." She spoke softly. It had been so long since he had shown any response at all that she felt a little self-conscious talking to him when they weren't alone.

Quint leaned over and gripped Jake's limp hand. "I'm Quint Lawrence, Mr. Mason — a friend of Elizabeth's." His voice was as firm as his handshake.

Jake's chin quivered. Elizabeth felt a tiny surge of hope that he might actually try to speak. But she had grown too fatalistic to feel disappointment when he didn't. She glanced around, spotting the dosage cup the nurse had left on the bedside table.

"Grandpa Jake, they told me you wouldn't take your medicine." She poured a glass of water from a plastic carafe and plucked the coated tablet from the cup. "Come on, now. How about it?"

Elizabeth held the tablet to his sunken lips, making encouraging little sounds, trying not to think of them as feeding-the-baby talk. When his lips didn't part, she tried pressing the tablet between them. It slid down his chin onto his hospital gown.

"My, my." Quint retrieved the tablet and moved around to the other side of the bed. "Stubbornness seems to run in the family."

She scowled at him.

Quint leaned down close to Jake's face. "Come on, Jake. There's nothing complicated about this. It's a simple open-and-shut deal."

He pressed a thumb hard against Jake's bony chin. Jake's mouth popped open, along with his eyes. Quint dropped the tablet onto the back of his tongue, and Jake's mouth snapped shut. Seconds later, his Adam's apple jumped.

"Nice job, Jake."

Quint slid an arm under the old man's frail shoulders and lifted him gently, holding out a hand for the water glass. Elizabeth handed it to him, watching in disbelief as Jake sipped from the plastic straw while staring up into Quint's face. She had an eerie feeling that they knew each other. But that wasn't possible.

Once he was sure that the tablet was washed down, Quint lowered Jake back onto the pillow. As Quint moved down toward the foot of the bed, Jake's eyes followed him. Elizabeth gaped at both men, shaken by the first real responsiveness that her grandfather had shown in eighteen long months.

"Jake!" She slid a chair close to the bed and grasped his hand, pressing it to her cheek. He didn't look at her, but she didn't mind. He was looking intently at Quint—staring at him. She could barely sit still in her excitement.

"Elizabeth," Quint murmured without taking his gaze off her grandfather. "Why don't you tell Jake about your inheritance?"

"Yes!" She scooted closer to the bed, fussing with the covers. "Grandpa Jake, do you remember Uncle Uri—Great-grandma's younger brother, in Budapest? He sent me the most wonderful—"

Jake's right hand suddenly rose from the blanket, reaching toward Quint. He made several garbled sounds and then, quite distinctly, "Tom."

Elizabeth sucked in her breath and looked at Quint. He gave her a questioning half smile that faded quickly when he registered her stunned expression.

"Tom . . . Tom . . ." Jake made clawing motions with his raised hand.

"Who's Tom?" Quint asked in an undertone.

She didn't really want to tell him, but she had to. She swallowed dryly. "Tom was my father, Quint. Grandpa Jake thinks you're his son."

For one long moment, Quint had the same five-mile stare she had seen at the carnival last Saturday night. Elizabeth watched him, not knowing what she should feel—embarrassment, regret, despair. Before she could make up her mind, he suddenly whirled and stalked from the room.

After Quint's hasty departure, Elizabeth watched helplessly as Jake subsided into his usual state of suspended animation. Confused, she fussed over his covers for a few minutes before hugging him goodbye.

She caught up with Quint leaning against his car in the parking lot. He looked a little hangdog as she pulled her cape close around her and leaned beside him on the car.

"I'm sorry I bugged out on you like that, Elizabeth."

"Don't be. I shouldn't have put you in such an awkward position. It's been so long since Jake has shown any awareness at all. I just never dreamed he would mistake you for my dad."

Quint's laugh was brittle. "That's only fair. Jake reminded me of someone from my past, too."

"Really? Who?"

He stared down at his feet for a while, the muscles in his jaw working fitfully. Finally he shook his head. "It doesn't matter."

Shoving away from the car, he turned to face her.

The jaundiced glow from the sodium lights that ringed the parking lot softened the sharp contours of his face. A biting north wind riffled through his hair, making the rest of him seem so . . . still.

Elizabeth gazed up into the infinite depths of his black eyes, knowing before he took his hands from his pockets that he was going to kiss her. She hadn't expected this. A tremor swept through her as she wondered what it would be like.

He cupped her cold cheeks in his hands, bracketing her mouth with his thumbs. As he lowered his face slowly, her lips parted and she sighed into him. His breath quavered. The tender kiss deepened, and the parking lot seemed to tilt under her feet. She slid her arms around his waist under his unbuttoned coat, struggling to keep her balance, losing herself in warm mist-shrouded desire.

Their lips parted suddenly before Elizabeth was ready for it to end. Quint pulled her against his chest. She stood listening to the powerful, driving rhythm of his heartbeat, trying to catch her breath. Her mind was still drifting in a gentle fog when he opened the car door a moment later and settled her inside.

Elizabeth retrieved her briefcase from under her desk and switched off the light. Fortunately the catering-service offices were deserted. She was in no mood to encounter Marge Holt or anyone else.

Considering the way Quint had sent her mind reeling and her knees turning to jelly in the nursing-home parking lot, he had seemed extraordinarily formal when he dropped her off at the hotel only minutes ago. Apparently feeling he had overstepped by taking their relationship onto such uncharted ground, he was backpedaling fast.

Still rattled by the unexpected heat of their kiss, Elizabeth had been stung by his sudden coolness. It was hard to admit his behavior made sense. But after all, he was a hotel client. There were rules. She left the offices and headed down the hallway toward the lobby, too strung out to think about it now. All she wanted to do was get home, put in a couple of hours of work and go to bed.

Halfway across the lobby, someone called her name. Elizabeth turned to find Nadine Elledge bearing down on her from the direction of the elevator bank, looking tense and put out. Elizabeth automatically glanced behind the older woman, but Nadine's ever-present shadow was absent.

"Good evening, Miss Elledge." She made an effort to sound pleasant. "Where's Nicky?"

"I was about to ask if you'd seen him." Nadine's lips formed a hard, uncompromising line. "When I find him, that boy is going to get a piece of my mind. He's supposed to be in his room doing his lessons."

"Well, you know what they say about all work and no play."

Nadine sniffed. "It isn't the play I'm worried about, don't you know."

Something in her tone snagged Elizabeth's full attention. "I'm afraid I don't understand."

"Well—" Nadine hesitated "—I don't suppose I should say this. But then, you are hardly a disinterested party, under the circumstances."

"Under what circumstances?"

Nadine smoothed the front of her designer suit and pointedly cleared her throat. "You see, Nicky has been known to . . . take things."

Elizabeth grew very still. "Surely, you aren't suggesting that Nicky stole Kasper."

" 'Stealing' is a rather harsh way of putting it."

"No matter what color you paint it, Miss Elledge, stealing is stealing and a thief is a thief."

"Yes, I suppose." Nadine flushed slightly. "But he is just a child."

Taken aback by the abrupt softening of Nadine's tone, Elizabeth was surprised to see tears well in the woman's pale eyes.

"It's happened before, don't you know." Nadine fingered a lace-trimmed handkerchief from her pocket and dabbed the corners of her eyes. "After my dear brother, Todd, died, Vivian became engaged to a banker in Philadelphia. A stuffy little man with grown children of his own—not at all like poor Toddy, who was so young and vital."

She averted her face and stood twisting the handkerchief tightly around one finger. "A week before the wedding, we attended a lovely lawn party at the gentleman's estate. The next day, we learned that a valuable gold watch had been taken from a collection case in his library. I searched Nicky's room—just to clear him of suspicion, don't you know—and there it was. Well, the gentleman was a banker, after all. He couldn't abide that sort of thing under his own roof, so the engagement was broken right then and there."

Elizabeth reached out and touched her arm, moved by the woman's distress. "I'm sure this will all work out for the best," she said lamely.

Nadine nodded. "I hope so. I truly do."

She turned and strode stiffly back across the lobby toward the elevators. Elizabeth watched her go, suddenly deeply depressed.

By late in the week, Elizabeth was beginning to feel like Henry Morton Stanley skulking around the Dark Continent in search of Dr. Livingstone. She hadn't set eyes on Nicky since her talk with his aunt Nadine. By now, she was convinced he was avoiding her. But she couldn't bring herself to go to the police with Nadine's suspicions until she had first confronted the boy. So she kept her eyes open for him, hoping for a chance encounter.

On the evening of the third day, Elizabeth finally ran into him in the ground-floor vending-machine alcove near the door leading to the hotel parking garage. When he saw her, Nicky looked as if he had been caught red-handed with the Hope Diamond, instead of a can of cream soda.

"Hello, stranger." Elizabeth leaned against the door frame, arms crossed. She needed to keep an open mind, but that was difficult. In spite of what she had learned from Nadine, she still liked Nicky, wanted to trust him. "Where have you been hiding yourself?"

"I haven't been hiding," he said too quickly.

*Lie number one.* It was written all over his face. Oddly, though, it set off an unexpected alarm in Elizabeth's head. A habitual liar ought to be better at it than Nicky was.

"Then I guess we've just been accidentally missing each other all week, right?"

He nodded too vigorously. She tried to put aside his overacting for the moment. "You've heard about Kasper being stolen?"

"Yeah." Nicky toyed with the tab on his soft-drink can, refusing to make eye contact. "I'm real sorry about that."

"Are you, Nicky?"

"Sure, I am."

"But you don't know anything about it?"

He did look up then, and she saw that his solemn face had gone ghostly white.

"I didn't take Kasper, Miss Mason. Cross my heart." He drew a big X across his thin chest with one finger.

Nicky couldn't seem to hold her gaze for even two seconds. She knew he had to be hiding something. Even so, she nodded slowly and said, "I believe you, Nicky." And she did.

His expression brightened a little. "Miss Mason, you said you'd teach me puppetry."

She considered that for a moment as disjointed phrases raced through her head. *Innocent until proven guilty. A promise is a promise. He knows more than he's telling.* In the end, it was the hungry look in his eyes that tipped the scales. She didn't

119

have the heart to go back on her word, not in the face of so much eagerness.

"Sure, Nicky. I still have four puppets. But they're very old, so we'll have to be careful with them."

"Oh, I would be!" Nicky promised, eyes shining.

"Go get your raggedy old hand puppet, and I'll give you a couple of pointers before I go home."

Nicky thrust the unopened can of pop into her hands and took off running toward the elevator. When he was out of sight, Elizabeth let out her breath in a whoosh. Was she being ten kinds of a fool to trust the boy? She didn't think so, but she couldn't be sure. She recalled how Quint had kissed her with such feeling on Monday evening, then abruptly shut her out. Lately, it seemed she couldn't be sure of anything.

Elizabeth smiled pensively. Puppets and fools. Trust and Quint. They all came together like pieces of a puzzle as she hit on a perfect idea for a theme for one of Quint's upcoming luncheons.

Grant Holbrook sat at his workbench, squinting through a magnifying glass as he carefully stroked a cotton swab over the puppet's wooden face. The paint was surprisingly bright for being 350 years old, give or take a decade or two. He was getting a real kick out of cleaning the antiques before contacting prospective buyers.

"She's rich—she's rich—Eliz-a-beth is rich." He laughed softly and tossed the cotton swab into the wastebasket, his expression growing wistful.

Elizabeth was distraught over the lack of progress

being made in finding Kasper. Grant didn't blame her. So far, the police hadn't turned up a clue. Even so, she had come alive lately. He could see a spark in her eyes of the sort he had never been able to kindle, and he had no doubt whatever as to what it meant. Elizabeth was falling in love, although Grant wasn't sure she knew that yet. He recognized the signs, because he was traveling down that same rocky-velvet road with Mandy.

Unable to figure out who was getting so deeply under Elizabeth's skin, Grant had made a few discreet inquiries among the employees of the Parkway Arms Hotel. From all indications, Quinton Lawrence was the lucky man. Grant chuckled, happy for her. Little Lizzie was swimming with the big fish now.

That showed, too, he thought, straightening the skirt on the puppet. Lizzie was changing, growing more confident. Her Uncle Uri had turned her life upside down with his priceless bequest. But a lot of her—the best part, close to her heart—was staying the same.

She needed time to sort out her life. In the meantime, Grant didn't think she should sell any more of her puppets. She should wait until she got both feet back on the ground—until she came home to herself.

Grant placed the puppet in an acid-free storage box and switched out the light over his workbench.

# Chapter Seven

"So far, Elizabeth, you seem to be giving Mr. Lawrence what he wants for his motivational luncheons." Marge Holt surveyed the banquet room as waiters clad in rented railroad-conductor coats and caps hurried around placing a mound of striped engineer caps at the center of each table. "Or so he claims."

Elizabeth stole a sidelong glance at her boss, wondering why the catering director felt compelled to be so grudging with her praise. Quint apparently had expressed his approval to Marge, or perhaps directly to George Keen. Anyone even slightly familiar with his credo knew Quint didn't hand out unearned plaudits.

Marge indicated the caps. "Why a railroad theme?"

"It complements Quint's—Mr. Lawrence's— luncheon topic for today. 'No Free Rides.' "

"Indeed." Marge nodded, then turned and walked away without another word.

Elizabeth returned her attention to the banquet-room preparations. Today began the second week of Quint's motivational luncheons. In spite of Marge's prickly disposition, Elizabeth thought she should feel elated that he was pleased with her work. But instead, she increasingly sensed that something vital was missing.

She sat in on Quint's seminar sessions whenever she could squeeze in the time, and was learning a lot. But she hadn't been alone with him since their visit to the nursing home last Thursday. Her fingers drifted to her lips, remembering. Elizabeth caught herself and jerked her hand down to her side. Considering the man's hot-and-cold behavior, perhaps it was best that she kept her distance. Eventually she was bound to get over feeling so miserable.

She began rearranging the caps on a nearby table. As she fussed, she couldn't dispel the restless, crazy notion that something important was missing in her life. She couldn't quite put her finger on it, but it nagged at her like an unquenchable thirst. With an impatient shrug, Elizabeth headed for her office.

At five minutes past one, she headed back to the banquet room to make sure the waiters' railroad-conductor coats were properly returned to the rental shop. She had just stepped out into the busy service corridor when Quint rounded the corner with a conductor's cap perched jauntily on his head. He broke into a wide grin when he saw her.

"Perfect!" Quint rushed straight up to her and planted a resounding kiss smack in the middle of her forehead. "The luncheon group got so involved with the program that they're wearing their caps back to the seminar this afternoon."

"Fine. I'll add the caps to your bill."

Elizabeth couldn't help grinning back at him. It seemed he was so energized by his own motivational speech that he couldn't stand still. The overflow of vitality spilled onto her. She tried to imagine what it would be like to be around Quint all the time and found the idea exhausting.

He went suddenly motionless, his gaze drifting down over her. "Say, is that another new dress?"

She glanced down at the understated lines of her new aqua wool coat dress with its matching wide, brass-buckled belt. She was still amazed by how comfortable she felt with the daring hemline.

"I went on a shopping spree over the weekend."

Quint arched an eyebrow, intrigued. Their gazes met, and for a few unsettling seconds, his coal-black eyes held the same almost wondering look she had seen just before he kissed her in the nursing-home parking lot last week. Then they both seemed to regain the awareness that they were not alone in the hallway.

"I have to run." He made no effort to move. A moment later, he shook his head as if to clear it. "Say, how about cocktails at my place Friday evening?"

Elizabeth drew in a slow, calming breath. It was difficult to think straight with his gaze wandering over her like warm, caressing hands. The thought of spending an evening alone with Quint made her giddy—which was reason enough to turn him down. The distance he had put between them ever since their kiss had left her feeling abandoned. She wasn't sure she was up to handling another loop on that roller coaster.

"Sounds lovely." The words popped out against her better judgment. Once said, however, Elizabeth felt no inclination to call them back. The decision seemed about as sensible as her hemline.

Quint whipped off his cap and clapped it over his heart. "You just made my whole week." He clicked his heels together and, spinning the cap on one finger, strode off down the hallway.

Seconds before the doorbell gonged softly Friday evening, Quint thought he heard the elevator open onto the private lobby outside his front door. He took careful aim at the number-four ball and missed an easy shot into a side pocket by a good two inches.

"It's about time you blew one!" George Keen chortled sinisterly, and began chalking his cue stick.

"Don't pay George any mind, Quinton." Eleanor Keen leaned back in her deep leather chair and glared good-naturedly at her husband across the pool table. "He just hates to admit he's met his match."

Quint grinned. "Take your best shot, George, while I get the door."

He left the hotel magnate contemplating a difficult bank shot and hurried toward the foyer. He'd been watching the clock for the past twenty minutes. When he pulled open the walnut-paneled front doors, he knew it was worth it.

Elizabeth stood in the marbled lobby, a black satin evening cloak draped casually over one shoulder. Except for the thin silver chain of her evening bag, the other shoulder was bare, the skin glowing softly in the muted light. She had on an incredible black dress with rhinestone buttons. The neckline seemed to be trying hard to join forces with the hemline. For a moment, he couldn't even blink.

*You were right. She had all the time she needed to get ready for this evening — and she's damn near stopped your heart.*

"You did say seven-thirtyish?" Elizabeth looked uncertainly at the pool cue in his hand.

"Uh . . . yes. Of course." Quint ushered her inside and took her cloak. "Come on back. We're all in the pool room."

A flicker of surprise crossed her face, followed by . . . disappointment? He wondered about that as they made their way past a row of dark walnut pillars and into a short hallway leading to the pool room. She paused to admire an eight-paneled oriental screen along the way. Quint didn't rush her as she paused to take in the adjoining high-ceilinged living room with its wide covered balcony and expansive view of the city lights.

While she looked, so did he. The plunging back of her dress convinced him he had the better view.

126

A certain spot between her shoulder blades reminded him all too vividly of their dance. Rubbing his fingertips down the sleeve of his suit coat, Quint gently prodded her on.

Her shoulders sagged slightly as they entered the pool room, then she seemed to brace herself. He realized too late that he'd failed to mention he'd also invited the Keens. He could have kicked himself. On second thought, however, considering what that incredible scrap of a dress was doing to him, Quint figured it was probably for the best he wasn't alone with Elizabeth.

Gracious to the core, the Keens greeted her as if she were a long-cherished friend. While she chatted with Eleanor Keen, Quint moved to the wet bar to pour Elizabeth a glass of wine. She looked elegant enough to fit in anywhere. As he handed Elizabeth the wineglass, he caught himself wondering if she would fit into his life. The idea jarred him.

"I hear you've done wonderful things with Quint's luncheons, Elizabeth," Eleanor said. "But it's a terrible shame about your puppet being stolen."

Elizabeth's eyes had lit up at the compliment, but the radiance died at the mention of Kasper. Quint wished Eleanor had quit while she was ahead.

"I keep telling George he ought to go ahead and promote you to catering director." Eleanor ran a bejeweled finger around the rim of her martini glass.

George shook his head. "Now, Eleanor, you know I'm leaving that entirely in Marge Holt's hands. Besides, from what I've heard about Elizabeth's inheritance, I rather expect she'll be taking herself out of the running for that job."

"Wrong." Quint was glad he could put that rumor to rest. "Actually, our poor little heiress wants to start her own catering service someday. She's eager for the seasoning she could gain as catering director."

"Indeed?" George offered Elizabeth a respectful nod that made her flush. "I admire your entrepreneurial spirit."

"Well, I'm personally rooting for Quinton, Elizabeth." Eleanor smiled and fingered her pearls. "He bribed me, you see."

Elizabeth glanced at Quint questioningly. "Rooting for *you?*"

Quint rolled his cue between both palms, cursing himself for not warning Eleanor to keep quiet about his wager with her husband. "Nothing, Elizabeth. Eleanor prattles."

Eleanor made good-natured indignant sounds, but he could tell she got the message. She settled back and sipped her martini, watching Elizabeth with interest.

"What the devil?" Quint belatedly noticed the empty expanse of green felt on the expensive regulation pool table.

"I ran the table while you were gone." George grinned innocently.

"In your dreams!"

George laughed, handing his cue to Elizabeth. "See what you can do, my dear. I'm afraid Quint is out of my league."

Elizabeth shook her head. "I have no idea how to play."

"I'm sure Quint can remedy that." George drew a gold cigarette case from his coat. "I believe I'll step out onto the balcony for a smoke."

Quint paused at the far end of the table, where he was busily racking the balls. "You'll freeze."

"Don't discourage him, Quinton." Eleanor hurriedly scrutinized Elizabeth and Quint, then rose and joined her husband. "George is trying to kick the habit. Limiting his smoking to the outdoors in the dead of winter is part of his strategy."

The Keens walked out of the room arm in arm, leaving Quint with the distinct impression that their strategy involved a good deal more than George's quitting smoking. Alone with Elizabeth, he rubbed chalk on the felt tip of his cue and positioned the cue ball.

"I'll break."

Elizabeth edged closer. "Break what?"

"Watch."

He leaned over the table and gave it his best shot. The cue ball rocketed down the felt-covered slate surface and slammed into the wedge of balls, dropping two into the corner pockets and evenly scattering the rest. Her little exclamation of surprise gave him an absurd charge.

"Your turn." Quint took a step back.

Elizabeth grasped her cue awkwardly and

leaned over to address the cue ball. Her hemline crept up a few inches.

Quint took a deep breath to steady himself. "Here. Let me show you how to hold that."

Aligning his body with hers, he cupped her outstretched left hand in his and gently shifted her right hand farther back on the cue. Her reddish-brown hair feathered against the side of his face. He took another deep breath, inhaling the intoxicating fragrance of her perfume. They took the shot together, and the nine ball dropped neatly into a side pocket.

Neither of them moved.

The silkiness of her hair against his cheek, the natural alignment of his body against hers, were exquisite torture. After what seemed like an eternity, Quint moved his right hand to her bare shoulder.

Elizabeth gasped and pulled away. They stood inches apart, both holding on to the polished rail of the pool table. He wanted to drag her into his arms and kiss her until their teeth ached. But when he looked into her wide hazel eyes, he saw both desire and fear. Afraid he might tip the balance in the wrong direction, he didn't dare move.

"I . . . I think I'd better go wash this chalk dust off my hands." She sounded strained.

Quint nodded, pointing toward the hallway. "Third door on the right."

With a silent groan, he watched her move away toward the door. He gripped the rim of the pool table to keep himself from going after her. Then he waited a couple of minutes before retreating to the bar to mix himself a stiff drink.

In the locked bathroom, Elizabeth fumbled shakily with the faucet knob, then thrust her wrists under the stream of cold water pouring into the clamshell sink. Slowly, the trembling subsided, along with the terrifying sensation that she was drowning.

"What is the matter with you?" she whispered harshly at the pale reflection in the mirror. A voice inside her head shouted back, *Quint — that's what!*

Plucking a small guest towel from the rack, she glanced around at the richly appointed bathroom. Gold faucets on the sink. Spotless black fixtures. Black marble floor. Mirrored walls with etched-glass inserts. A wall phone tucked away in one corner.

The trappings of wealth — and Quint's home. But he was rarely there. He traveled with his work, living out of hotels for weeks on end. *He steals into people's hearts,* she thought, *but he doesn't stay.* Money had bought him that freedom. But what had her newfound wealth bought her, besides relief from unrelenting financial worry?

Now that the means to fulfill her dreams were within her grasp, something inside Elizabeth seemed to be shifting. Fantasy dreams weren't the same as those built on reality. Owning her own catering business had always been her goal, and now it seemed, with the money made from selling the puppets, it could become reality. And yet, since Kasper was stolen, an invisible force seemed to be pulling her in a direction that had little to do with catering.

She remembered all those times she had borrowed Grandpa Jake's old marionette, Juniper, for her puppet performances during college. Elizabeth could almost feel the strings running smoothly through her fingers, the heat of the stage lights, the heady rush of adrenaline at the first patter of applause. The make-believe world of the little wooden people wasn't just in her blood, it was in her soul. She could no more turn her back on it than she could stop breathing.

Elizabeth stared hard at her reflection in the mirror. For the first time, she realized that embracing puppetry had already become more than just a dream for her. It was a hunger. An impractical hunger, at that. She was becoming obsessed with puppets.

Feeling trapped between *two* wildly conflicting desires — one for Quint, the other for the world of puppets — Elizabeth somehow endured the remainder of the evening in a troubled haze. By the time she left, she knew she wasn't going home. Instead, she drove to the nursing home, needing to be with Jake.

A night-light dimly illuminated the room and the sleeping figure on the bed. Elizabeth was halfway across the room when a tall figure moved toward her out of the shadows. She jumped.

"Sorry, Lizzie. I didn't mean to startle you."

"Grant! What are you doing here at this hour?" Besides Elizabeth, Grant was the only other person whom the night staff allowed in to see Jake after visiting hours. Her grandfather had always considered him part of the family.

He ducked his head, smiling softly. "Oh, I just had this crazy urge to tell Jake I was getting married this summer."

"You and Mandy finally set the date?" Elizabeth threw her arms around Grant and gave him a sisterly hug. She had to blink back tears, knowing how Jake had always hoped she and Grant would end up together. Maybe someday she would stop feeling disloyal to Jake for not having fallen in love according to his script.

Grant eased her toward the door, speaking in an undertone. "Say, I haven't been by in several weeks. But Jake seemed . . . different, this time. More alert."

Her fingers shot to her mouth as she glanced back toward the bed. "Still?"

Grant looked at her questioningly, and she told him about bringing company with her one evening last week. He smiled and seemed to nod to himself when she mentioned Quint Lawrence, but looked astounded when she described how Jake had mistaken Quint for her father.

"That's wonderful, Lizzie!"

"No, Grant. It was awful."

"But don't you see? It was the first real rise you've gotten out of Jake since his stroke. It's a

133

step—a giant step. I'd say you and this Lawrence guy make a fantastic team."

She shook her head almost before he finished. The memory of how Quint had reacted to Jake's "giant step" was all too vivid. "I don't think Quint is the sort who would risk commitment to anyone, Grant. I'm pretty sure someone burned him badly once. Now he seems totally committed to his work."

Grant chucked her playfully under the chin. "Come on. A good woman can change all that."

Elizabeth shook her head again, suddenly too charged with emotion to speak. Quint owned a palatial apartment, to be sure. A gold-plated toilet handle, for heaven's sake! But he lived out of a suitcase most of the year. Something felt terribly wrong about that. A gloomy sense of dread seized her. She couldn't help wondering if wealth was a lonely affliction.

Half an hour later, Elizabeth pulled into her parking slot, glad to be home. The evening had been strangely exhausting. And yet she felt keyed up, like an overturned vehicle with a still-racing engine. She was vaguely aware of the smell of snow in the frigid night air as she got out and hurried across the quiet parking lot. She pulled up short when she spotted Quint leaning against a post near the locked rear entrance to her apartment building.

"Doesn't anybody sleep?" she wondered aloud.

"I was thinking the same about you." He shoved

off from the post and walked toward her. "I've been waiting almost an hour."

He seemed to expect her to tell him where she had been. Elizabeth debated a moment, then did.

Quint frowned. "You should have said something. I could have gone with you."

She let that pass. Only now did she realize that she had fled to Jake that night in search of a calming refuge from Quint. But now that she was with Quint again, her emotions felt as hopelessly tangled as ever.

He reached out, not quite touching her, then motioned back toward the parking lot. "Will you go someplace with me?"

"It's late, Quint. I'm very tired."

"So am I. This won't take long. I promise."

Elizabeth hesitated, wanting to resist, wanting to give in. Just being around Quint seemed to generate an endless necessity to make emotionally draining choices. Finally she let him guide her to his car.

As they pulled out of the parking lot, she leaned back and closed her eyes. The throaty roar of the sports car's powerful engine was oddly comforting. When she opened her eyes again, they were speeding east on the interstate.

Thin patches of ice shone on the pavement. She tensed, reminding herself that the plastic lamination on Quint's driver's license had barely had time to dry. But he had the hand-eye coordination of an athlete. Maneuvering a car already seemed to have become second nature to him. He slowed as they approached a cutoff, and Elizabeth suddenly knew where they were going.

Minutes later, they entered the vast deserted parking lot outside Arrowhead Stadium. Quint drove straight to a service entrance on the southwest corner, tapped the nasal-sounding car horn, and got out. By the time he had strode around to help Elizabeth out, a night watchman was unlocking the gate to the stadium.

The gate opened barely enough for Quint to usher Elizabeth through. "I appreciate this, Smitty."

"Anytime, Dutch." The grinning night watchman tipped his cap at Elizabeth, revealing a snowwhite crewcut.

She looked at both men. "Dutch?"

Smitty laughed heartily. "Yes, ma'am, that's what we used to call him — Dutch. You see, whenever the Chiefs got into trouble during a game, you could always count on Quint Lawrence to plug the leak in the dike, just like the little Dutch boy."

"I see." Elizabeth peered up at Quint, who seemed embarrassed.

They left Smitty locking the gate and moved down the ramp into a cavernous tunnel. Quint paused when they reached a second tunnel branching off to the left.

"This is the visiting team's locker room." He pointed to a nearby door in the adjoining tunnel. "The Chiefs' training room, showers, and whathave-you are on down that way."

He made no move to show her through those areas. Elizabeth concluded that the object of their visit to the stadium wasn't a grand tour. They continued on down the sloping tunnel. Quint had tucked her hand into the crook of his elbow. As they approached the end of the tunnel, she felt him tense. When they emerged from the far end, she halted, spellbound.

She had attended pro football games at Arrowhead Stadium a couple of times, but had never seen it from this perspective. They had entered the playing field at the south end. The huge stadium rose clifflike around them. Rows and rows of bright red seats seemed to climb all the way to the low-hanging clouds. She imagined what it must be like to run down that field amid the deafening thunder of nearly eighty thousand roaring fans. The thrilling image sent a shiver of excitement through her body.

"It does get to you, doesn't it?" Quint spoke softly, gazing up at the endless vacant seats.

"I never dreamed . . ." She could barely manage a whisper. "At night, deserted like this, it's almost like being in a temple."

He looked down at her for a long moment, then nodded slowly. They moved across the wide rubber track bordering the playing field, then onto the artificial turf. Quint led Elizabeth upfield to the forty-yard stripe. A half-dozen yards from the far sideline, he stopped and turned to face her.

A brilliant security light shone high behind him, like a small distant moon. She stared up at Quint's silhouette, more conscious than ever of his size. She found herself mesmerized by the vaguely enchanted quality of the moment, wishing she could capture it to keep with her always.

"This is the exact spot where my football career ended." Quint toed the ground. "We were one touchdown away from a slot in the playoffs. I took a handoff from the quarterback, shook a lineman with a head-fake, and took off running like a bat out of hell. Thought I was home free. Then the lights went out. I don't even remember getting clipped."

His chuckle sounded ironic. "I also don't recall the half ton of defensive beef that piled on top of me before the referee whistled the ball dead. But I do have a vague recollection of being scraped off the field onto a stretcher, with sandbags around my head to stabilize my broken neck."

Elizabeth gasped.

"Yeah, it got my attention, too. it was a miracle my spinal cord wasn't damaged, but the doctors warned I'd risk permanent paralysis if I ever took another bad hit. I spent a long time in traction and rehab. By the time I threw away the neck brace, I was already half-finished with my first book. And I knew just where I was going."

Quint turned, gazing up at the seats. As he faced the light, she could see his almost savagely intent expression. He smiled—the kind of smile a football player gave his opponent just before the ball was snapped.

"The transition must have been rough on you,

Quint." A gross understatement, she thought.

"Not at all. Once I was on my feet again I never looked back." He grasped her shoulders. "That's what I'm getting at, Elizabeth — why I brought you here. I want to impress on you how important it is that, once you've set your goals, you don't let anything sidetrack you, no matter what. That's the only way you can make good things happen for you."

Quint stroked her cheek with a thumb. But his intensity disturbed her, as well as the unspoken message. He seemed to be backhanding her growing obsession with puppetry.

She started to mention that it was her own past, her heritage, that had brought her a stunning fortune in the form of seven winsome old puppets. But she didn't think there was any way Quint would understand how, with each passing day, her yearning to look back grew stronger. Even now, as she recalled the endless hours she had spent learning how to make Juniper walk and talk and dance a jig, she sensed invisible strings pulling her back.

*You and Quint are on different tracks. He has wilfully turned his back on his past, even as you reach out to yours.*

As they retraced their path across the field toward the tunnel, Elizabeth hugged herself, trying to shake the oppressive feeling that they were racing pell-mell in opposite directions.

# Chapter Eight

"Don't bother getting out, Quint." Elizabeth placed a restraining hand on his arm as he killed the engine beneath the drive-through portico of her apartment house. It was altogether too late at night for chivalry. Besides, she was ready for the long evening to end.

She reached for the door handle, then jerked her hand away when someone tapped the tinted window glass inches from her face. When she saw who it was, she slumped back against the seat. Quint pressed a button on his door panel and her window glided down smoothly.

"Mr. Cooksey, you scared the daylights out of me!" She smiled stiffly at the apartment-house security guard.

"Sorry, Miss Mason." Cooksey leaned down and gave Quint a courteous nod. "I was making my rounds when I saw you drive up. Thought you might want to know you had a visitor a little while ago. A boy—about ten or eleven, I'd say."

Elizabeth exchanged glances with Quint. "Nicky Elledge?"

"When I told him you were out, he wouldn't give me his name." Cooksey tucked a utility flashlight under one arm and shoved his hands into the pockets of his insulated uniform coat. "A kid that age shouldn't be roaming the streets at night. But while I was trying to figure out what to do with him, he just up and vanished on me."

Quint drummed his fingers on the steering wheel. "Elizabeth, why would Nicky—or anybody—come calling on you at this hour?"

She looked at him askance. "You might ask *yourself* that question, my friend."

"He didn't say what he wanted." Cooksey frowned. "But he sure did seem agitated about something."

Ever since Elizabeth had run onto Nicky at the pop machine the previous evening, she'd been convinced he was hiding something. She couldn't ignore the real possibility he might be hoarding a dirty little secret about Kasper. If that were the case, he might have trekked all the way over from the hotel to bare his soul to her. She regretted having missed him. At the moment, however, she was far more concerned about his safety.

"Quint, it has to have been Nicky. Do you mind running me over to the hotel to make sure he got back safely?"

"We're on our way."

He turned the key in the ignition and shoved the floor stick into gear. Elizabeth waved good-bye to Mr. Cooksey as the sports car tore out of the portico.

Elizabeth raced into the deserted lobby of the Parkway Arms Hotel, then abruptly slowed to a walk. Nicky would have been hard to miss even if she hadn't been looking for him. He hunkered in his coat on a green leather couch facing the banquet-room corridor, looking dismally alone. The backrest of the couch rose several inches higher than his head, so his presence apparently had gone undetected by the bored night clerk at the front desk.

Elizabeth slid onto the cushion next to him. His eyes grew round, but he stared straight ahead without looking at her. His coat and shoes were still damp with melted snow.

"You're up a little late, aren't you, Nicky?"

He shrugged.

Quint strode in through the main doors, saw them both on the couch, and detoured toward the vacant concierge desk across the lobby. Elizabeth was grateful to him for not barging over and driving Nicky deeper into his shell.

"Mr. Cooksey said you came to visit me." She gently smoothed a lock of blond hair off Nicky's forehead. "How did you find out where I live?"

Nicky's only answer was a shrug. Her patience was wearing thin, but not her concern. "I guess you must have something pretty important to talk about, to walk all that way through the cold in the middle of the night."

He sucked in his lips and still didn't speak. She couldn't decide whether he was trying not to cry or was just being bullheaded. She glanced toward Quint in exasperation. Quint began drifting casually toward the couch.

"Nicky, I know you're hiding something from me." The way he paled and turned his face away from her told Elizabeth she had scored a bull's eye. "Is it about Kasper?"

Not a peep.

Quint stopped at the end of the couch and studied the boy for a moment. Then he reached down and took Elizabeth's hand.

"This isn't a civilized hour for you to be on the prowl, son," he said firmly. "Why don't you trot on up to your room and hit the sheets?"

Nicky's fixed gaze shifted slightly to focus on Elizabeth's hand cradled in Quint's, but he didn't budge. Elizabeth started to ask again about Kasper, but Quint's sudden squeeze of her hand made her stop.

"The boy seems to have gone stone deaf, Elizabeth. Maybe we should find out if his mother knows where he is right now."

Nicky looked glumly at Quint. After a moment, he slid off the couch without a word and scuffed off toward the elevator bank.

Elizabeth felt pretty gloomy herself as she watched him go. "Quint, I wish you hadn't sent him packing that way. If I'd had just a little more time, I might have found out what's bothering him."

"Not tonight. Once he figured out I was with you, he dummied right up—I could see him do it clear across the room. The kid didn't like my looks a pound."

Elizabeth glanced up at him in surprise. "Why not?"

"He's jealous."

She almost laughed outright. "Jealous? Come on, Quint. The child is barely eleven years old."

Unsmiling, he bent and brushed his lips across the backs of her fingers. "Elizabeth, you have a lot to learn about men."

The Monday-morning seminar was already in full swing when Elizabeth crept into the crowded Royal Ballroom, notebook in hand. But her intention to sit in on a few minutes of Quint's lecture on time management quickly fell by the wayside when she got a look at the front row of seats.

Nicky Elledge sat in the third chair from the left. Clad in a charcoal-gray suit and a red-and-gray-striped tie, his hair slicked down, he looked like a miniature Wall Street broker. His feet didn't quite touch the floor. He stared raptly at Quint, who was demonstrating what appeared to be a complex time-management concept, using a large chart propped on an easel at the back of the low stage.

Elizabeth eased back out the doorway, fuming. The gall of the man, recruiting a child! Nicky had little enough of a childhood, being dragged around all over the world in the company of adults, without Quint trying to turn him into a pint-size business tycoon. She whirled and stalked off toward her office, muttering to herself.

She passed the entrance to the shopping concourse just as Nadine Elledge emerged from one of three small coffee shops located on the ground floor. Elizabeth kept going for a few paces, then did an about-face and strode back to where Nicky's aunt stood buttoning her coat.

"Miss Elledge, do you know where Nicky is?"

Nadine seemed momentarily nonplussed. Then she resumed buttoning her coat, slowly. "He's attending Mr. Lawrence's seminar."

Elizabeth pressed her lips together, struggling to keep her temper from boiling over. Marge Holt would have her head on a platter if she offended an important client, no matter how much Nadine deserved a good tongue-lashing.

"Well, then, do you have any idea where Nicky was at one o'clock Saturday morning?"

Nadine stopped fiddling with her coat buttons. "Why, in bed, of course."

Elizabeth's smile felt starched. "Miss Elledge, I think it would be a good idea if we sat down over a cup of tea and had a little discussion about your nephew's night life."

The older woman started to speak, then seemed to think better of it. With a sigh of resignation, she nodded.

Just before noon, the seminar participants rose as one and headed for the exits. Quint busied himself with the charts at the rear of the stage, keeping a surreptitious eye on Nicky Elledge, who remained glued to his seat.

The kid had dumbfounded him by showing up bright and early that morning, dressed like a banker and wanting to sign up for the session. Quint had started to tell him that the seminar was sold out, and that it was hardly suitable for a kid, in any event. But something about the boy's demeanor had given him pause. He ended up calling the Elledge suite to make sure it was all right, then had an extra chair brought in.

With Nicky sitting right there under his nose, at least he could keep an eye on the little thief. And if he didn't stay still, Quint could always evict him. That was the game plan, anyway. As it turned out, however, Nicky had been a model of studious attention right on through the lengthy question-and-answer period. Quint couldn't help being impressed by the kid's adult attention span and obvious intelligence.

He slid the last of the charts into their custom-made carrying case and stepped off the low stage. Nicky stood up and took a tentative step toward him.

"Well, Nick. What did you think?"

The boy squared his shoulders and clasped his hands behind his back. "It was excellent, sir."

Quint didn't pay much attention to the "excellent," that word being such an overused figure of speech among kids these days. But he was favorably impressed by the way Nicky called him "sir."

"I'm glad you liked it." Quint wished he had time to hang around and pick the boy's brain. He started toward the door, trying to shift his thoughts onto the upcoming luncheon speech.

"Mr. Lawrence?"

"What?" Quint glanced back, still walking, and saw the impatience in his tone reflected in the boy's widening eyes. He had forgotten how painfully shy Nicky could be. "I'm sorry I barked at you, son. I was thinking about the speech I'll be giving in a few minutes, and that always makes me nervous as a cat."

"Really?" Nicky looked amazed.

"Sure. I get butterflies as big as bats in my stomach."

The size of Nicky's sudden grin brought Quint to a complete halt. Apparently, nobody had ever bothered to inform the poor kid that only idiots and fools never got scared.

"Fear is a good thing, Nick. It causes your

body to produce adrenaline, which makes you stronger and faster. But it's what you do with that strength and speed that counts. If you don't do anything at all, well, that's when it gets bad."

"Like if you run away?"

Quint scratched his jaw. "No. sometimes running away is smart. For instance, you wouldn't want to hang around trying to look brave if a tree was about to fall on you, would you?"

Nicky shook his head, frowning, one eye squinted. Quint could almost see him sizing up other situations in his mind. The kid was a thinker, all right.

"Did you want something, son?"

"Oh . . . yes, sir." Nicky chewed his lip nervously.

Quint smiled. "Here—give my scared-stiff remedy a try. First, tell yourself that you really *want* to do this. Then take two deep breaths, count to three real fast, and spit it out."

Nicky stood very still for a moment, then panted quickly, closed his eyes, and blurted, "Will you let me come back this afternoon?"

"Great job!" Quint reached out and tousled the kid's slicked-down hair. "Sure, you can come. But you have to swap that suit for jeans and sneakers, and bring a note from your mom giving you permission."

Nicky looked crestfallen. "Mom is in Independence, visiting relatives all day."

"How about your aunt?"

"Shopping."

Quint cursed silently. No wonder the kid had serious problems. He was too damned far down on his family's list of priorities.

"Okay, I'll tell you what, Nick. I'll take responsibility for you this once. You go get out of that monkey suit, and I'll find you a place at today's luncheon even if I have to feed you under the table. Then you can bring a note from your mother tomorrow."

"Tomorrow? I can come tomorrow, too?"

"Only if you bring a note."

Nicky shot past him toward the door, tearing at his tie as he went. Following in his wake, Quint hoped he wasn't making a mistake. But he had a gut feeling that, in spite of Nicky's reputation, the kid needed a friend more than he needed a warden. Even if he was wrong, keeping Nicky around close might at least give Quint an opportunity to find out something about Kasper for Elizabeth.

The three doors to the dining room opened all at once. A raucous horde of luncheon guests poured out into the corridor, jostling each other as they sought elbow room for their yo-yos. Elizabeth stood her ground, and they flowed around her as if she were a pillar.

Her eyes narrowed when Nicky emerged near the middle of the crowd. But he, too, strolled right past without noticing her, concentrating intently on getting his orange glow-in-the-dark model to "sleep" at the end of its string.

Quint was the last to show his face. He strolled out with his suit coat thrown over one arm, grinning. Unlike the others, he noticed Elizabeth at once. His grin broadened. He stopped and flicked his wrist at her. A yo-yo shot out to within an inch of her nose, hanging there for a few seconds before whipping back to his cupped hand, striking his palm with a solid *pop*.

She didn't even blink.

His smile became guarded. "Terrific idea of yours, matching the yo-yos-and-hotdogs theme with my 'Getting Back to the Basics' topic. I'll bet you didn't know I placed second three years running in the Greater Kansas City Open when I was a kid."

Still no response.

"It was the first time I'd ever come up against a girl I couldn't get the better of. Flame-red pigtails, freckles, braces—and a rocking-the-cradle maneuver that'd knock your socks off. I flat fell in love with her. It was a very humbling experience."

Quint began to get the news that Elizabeth was seriously ticked off at him. He worked the loop of string off his finger and slipped the yo-yo into his pocket out of sight.

"Let's have it, Elizabeth. What's the problem?"

"What was Nicky doing in your seminar session?" She glanced back at the crowd receding down the corridor. "And at the luncheon?"

"Oh, that." His playful smile returned. "I figure as long as I can hold the attention of an eleven-year-old, I have a grip on the entire room."

"This isn't a game, Quint. How can you stoop to . . . to *using* a child?"

"Using?"

His smile faded. She could tell she had jolted him. His face reddened slightly. She thought it was from embarrassment, until he grabbed her by the arm and marched her angrily up the hallway.


The third room that Quint checked turned out to be empty. He pulled Elizabeth inside and closed the door. He didn't like the me-Tarzan-you-Jane tactics, but she hadn't given him a lot of choice.

Now that he had her alone, however, he didn't quite know what to do with her. He knew what he would *like* to do—her new wardrobe was getting more adventurous by the day. A trickle of sweat coursed down the hollow of his spine as he took in the soft peach blouse and skirt that hugged her in all the places he wanted to.

First things first. There were two males in the current equation, as far as Elizabeth was concerned. He needed to get rid of the pint-size one.

"Elizabeth, I do not *use* people." The itchy thought that he was using Elizabeth to win his wager with George Keen made his stomach twitch. But that was different. Quint was helping her to achieve her own goal of gaining Marge Holt's job.

"Then what was Nicky doing there in the front row this morning?"

Quint shrugged. "Maybe he was just sizing up the opposition."

"Oh, right. This is part of your jealousy theory."

He exhaled through his teeth and shook his head. "Don't tell me you've never had two men with a crush on you before."

"A crush? *You* have a crush on me?"

She looked stunned, which was a marked improvement over angry. But how could she possibly not know how he felt about her after the way he had kissed her that night outside the nursing home?

"Be reasonable, Elizabeth," directing the subject back to the boy. "Nicky seemed to enjoy himself, so I'm letting him stay. What harm can it do? His own family admits he's a troubled kid. I figure that anyone who can keep him out of further mischief is doing him a major favor."

Elizabeth seemed to be coming out of her momentary fog. She had not yet recovered her power of speech apparently, but the warmth in her eyes drew Quint closer. He cupped a hand around her neck under her silky hair, tracing his thumb gently along the delicate line of her jaw. Their one kiss had been such an incredible, falling-through-space sensation. Not a day had passed since that he hadn't wanted to take that leap again. But he hadn't, because that kind of involvement was a dangerous ingredient in a business relationship.

Of course, the involvement was already there—for both of them. He could feel it in his own body and see it in the pulsing vein on the side of her neck. The desire. He could kiss her now and tell her all about his wager with Keen. Or he could keep on denying what he wanted body and soul.

He was still trying to make up his mind when the door behind Elizabeth swung open. Nicky Elledge ducked into the room, still clutching his orange yo-yo. Quint quickly dropped his hand from Elizabeth's neck, but not before the boy noticed.

"What's the problem, Nick?" Quint asked. He couldn't quite manage a smile.

"No problem." Nicky glanced back and forth from Quint to Elizabeth. "Just thought I'd come tell you we're all ready for the afternoon seminar."

Quint nodded. For the first time he could remember, his work seemed like an intrusion.

"Thanks. I guess I'm going to have to hire you as my official timekeeper."

Nicky brightened. Elizabeth frowned. She was still doubting Quint's motives. That was one thing he intended to nip in the bud, at least where the boy was concerned.

"Look, Elizabeth, just to prove I'm not out to exploit the young and innocent, how about the three of us—you, Nicky, and I—spending next Saturday exploring the plaza together?"

Nicky's jaw dropped open, which made Quint surprisingly happy.

"I don't know, Quint." Elizabeth seemed to be fighting a war within herself.

"It's all three, or none." Quint looked straight into her eyes and smiled, daring her to disappoint the boy. If he'd been thirty years younger, he would have crossed his fingers behind his back.

Elizabeth started to shake her head. Then she looked at Nicky. "Oh, all right."

Nicky chomped down on his lower lip, his eyes glowing. Quint got out his yo-yo, looped the cotton string around his finger, and spun the yo-yo to the floor at his feet. Without moving from where he stood, he walked the yo-yo across the carpet and up Nicky's right leg before a tiny jerk of his finger brought it whipping back into his hand. Nicky looked at him worshipfully.

Quint winked at Elizabeth. "If you think that's

154

something, wait until Saturday. You ain't seen nothin' yet."

She rolled her eyes toward the ceiling. "I can hardly wait."

He laughed and clamped a hand on Nicky's shoulder. "Come on, my man. We have a seminar to conduct."

Quint radically shortened his gait so that he and Nicky walked out the door in lockstep. He felt high, almost intoxicated. But leaving Elizabeth alone there in that empty room was the hardest thing he had done in a long, long time.

# Chapter Nine

"Quint, it's seventeen degrees out here. I'm freezing to death!"

Elizabeth inched stiffly along the ice-crusted sidewalk between windrows of freshly-shoveled snow. Nicky had skittered on ahead to the corner and was now on his way back to meet them. If he skidded into her the way he had the last time, she was going to end up flat on her behind.

"We're having too much fun to quit now." Quint shuffled along beside her, trying to skate in his insulated boots. "Do something to warm up."

"Such as?"

Quint waited until Nicky was a few feet away, then said, "This."

He lunged forward and jerked Nicky's knit cap down over his eyes. Before the boy could recover, Quint picked him up and dunked him headfirst into a snowbank. By the time Nicky wriggled free, Quint was sprinting toward the corner. Nicky took off after him, screaming like a Comanche warrior. Slipping, sliding, and clawing air, the pair disappeared around the corner.

156

Elizabeth smiled in spite of her chattering teeth. It was good to see Nicky cutting loose and having fun. Their tour of the plaza had gotten off to an oh-so-proper start an hour ago, with all three of them on their best behavior. That was before she caught Quint squarely on the back of the head with a snowball. Ever since, they'd been conducting a roving free-for-all. She had snow down her neck, in her boots, and up her sleeves. Unlike her, however, her two macho companions showed no signs of slowing down.

She was still trudging toward the corner, trying not to whimper from the cold, when Quint and Nicky came back into view. Nicky was holding a steaming paper cup in both hands, concentrating on keeping his feet under him. Quint had a cup in each hand, holding them way out to the side so he wouldn't get splashed if he lost his footing.

"There sure are a lot of statues and things around here." Nicky handed Elizabeth his cup.

"About a million dollars' worth right here in Country Club Plaza." Elizabeth gratefully accepted the cup of hot chocolate. She deftly slurped the partially melted marshmallow off the top.

Quint gave Nicky one of his cups and tucked Elizabeth under his free arm. They stood with their backs to the north wind, sipping the rich concoction. With more snow threatening, there was little pedestrian or street traffic for a Saturday afternoon. They had the plaza almost to themselves.

"Better?" Quint gathered their empty cups and tossed them into a nearby receptacle.

"Much." Elizabeth patted her mittens together. "I can actually feel my fingers now."

"Good. Let's go see old Ben." Quint took her elbow and steered her across the street.

Elizabeth moaned pitifully as they passed a sweet shop—trying to stay warm was using up a lot of energy. But Quint refused to stop, even when she mentioned that the shop sold freshly baked chocolate-chip cookies. As they turned onto Jefferson, he dug out a pocket camera.

"Okay, guys," he said. "It's time for the official picture-taking."

He halted in front of a life-size bronze statue of Benjamin Franklin lounging on a park bench. Elizabeth dutifully brushed snow from the bench and Ben's lap while Nicky dusted off the statesman's spectacles. They settled onto the bench beside him, struck a comically dignified pose, and Quint snapped the shutter.

"My turn!" Nicky sprang off the bench and reached for the camera.

Quint gave him a few quick instructions before sitting on the bench beside Elizabeth. He pulled her snugly against his chest and locked both arms around her. Nicky fumbled awkwardly with the camera. Elizabeth didn't mind the delay. Quint was holding her tighter than he needed to, and it felt good. He leaned down close. She could feel his warm breath on her ear. For the first time in nearly an hour, she forgot about the cold.

Finally the camera shutter clicked. Quint gave her a little hug before he let her go, as if to tell her he might have behaved less circumspectly had they been alone. She dared not meet his gaze for fear that her response to the heady combination of fire and ice was written all over her face.

Quint tucked the camera away. The pale winter sun broke through the clouds for just a moment, casting long shadows across the plaza. As if by silent agreement, they started working their way back in the general direction of the Parkway Arms Hotel. Their boots made soft munching noises in the snow.

"Wait, guys." Elizabeth stopped next to a square of virgin snow covering a parking lot. "One last thing." She stepped gingerly onto the unblemished snow, turned around and plopped onto her back. She began fanning her arms and legs.

"Snow angels!" Quint romped onto the parking lot and flopped onto his back, too, followed by Nicky. Within minutes, the three of them had covered the virgin snow with graceful, winged impressions of their bodies.

"You still have a lot of little boy in you, Quint." Elizabeth brushed snow from his back as Nicky swatted and pounded at hers.

"If you've been paying attention at my seminars, Elizabeth, you know how important it is to let yourself go—to search for and experience the poetry in life."

She stopped brushing, dreamily transfixed by the delicious thought of letting herself go with

Quinton Lawrence. Then she frowned, annoyed that he had found a way to bring his blasted seminars into the afternoon of play. Without thinking, she scooped up a handful of snow and crammed it down the back of his collar.

He bellowed. "No fair!"

"No fair turning fun into a lecture!"

She took off running, making it a dozen yards before her feet flew out from under her. She careered into a snowbank a split second before she was hit by a barrage of snowballs. Nicky had joined the battle, enthusiastically taking Quint's side.

"Traitor!" Elizabeth heaved a gargantuan chunk of snow at Nicky. He looked shocked, then collapsed in hysterical laughter.

"Take no prisoners!" Quint dove on top of her, holding a fistful of snow and tugging at the collar of her coat. She yelped and kicked, squirming under him. He pinned her arms to her sides, snarling.

Suddenly he went very still. Elizabeth stopped struggling and looked up into his dark eyes, mesmerized by their smoldering heat. Her lips parted, waiting for the kiss they both knew was coming. Then they remembered they weren't alone. A look of tremendous pain crossed Quint's face as he rolled off her and sat up in the snow.

Still laughing, Nicky helped them both up. As they walked back toward the hotel, Elizabeth felt almost mellow. She realized she hadn't had a worrisome thought for hours. Not about Jake, nor

ZEBRA HOME SUBSCRIPTION SERVICES, INC.
LUCKY IN LOVE
120 BRIGHTON ROAD
P.O. BOX 5214
CLIFTON, NEW JERSEY 07015-5214

This is your best chance to get "LUCKY IN LOVE". Fill in the coupon and mail this postcard today. (See inside for FREE OFFER.)

# FREE BOOK CERTIFICATE

## LUCKY IN LOVE

Zebra Home Subscription Services, Inc.

P.O. Box 5214    120 Brighton Road Clifton, New Jersey 07015-5214

**YES,** I want my luck to change. Send me my gift of 4 Free LUCKY IN LOVE Romances. Then each month send me the four newest LUCKY IN LOVE novels for my Free 10-day preview. If I decide to keep them, I'll pay the low preferred Home Subscriber's price of just $3.00 each; a total of $12.00. This is a savings of $2.00 off the publisher's cover price. Otherwise, I will return them for full credit. There is no shipping and handling charge. There is no minimum purchase amount and I may cancel this arrangement at any time. Whatever I decide to do, the Free books are mine to keep.

NAME

STREET ADDRESS                                                            APT.

CITY                                            STATE            ZIP CODE

( )
TELEPHONE NUMBER                    SIGNATURE (if under 18, parent or
                                                            guardian must sign.)

Prices and terms subject to change without notice. Orders subject to acceptance by Zebra Home Subscription Services, Inc.

**LILBOB**

Change Your Luck Today. Fill-out And Mail
The FREE BOOK Certificate. We'll Send You
Your Free Gift As Soon As We Receive It!

**"Lucky in Love"—a new concept in contemporary romantic fiction.**

Now you can start to experience the romantic adventures of modern women whose dreams come true with 4 FREE BOOKS (a $14.00 value).

Did you ever dream of winning the jackpot in the lottery or suddenly inheriting a fortune from someone you hardly knew or finding out that the "junk piece" of jewelry your mother gave you is worth over a million dollars? How would your life change?

Now you can share this fantasy, as Zebra, the leading publisher of romantic fiction, proudly brings you LUCKY IN LOVE. You'll go on exciting romantic adventures with heroines who learn that good fortune is not enough until they find true love.

**CHANGE YOUR LUCK WITH 4 FREE BOOKS!**

To start your home subscription to "LUCKY IN LOVE", Zebra will send you the first four novels absolutely FREE. There is absolutely no obligation.

**GET LUCKY WITH FREE HOME DELIVERY AND BIG SAVINGS!**

Each month, we'll send you the latest LUCKY IN LOVE titles for you to preview FREE for 10 days. If you like them, keep them and pay the low Preferred Home Subscribers price of just $3.00 each. That's a savings of $2.00 off the cover price each month. Plus, Free Home Delivery means there are never any ship- ping, handling or other "hidden charges"— so your savings are even greater.

And remember, you can return any shipment within 10 days for full credit, no questions asked. There is no minimum number of books you must buy, and you may cancel your subscription at any time.

EVERYONE CAN BE "LUCKY IN LOVE"
WITH OUR GIFT OF
**4 FREE BOOKS**
(A $14.00 VALUE, NO OBLIGATION)

about Kasper. She wasn't sure if the all-pervasive stress she'd lived with for so long had faded because of her inheritance, or because of the company she was keeping that afternoon.

One thing was for sure, however. As they crossed Ward Parkway, she suddenly couldn't bear the thought of the day petering out into nothing. When Nicky ran ahead across the hotel parking lot, she slowed her pace slightly. Assuming she was having difficulty with her footing, Quint put an arm around her waist.

"I can't tell you how much I've enjoyed this afternoon, Quint."

"So have I. Sometimes, it takes a kid to show us what we're missing."

"This is the second time you've taken me on a memorable outing. I'd like to repay you."

He stopped abruptly. "You don't have to repay me, Elizabeth."

"I was thinking in terms of dinner at my place. Tonight, about eight." It was the only way she could think of to get him alone. "Cornish game hens. Pecan pilaf. Hot buttered rolls."

"Say no more. I'll be there."

"Are you sure you don't have something else planned?"

Quint smiled and brushed the tip of his gloved finger across the cold-reddened end of her nose. "As a matter of fact, I do. But I'll have it canceled in about two shakes."

Elizabeth felt something inside her leap joyfully, followed by a jittery wave of nervous tension. All of a sudden, eight o'clock seemed to loom very near.

As soon as he spotted Nadine Elledge pacing the hotel lobby in apparent anticipation of their return, Quint bussed Elizabeth on the cheek and abandoned ship. Watching Nadine come steaming toward them in a battleship-gray suit, Elizabeth didn't hold Quint's hasty departure against him. The woman wasn't exactly a welcome sight for her, either.

"Nicky, you get upstairs and change clothes right this minute," Nadine said without preamble. "You're soaking wet."

"Yes, ma'am." Nicky hunched his shoulders and headed across the lobby.

Halfway to the other side, he glanced back and winked at Elizabeth. She smothered her smile, because Nadine was looking straight at her. But she was glad that his aunt's uncompromising attitude hadn't spoiled the afternoon for Nicky.

"If I didn't know better, I'd think Mr. Lawrence has taken on my nephew as some sort of personal project." Nadine's tone made it clear she wasn't sure she approved of such a notion.

"I'm sorry we're late, but the time got away from us." Elizabeth glanced at the antique railroad clock over the front desk, and did a double-take as eight o'clock seemed to take a giant step closer.

"The man doesn't know the situation," Nadine

162

sniffed, ignoring Elizabeth's tactful effort to skirt the issue.

"Mr. Lawrence has no intention of becoming a father figure for Nicky, if that's a concern to you." Elizabeth strained to keep her voice even. Where Nicky was concerned, Nadine Elledge had the flexibility of a fence post. "Besides, as soon as his mother marries Byron Thompson, Nicky will have a real father to look after—"

"Miss Mason, Nicky already has a real father!" Nadine snapped, cutting her short. "My poor dear brother, Toddy, was all the father any boy could ask for."

*Unfortunately poor dear Toddy is dead,* Elizabeth wanted to say, taken aback by Nadine's intensity. She realized that the older woman was struggling to blink back tears. Before Elizabeth could decide how to deal with what was, for Nadine, an extraordinary show of emotion, the woman whirled and stalked away, her back as stiff as an iron rod.

At precisely eight o'clock that evening, Quint planted his feet squarely on Elizabeth's immaculate welcome mat and pressed the doorbell. He resisted the urge to fidget with his sport coat and open-collar shirt during the seconds when he knew he was under observation through the peephole in the door. Fidgeting was a sign of insecurity, and he wasn't prepared to admit he had been reduced to that pathetic condition.

163

The door swung open. Elizabeth stood before him in a cloud of pale lavender silk. He had never seen a more enticing jumpsuit and hoped he never did. This one seemed to be all he could handle without doing serious and irreparable damage to his mental health. Quint just stared at her for as long as the rules of polite society would permit. Then he cleared his throat.

"Smells delicious." He sounded hoarse.

Elizabeth did a little curtsy, assuming that he was referring to the mouth-watering aromas wafting from the kitchen. But Quint noticed those only belatedly, after first inhaling the far more bewitching fragrance of her perfume.

She motioned him inside and took his coat. He didn't know whether or not to kiss her. And if he kissed her, should he stick with her forehead? Her cheek? The succulent fruit of her lips? She drifted away before he could solve the dilemma.

Quint moved farther in to her tiny apartment, sparing the efficient cubbyhole of a kitchen barely a glance as he passed the doorway. In the dining area, the glass-topped table had been set for two, with pink dinner napkins precisely fanned on the black-and-white china plates. A silver-and-crystal candle holder held an unlighted pink taper. The table looked fussed-over. He was both flattered and beguiled that Elizabeth had gone to so much trouble for him.

As he stood considering the table, Quint found his attention drawn past the nearby sitting area toward the bed alcove. His mouth went dry as he took in the puffy comforter and a double layer of ruffled pillows mounded against the headboard. His imagination all too readily conjured up an image of Elizabeth lying there—next to him.

Ten minutes after showing Quint into the sitting room, Elizabeth was still rattling around in the kitchen, trying to sound busy. Trying to settle her nerves. Trying to pretend she hadn't noticed the way his attention had fixated on the bed.

Her tiny apartment had suddenly acquired an almost palpable aura of intimacy. She couldn't quite figure out how that had happened. She hadn't intended the dinner table to appear so cozy. And she certainly hadn't intended to leave the bedside lamp shining like an unspoken invitation. Had she?

She shoved the thought from her head and reached into the cabinet for her new crystal wineglasses. She had bought just two last week, telling herself she was being frugal for Jake's sake. She couldn't help wondering now if, even then, she had been influenced more by subliminal visions of a specially-catered dinner for two than by duty. After all, she hadn't exactly been a paragon of thriftiness when she splurged on the jumpsuit.

Elizabeth peeked through the louvered shutters screening the pass-through counter. Her guest had migrated to the foot of the bed, where he stood admiring her new bird-of-paradise comforter. And he was smiling!

She clamped her eyes shut. The wineglasses, the candle, the silk jumpsuit that concealed a froth of lace lingerie. What had she been thinking? Well, whatever it was, Quint was definitely taking it all to heart. She closed the shutter louvers tightly, thinking, *Will you grow up? It isn't as if you've never had a man to dinner before.*

Only, Quint wasn't just a man. He was . . . Quint. And while she wanted this to be a special evening for him, she hadn't yet allowed herself to consider what she wanted or expected for herself.

Her hand shook as she reached into the wine rack under the small butcher block counter—and came up empty. Elizabeth ducked down for a better look, swallowing a sinking feeling.

"Oh, no!"

Quint quickly appeared in the kitchen doorway. "Problem?"

She threw up her hands. "I thought I had wine."

He glanced at the two wineglasses on the counter. Then his gaze locked with hers. He didn't look at the table or the bed. She was pretty sure he was being discreet about that.

"Hey, no problem." He snatched his coat from the entryway closet. "I'll be back in two shakes."

Elizabeth leaned against the refrigerator as Quint hurried out the front door, feeling trapped in a syrupy quagmire of her own making. He was obviously reading too much into her dinner preparations—because she had written too much into them. How was she going to erase the part that was threatening to get her in over her head?

166

*The best part,* a mocking little voice added.

A moment later, the doorbell rang. She started. Quint couldn't be back so soon. He'd barely had time to get down to his car. Elizabeth hurried to the door.

"Nicky!"

The boy stood with his hands jammed in his coat pockets, his cheeks ruddy from the cold. His coat and cap were damp from the powdery snow that had been falling intermittently all evening. She realized he must have walked all the way over from the hotel again.

"What on earth are you doing out on a night like this, Nicky?" Elizabeth winced. She hadn't meant to sound so much like Nadine.

She dragged him into the entryway and cupped her hands over his reddened ears. He stared at the floor, his lips twitching. She didn't have the heart to continue scolding him. "Well, come on in and get warmed up."

He slowed as they passed the dining table, eyeing the candle and the intimate double place setting. She steered him to the settee in the sitting room. Beneath the blush of cold on his cheeks, he seemed to blanch when he noticed her four remaining puppets lined up on the parson's table against the wall.

Nicky hadn't uttered a word since she opened the door. His loose carefree behavior of the afternoon had vanished. He seemed tense, as if he had something bottled up inside. Elizabeth settled close to him, puzzled.

167

"What's on your mind, pal?"

He shrugged.

*Not that again,* she thought, alternately rubbing his icy hands and ears. "Is your aunt upset with you?"

Nicky hesitated, then shook his head.

"How about your mom?"

He shook his head again. Elizabeth struggled to rein in her frustration. At times, getting Nicky to talk required the talent of a Perry Mason.

"I bet you're a little anxious about getting a new stepfather in a few weeks." If that was the case, she was prepared to offer plenty of reassurance. She liked what she had seen of Byron Thompson. He reminded her, in fact, of Grant.

But Nicky offered another shrug and murmured a lukewarm, "Oh, he's okay."

"Just okay?"

"Well, not as nice as Mr. Lawrence." His eyes brightened for a few seconds. Then the light died away, and he sat staring morosely at his lap.

Elizabeth tried to wait him out. When it became obvious the boy wasn't making any headway, though, she gave him a gentle nudge.

"Nicky, I know you didn't trek all the way over here in the cold just to sit. You have something you want to say. But I can't read your mind, so how about at least giving me a hint?"

He cut a sidelong glance at the puppets on the parson's table. Elizabeth held her breath. She had been convinced for days that Nicky knew something about Kasper's disappearance. Was he finally going to open up to her?

She stroked his cheek and said softly, "Does it have to do with Kasper, sweetheart?"

Nicky shifted his gaze to her, his expression suddenly rigid with determination. He took two quick deep breaths and opened his mouth. But nothing came out. He looked at her helplessly for a long moment, then lowered his eyes and shook his head.

She tried not to let her frustration show, but it was hard. Nicky was obviously anxious to tell her something. What was keeping him from spitting it out? Whatever it was, though, she had a feeling she'd find out tonight.

"What the blazes?" Quint pushed open the front door, which Elizabeth had failed to pull to, and strode into the apartment with a sack tucked under one arm.

Elizabeth spun around on the settee. Nicky bolted to his feet, his eyes round, as if he'd been caught red-handed in some heinous crime. Her heart sank. She felt a golden opportunity to find out something about Kasper slip through her fingers.

Nicky sat scrunched down in the leather seat, not enjoying the ride back across the plaza to the hotel in Quint's snazzy sports car. How could he when Quint was so ticked off at him?

He stole a miserable glance at the big man.

Quint was trying to be nice about it, but Nicky could tell he was really steamed about having his evening messed up. If he'd known Quint and Elizabeth had a date tonight, he never would have walked across the plaza to her place.

Nicky chewed his lip, savagely biting back tears. He was too old to bawl. If he did, Quint would think he was nothing but a big crybaby, and that would be really awful. Nicky barely remembered his father, but he liked to think he'd been a lot like Quint. Big. Smart. Fair. A good sport. He liked Quint and Elizabeth a lot. And he wanted them to like him, just like he wanted Byron Thompson to. But it seemed that something always got in the way. That's what made him feel so rotten.

The tire chains chattered across Ward Parkway. Nicky sighed tightly and leaned his head against the backrest. He had almost told Elizabeth his secret tonight. Maybe he should have gone ahead and told both of them. But he couldn't. He just *couldn't*.

Tasting blood in his mouth, Nicky released his lip. There wasn't anyone he could talk to about it. The secret felt like a huge monster sitting on his chest. And it got bigger and meaner every day.


The doorman came striding out, bundled in a heavy, gold-braided topcoat, as the sports car pulled up in front of the hotel. Quint waved him off, leaving the engine and heater running. Through the double doors, he could see Nadine Elledge pacing the brightly lighted lobby.

"Your aunt looks ready to chew nails, sport. You shouldn't worry her this way."

He prodded Nicky's arm. The kid hadn't let out a peep since Quint returned from the wine shop and found him sitting in Elizabeth's apartment.

Nicky nodded, but didn't look toward the hotel entrance. He was sitting on his hands, his shoulders hunched up around his ears, as if he was prepared to park himself there all night. But that wasn't going to happen. Quint wasn't about to let this pint-size glitch wash out his evening with Elizabeth.

The kid's cheek twitched, his eyes glistening in the muted light from the hotel portico. The realization that the boy was nearly in tears caught Quint by surprise.

"Hey, there." Quint reached over and massaged the back of Nicky's neck, the same way he rubbed his own when he was under stress. For a moment, he felt the boy's loneliness and distress almost as if they were his own.

*Isolation is a terrible thing.* The thought startled Quint. The exact opposite had been his credo since college, when he was betrayed by the man he most trusted. His professional life had become a three-ring circus, but he had always guarded his personal privacy with almost monastic zeal. It struck him as bizarre that he should suddenly see his self-imposed isolation as a kind of affliction. He had a feeling that a certain Elizabeth Mason had a great deal to do with that.

"It looks pretty stormy in there, Nick." Quint

peered past the boy toward the lobby, watching Nadine move back and forth like a great gray battleship. "Maybe I should go in with you—see if I can pour some oil on the troubled waters."

Nicky quickly shook his head and grabbed for the door handle. "Aunt Nadine's okay—honest. She's always been real nice to me, even when I mess up and get Mom upset. It's just that she's been sorta . . . watchful lately."

Quint stopped him from getting out. The mere suggestion that he might go in and talk to Nadine seemed to have struck a major nerve with the kid. But Nicky's earnest defense of his aunt was what really got Quint's attention. Nicky painted a completely different picture of her than the harsh one Quint had drawn, based on the things he had heard her say about her nephew. It might be worthwhile, he thought, to take another look at Nadine Elledge, if the opportunity presented itself.

For the moment, however, he focused his attention on Nicky. "I wonder why she's so watchful, Nick."

A tear stole down Nicky's cheek. He tried to turn his face away so Quint wouldn't see it. Quint hesitated, then took him by both shoulders and gently but firmly twisted him around till they faced each other.

"Nick, I once told you that it was all right for a man to be afraid. Remember?" Quint waited for him to nod. "Well, it's also all right for a man to cry. I've been known to do it myself."

172

Nicky's head snapped up. "You?"

"Sure. I'm a sucker for sad movies. And once when I was about your age, there was this infuriating little red-haired girl who always beat me in yo-yo tournaments."

"You cried because you lost?"

"No. Because she moved to another city."

Quint thumbed away the boy's tear. A second one slid down to take its place. Something about that took Quint back farther than he wanted to go. He pulled Nicky into his arms and gave him a rough hug. When he let go, the kid was smiling through his tears. And damned if that didn't bring a lump to Quint's throat.

Quint leaned back, giving them both space. "Nick, do you want to talk about what has you all tied up in knots?"

"No, sir." Nicky took a deep breath and looked him in the eye. "I can't."

"Well, if you change your mind, I'll be around."

Nicky dried his face on his sleeve, clawed his fingers through his damp hair, and got out. Quint rolled down the passenger window and watched him trudge up the walk. At the lobby doors, Nicky turned and looked back at him. Quint gave him an encouraging thumbs-up. Nicky grinned crookedly and returned the gesture. As he entered the lobby alone Quint felt sorry for the kid—and intensely proud of him.

173

# Chapter Ten

Quint held his wineglass to the candlelight. The flame-glow danced through the etched crystal, swirling like minute water sprites in the pale liquid. Elizabeth assumed that some conscious or subliminal whim had driven him to select a wine color to match the taper. But it was nice to imagine that Quint had intuited that pink Zinfandel was her favorite.

"This was an incredible dinner, Elizabeth. Well worth waiting for." He tilted the glass toward her in a silent toast.

She smiled warmly. After a rocky beginning, the evening had smoothed out nicely. Having some time alone while Quint transported Nicky back to the hotel had worked wonders on her nerves. By the time he returned, just as she took the roasted game hens from the oven, she was in complete control again. He'd drawn the cork from the wine bottle, then offered to help put the finishing touches on the avocado-and-grapefruit salad. But Elizabeth had firmly chased him from the kitchen, unwilling to share the hatching of her special culinary presentation even with Quint.

"I'm glad you liked it." Elizabeth shook her head when he reached for the wine bottle again. She dared not risk another glass of zinfandel. Sitting across the table from Quint for the past hour was already going to her head.

Quint refilled his own glass. "It can't have been much fun for you, cooking on your day off."

"Actually, it was. I think I was born to play with food."

"Too bad you don't enjoy eating it. You've barely touched your food."

She shrugged one shoulder, as if being a picky eater was an everyday thing for her. That was easier than confessing that every time he looked at her across the flickering candle, her stomach fluttered and slammed the door on her appetite.

"Hazelnut coffee?" she asked.

Quint nodded, pushed back his chair, and glanced over at the settee. "Mind if we get comfortable?"

Elizabeth's fluttery stomach performed a couple of full-blown somersaults. She recalled the quick hug he'd given her while they sat next to Ben Franklin in the snowy plaza that afternoon—the subtle promise of much more. The room suddenly felt terribly warm.

"Fine," she managed.

She rose to clear the table. But the dishes clattered in her hands, so she left them and retreated to the kitchen to prepare the coffee tray. When she returned, Quint had moved into the sitting area. He took the tray from her and placed it on the low table in front of the settee, then sat down next to her. Their knees touched. Elizabeth was glad she'd had the presence of mind to switch off the nightstand light in the bedroom alcove while he was driving Nicky back to the hotel.

"How do you like your coffee, Quint?"

He smiled, sliding one arm across the back of the settee behind her shoulders. "With breakfast."

His gaze locked onto hers. Her heart skipped a beat, a nervous tremor seizing her as she realized he meant morning-*after* breakfast. His smile widened playfully until the ice broke and Elizabeth broke down and smiled, too. He leaned over and touched his lips circumspectly to her forehead, as if to reassure her it was just a joke.

"Sweet and blond." Quint settled back to watch her pour.

*He's just handed over the controls to you,* she thought, a little surprised. *You can go fast, slow, or come to a dead stop. What do you want it to be?* And then, another thought—how deeply did she dare to wade in with a man who could steal her heart, but who wouldn't stay? At the moment, it didn't seem a question that could stand serious consideration.

Elizabeth added cream and sugar to his coffee, her hand now steady as a rock in spite of her taut nerves. She passed him his cup. They sat quietly for a moment, pretending they were relaxed enough together not to require conversation. She watched Quint's gaze drift around the apartment, snagging briefly on the puppets lining the parson's table against the wall.

After a while, he placed his empty cup on the table. "Do you mind my asking why your great-great-uncle left you such a valuable bequest?"

Elizabeth shook her head. "I've wondered that, too. We'd never met, nor even communicated. But he and Jake used to exchange letters every few years, and Uncle Uri must have known Jake had a granddaughter with at least a passing interest in puppetry. I guess the family line in Europe was petering out, and he had to leave them to someone."

"Have you sold any more of the puppets?" His arm had returned to the back of the settee. He stroked the silken fabric of her collar, creating tiny shock waves of pleasure when his fingertips brushed her neck.

She struggled to keep her thought processes from drowning in a rising tide of physical sensation. "No. I've decided to hold on to the rest of them for the time being." She didn't mention Kasper.

"This is a nice place." He raised his hand in a gesture that took in the apartment. "But I imagine you'll be moving into something bigger now that you have real investment capital."

"How much room does one person need?" She bit her tongue, hoping he didn't take that as a slap at his own sumptuous abode. "Besides, I want to let things settle before making major life-style changes." Changes that she might have to forgo if ransoming Kasper became a real possibility.

"Sensible."

His fingers drifted back to her collar, stroking. She gazed blindly into her untouched coffee. After a minute, Quint took her cup from her hands and placed it on the table. His hand settled on her thigh. She stared at it for a long time, waiting for it to move. It didn't. When she finally looked up, he smiled at her tensely, questioningly.

*Your move.*

She swallowed. Then, before she realized what she was doing, Elizabeth had glided into his arms. He bent and kissed her softly, almost tentatively, on the neck below her ear. She gasped, turning her face to him. His lips found hers and he pulled her against him with a shuddering sigh that spoke more clearly than words of just how much he had been holding himself back. She felt as if she were falling, falling into a warm enveloping cloud. He cradled her head in one hand, the other stroking her back, her hip, her thigh. When it drifted up to her breast, she moaned softly and curled her arms around his neck. He pressed into her, bending her slowly back against the rolled arm of the settee. They remained that way for a long time, sinking deeper and deeper into a kiss that could not sate their increasingly feverish desire.

"Oh, Elizabeth, Elizabeth . . ." He whispered her name over and over, bathing her face in his ragged hot breath. "I want to make love to you."

Every atom of her body screamed *yes!* But when she felt his fingers fumbling with the top button on her jumpsuit, an alarm went off inside her head. *He'll steal your heart, but he won't stay.* Elizabeth stiffened and grabbed his hands.

Quint froze. She could feel his heart pounding, but for an interminable moment, he seemed to stop breathing. She clamped her eyes shut, not wanting to witness the change in his expression. After what seemed like hours, he slowly straightened. The deep settee cushions shifted as he rose.

Elizabeth opened her eyes and watched him move to the French door. He stood looking out over the lights of Country Club Plaza, his hands stiffly at his sides. Tugging at her disheveled attire, she felt an intense surge of embarrassment.

"I'm sorry, Quint."

He turned toward her. "Why?"

179

His voice sounded husky. The flush of passion still gave a ruddy cast to his face. The heat of it smoldered in his dark eyes, and his hair was tousled from her fingers. Elizabeth realized with a dull ache that she still wanted him every bit as much as he wanted her.

"I'm sorry that going to bed with you would be so easy—and so wrong."

"Wrong?" He shook his head, uncomprehending.

"I don't believe in one-night stands, Quint."

"One night . . ." He spread his hands, shaking his head again. "What on earth are you talking about? I thought—"

"Making love isn't making a commitment." She paused, having trouble finding the right words. "In a few weeks, you'll leave on an extended book tour. And then there will be other seminars in countless other cities. You'll go. I'll stay." Perhaps that was even for the best, Elizabeth thought, although she already felt an almost overwhelming emptiness at the prospect.

"I'll come back," he said evenly.

"Not to stay."

He stood very still, as if turning that over in his mind. Finally he nodded. "It's what I do."

She didn't let him see how sharply his last words stung. Elizabeth had hoped he would protest. His ready agreement convinced her that he would never change. And she had no right to make him try.

"That's why I don't want to start something between us that has nowhere to go, Quint."

He startled her with a burst of sardonic laughter. He planted his fists on his hips and looked down at the floor, his lips set in a hard line that might have been a smile.

"I'm sorry," she said again.

"Don't be. I guess it isn't your problem."

She wasn't sure what he meant by that. Because if loving a man she could never have wasn't her problem, Elizabeth couldn't imagine what was.

They seemed to have reached a dead end. When the silence became awkward, Quint moved to the dining table and began stacking dishes. Elizabeth got up and joined him. She had neither expected nor wanted Quint to help with the cleanup. But they couldn't go back to the settee, and in spite of their discomfort, she wasn't ready for him to leave. So, while she scraped plates and pans, he tucked a dish towel into his belt and loaded the dishwasher.

They didn't talk as they worked, and scrupulously avoided brushing against each other in the cramped kitchen. Quint guessed at where items went in the cabinets and refrigerator, and she tried to remember where he put the items so she could find them later. To Elizabeth, the scene had a painfully mocking air of domesticity about it.

When they were almost finished, Quint cleared

his throat. "How do you rate your chances of replacing Marge Holt as catering director when she transfers to the West Coast?"

"I wouldn't bet the baby shoes." Elizabeth smiled wanly, aware that he was trying to meet her on neutral ground. "But I'm not so concerned about that anymore."

He popped the butter dish into the refrigerator and turned to face her. "Why not?"

"I'm having second and third thoughts about starting my own catering business."

Quint looked as if he'd been slapped. Elizabeth hadn't expected him to take it so personally. What possible difference did her future make to him?

"It's the puppets, Quint. Until Uncle Uri left them to me, I guess I'd never realized how much puppetry was in my blood. I don't expect you to understand that."

"It's a damn good thing, because I don't."

Elizabeth turned her back to him, ostensibly to wipe the stove. She could feel his gaze burning into her back across the bridgeless gulf that seemed to have yawned between them since they left the settee. A peak of pleasure, swiftly followed by a deep valley of despair. It had happened the night he took her to the winter festival—the night Kasper was stolen. It was happening again.

"So, you're going to chuck everything you've worked for and spend the rest of your life resting on your inheritance?" Quint's gaze swept up and down her expensive silk jumpsuit. "I have to tell you, Elizabeth, I'm disappointed."

She whirled back toward him, a flash of anger erupting from the depths of her pent-up emotions. "You're disappointed? Well, don't be, Quint. Because I don't intend to *rest* on anything, much less my inheritance. Which, by the way, I'd trade for Kasper right this second."

"You'd what?"

"That's right. If I could find the low-life thief who took him, I'd swap the other four puppets for Kasper and never look back." An image of Jake's old puppet, Juniper—Kasper's near look-alike—brought sudden tears to her eyes. Elizabeth blinked them back, angry at herself for being so maudlin. "But he's gone, and he's probably never coming back."

Elizabeth mentally tripped over the word "he." Was she referring to Kasper? Jake? Juniper. *Quint?* The horrible reality struck her—she meant all of them.

"Come on, Elizabeth. I know the dummy meant a lot to you, but . . ."

Quint took a step toward her, but she held up both hands. She didn't want him to touch her. She was afraid that if he laid a finger on her, she would shatter into a million pieces. Or she would simply surrender herself to him. Either way, she would be destroyed.

"No, Quint. You were right—you don't understand. You go on and on about how important it is for people to commit themselves to taking risks. And all the while, you aren't prepared to risk yourself with a commitment."

His expression hardened. She could tell she had struck him in a soft spot, perhaps even wounded him. The discovery that Quint was that vulnerable came as a jolt.

"I have my reasons," he said quietly.

Elizabeth nodded slowly. "We all do."

They stared at each other across the kitchen. His shoulders sagged. He raked a hand through hair that she had fondled so passionately just a short time ago.

"I'll concede the point, Elizabeth. But please, promise me you won't turn your back on everything you've worked for until you've given it plenty of thought."

"I've already made that promise to myself."

He pulled the dish towel form his belt, folded it carefully, and placed it on the counter. "Well, then . . ."

He was leaving. At no time during the entire evening had Elizabeth prepared herself for this moment. She certainly hadn't expected it to arrive so weighted with tension—and a sense of finality.

"It's been . . . interesting." Quint moved toward the door.

Elizabeth followed. None of the usual inanities seemed to fit. *Hope you enjoyed yourself. Don't rush off. Come back anytime.* She fetched his overcoat from the closet. He tossed it over his arm and opened the apartment door. For a moment, it looked as if he was going to just walk out. But he turned in the doorway and looked down at her.

She felt the heat of his gaze and sensed he wanted to say something. Neither of them spoke. Finally he cupped her cheek in one hand, bent, and lightly brushed his lips over hers. A drop of rain in the desert.

And then he was gone.


"You unmitigated jerk!" Quint jabbed a thumb into the elevator button, then flung his overcoat onto the floor, furious with himself.

Elizabeth claimed she didn't want to start something between them that had nowhere to go. Well, something had already gotten started in a big way. Something that couldn't be turned off or shoved away in a drawer. And he had fumbled it. He paced the cramped confines of the elevator cubicle, alternately rubbing his neck and kicking the walls.

"Who the hell said anything about a one-night stand, for crying out loud?" He certainly hadn't. He was in love with the woman, dammit. As far as he was concerned, that meant a long-term relationship.

*Make that permanent, jerk.* The concept rattled him. Quint had never in his life seriously considered that kind of move. The thought of trusting anyone but himself that much scared the daylights out of him. But he kept thinking about it right up until the elevator doors slid open at the ground floor.

He snatched up his overcoat and strode outside to the parking lot, too worked up to feel the biting cold. He never should have let himself fall for the woman. It was insane.

"But not half as insane as trashing her entire career for a bunch of damned dummies!"

From Quint's point of view, Elizabeth's recently acquired wealth should have nothing to do with her work attitude. After all, since his books took off, he no longer had to lift a finger if he didn't want to. Establishing goals was the important thing. Having spent his entire life searching out new mountains to climb, he couldn't believe Elizabeth would even consider frittering herself away chasing dumb puppet rainbows.

Quint stopped suddenly, frowning, as an unpleasant thought wormed its way to the front of his mind. The thought left a bad taste in his mouth and made him pause for a good hard look inside himself. How much of his disappointment in Elizabeth's life choices, he wondered, was tangled up in his under-the-table wager with George Keen?

* * *

Vivian stood on tiptoe just inside the hallway door, her arms locked around Byron Thompson's neck. Their kiss lingered on and on. She didn't want it to ever end. With a pleasurable moan, Byron lifted her right out of her shoes and turned slowly. She lost herself in the warm, cloudlike haze of their passion dance.

He murmured softly, tickling her ear with his lips. Vivian heard the almost childlike gaiety of her own laughter, knowing this was a magical time for them both. Her knees felt weak. And yet she felt stronger, more whole, than she had in years.

Too soon, Byron released her. She watched him walk away down the corridor, then closed the door and set the lock. She stood there for a moment, eyes closed, smiling dreamily in the afterglow of their kiss.

Life was nothing more than a crazy game of chance, she thought, recalling the day they had first met. She had caught an evening shuttle flight from New York to Boston one damp day last spring, cutting short a weekend shopping trip because of the sudden onslaught of a bad head cold. As luck would have it, her seat was next to a charming gentleman who just happened to be suffering the same affliction. By the time the flight touched down at Logan, their mutual misery was hardly worth noting. They were too busy trying to deny to themselves that there really was such a thing as love at first sight. As luck would also have it, they both were wrong.

With a heavy sigh, Vivian turned. "Oh, Nadie!" She started. "Are you still up?"

Vivian's former sister-in-law stood across the room, tugging the belt of her quilted robe tighter around her thickened waist. She wondered with a tiny ripple of annoyance how long Nadine had been watching her. With a shrug, she cast the thought aside, unwilling to let anything spoil her evening.

Scooping up her sling-back pumps, Vivian performed a graceful pirouette, her shoes dangling from one finger. She suspected that she didn't have a trace of lipstick left and that the residue of a deep blush still warmed her shoulders and cheeks. She must be a sight to behold, she thought. But she didn't care as she seemed to float across the sitting room of their suite. Being in love made her feel fifteen years younger.

Nadine followed her into her room, still tugging at the belt to her robe. Vivian unzipped her strapless evening dress, letting the velvet-trimmed garment fall to the floor. She stepped out of it and kept walking toward the dresser. As she removed her earrings and bracelets, she smiled happily at Nadine's reflection in the tall dresser mirror.

Vivian's smile changed into a quizzical frown. She turned and looked at Nadine. "Is something wrong?"

Nadine settled stiffly onto the foot of Vivian's bed and patted the mattress beside her. "Come and sit, Vivian. We need to have a talk."

Worried, Vivian crawled onto the bed in her lace slip and sat back on her heels. She still had the figure of a girl, small and firm of hip and breast—as Byron continually reminded her. But the delicate, almost fragile appearance of her body was deceptive. She possessed an inner strength that sometimes surprised even her. She felt that kick in as she studied Nadine's troubled expression.

"It's Nicky, Vivian." Nadine paused, her fingers plucking nervously at the bedspread.

"I know what you're going to say." Vivian reached over and pressed Nadine's arm. "Nicky hasn't warmed up to Byron the way we'd hoped. But he will, Nadie. You'll see. Byron will be a good father to him."

A muscle twitched in Nadine's cheek. She wasn't wearing makeup. Her face looked pale and drawn in the lamp light. Vivian's worry deepened. She had been so caught up in Byron she had failed to notice that Nadine seemed to have visibly aged these past weeks.

"Vivian, I'm not sure Byron—"

"It's been so long, Nadie," Vivian interrupted, anxious to assuage the older woman's concern. "I didn't think I could ever feel this way again. But Byron is special."

"So was Toddy."

Vivian tensed, then sighed. Nadine couldn't let a mention of Byron go by without bringing in Todd. For once, however, Vivian was glad the subject had been broached. "I know. Todd wasn't just one in a million. He was totally unique in the whole world. That's why it's been so difficult to go on these past years."

As Nadine continued to pluck at the bedspread, Vivian realized she hadn't talked freely about Todd since his death. It hurt both of them. But Vivian looked at it as a necessary, healing pain. She gathered up her courage and continued.

"I never told you, Nadie, but I made a vow to Todd after Nicky was born."

"Vow?"

"Yes. He made me promise to remarry if anything every happened to him." Vivian smiled sadly. "Of course, we never dreamed that anything would. We were both so young and . . . immortal. And then he was suddenly gone, and I was left with that stupid promise."

Tears filled Nadine's eyes. She blinked them back and put her arms around Vivian. They leaned on each other for a moment, sharing the pain of memory and loss.

Then Vivian straightened. "Sometimes I think the fiasco with that other engagement was a blessing in disguise."

"How can you say that?" Nadine drew back, clearly appalled. "After what Nicky did!"

"Well, I haven't forgotten *that*." Vivian made it sound like the understatement of all time. "Still, the man was so awfully stuffy. And he would have made a terrible father to Nicky. I must have been blind not to have seen that then."

"Yes—he wasn't at all like Toddy."

"Neither is Byron, Nadie. That's just it—he's good and sweet and kind, but different. I love him, heart and soul. This is the first time I've really wanted to keep my promise to Todd." Vivian clasped Nadine's hands in both of hers, her eyes shining. "Nadie, he's the first man I know—*I know*—Todd would approve of. It's almost as if Byron is the answer to a prayer—Todd's prayer for Nicky and me."

Nadine sat perfectly still, staring into the middle distance that separated them. Her pale face suddenly looked waxen. Little hitching sounds came from her parted lips, as if she were unable to draw a breath. After a while, she slowly shook her head, as if she had just glimpsed something too awful to bear.

## Chapter Eleven

Just before noon on Wednesday, Quint rushed from the Royal Ballroom a few strides ahead of a wave of excited morning-seminar participants. He had fifteen minutes in which to track down Elizabeth. This time, he was determined to bag his quarry, even if he had to have her paged over the hotel's emergency public-address system.

Quint had caught only fleeting glimpses of her since he'd left her place Saturday night. Elizabeth had been charging around the hotel at a dead run all week, engrossed in her catering projects to the exclusion of all else. Last weekend, he'd had the audacity to criticize her apparently waning commitment to her work. But she'd been a whirling dervish of activity ever since. He was beginning to suspect he'd created a monster.

"Damn right, you did," he muttered. The monster was named desire, and it was eating him alive.

He stalked down a service corridor near the hotel kitchens and was about to hang a right toward her office when he heard a familiar voice.

Quint stopped, listening. Backing up a few paces, he glanced through a partially open door into a small employee lounge.

Elizabeth stood on a chair behind a long utility table littered with scraps of bright cloth. He watched her walk what appeared to be a brand-new marionette slowly down the length of the table, her hands moving the control strings with the nimble grace of a pianist.

"Rod puppets have become very popular lately, because of Jim Henson's Muppets," she said. "But I learned puppetry with these string marionettes. My grandfather had one that looked almost exactly like Kasper. His name was Juniper."

Assuming she wasn't talking to herself, Quint eased the door open wider to check out her audience. Nicky stood on a chair at the end of the table, awkwardly trying to mirror Elizabeth's movements with another puppet. Quint smiled. He had noticed the boy slipping out of the seminar room about an hour ago.

Elizabeth glanced up and saw Quint leaning against the door frame. She hesitated on the brink of a smile, then seemed to think better of it. "Hello, Quint. I'm giving Nicky a quick lesson in puppetry."

"I can see that. You handle the thing like an expert."

She accepted the compliment with a shrug. "I am an expert, albeit a slightly rusty one. Did you need something?"

He shook his head, trying to look casual, as if he had all the time in the world. "I just thought you might like to know the luncheons are still drawing raves. I'm beginning to wonder if people are showing up to hear my motivational spiels or to see what you're going to come up with next."

She looked pleased, and that pleased Quint. He had a lot of other things he wanted to say to her — but not in front of Nicky.

Elizabeth glanced around at empty packing boxes stacked against the wall almost to the ceiling. They all bore orange Puppet Factory labels. Then she winked conspiratorially at Nicky and sent the puppet into a rambunctious little jig. "If you liked the other luncheon themes, Quint, wait until you see today's." She grinned. "You ain't seen nothin' yet."

He raised a brow, but Elizabeth didn't elaborate. Clearly intending the day's offering to be a surprise, she returned to putting the puppet through its paces for Nicky. As far as Quint could see, the siren song of puppetry was beckoning to her strongly — and Nicky appeared to have become an eager disciple. Quint found himself feeling absurdly jealous.

"Have you heard anything from the police about Kasper?" Quint hoped to establish a beachhead between the two.

"Nope," Nicky answered for her. Neither of them looked up.

Quint glanced at his watch and rubbed the

back of his neck. He was running out of time before the day's luncheon began, and so far he hadn't accomplished a damn thing. He couldn't even tell for sure if Elizabeth was still upset about Saturday evening. But he figured she must be, because *he* still was. As long as Nicky was sitting there, however, Quint didn't know what he could do about it.

"Ahem."

He glanced over his shoulder. Nadine Elledge stood close behind him, lips pursed like a prune, waiting to get past. Quint stepped aside, wondering irritably if he could muster up a brass band to march through the room, as well.

Nadine halted abruptly just inside the door as she spotted Nicky. Instead of sending the boy packing as Quint had expected her to, she turned to Elizabeth. "Miss Mason, we have a problem with the napkin colors. Vivian has bought a new dress for the prenups, so orchid simply will not do."

Quint shifted his feet impatiently while Nadine went on at length about cool colors versus warm ones. There was something about the brittle tone she used toward Elizabeth and the way she kept shooting glances at Nicky that set his teeth on edge. After a couple of minutes, Quint finally figured out what it was. Damned if Nadine didn't seem to be jealous of Elizabeth.

*Hell's bells,* he thought in exasperation, and ducked out the door.

An hour later, Elizabeth sat flipping through color charts at her desk, trying hard to concentrate. Vivian Elledge's prenuptial bash was only nine days down the road, and there were still a million loose ends to nail down.

Since her tense parting with Quint on Saturday evening, she had thrown herself into her work with a vengeance. That was what he wanted, and that was what he was going to get. Not until he stopped by the lounge while she was giving Nicky a puppet lesson, however, had Elizabeth finally allowed herself to consider what *she* wanted.

The sad truth was that what she wanted was turning into a triple-decker impossible dream. She wanted Jake and Kasper and Quint. No amount of money could buy any one of the three, with the possible exception of Kasper, and that was looking more remote with each passing day. Without them, she felt like an emotional quadraplegic. She had no idea how, or even if, she could ever learn to exist without them.

With a sigh, she reached for a sketch of two graceful ice flamingos that would grace the main buffet table at the Elledge-Thompson prenup. She made a quick note to ask the sculptor if he could tint the ice pink.

"Very, *very* funny."

Elizabeth glanced up, astonished, as Quint

stormed into her office clutching a giant, four-foot tall marionette by the strings. He flung the loose-limbed puppet onto a chair. It collapsed, arms and legs akimbo, looking like a wide-eyed, leering wino in patched coveralls. Quint planted his fists on his hips and glared murderously at her.

"That's a loaner from the Puppet Factory, Quint. It's one of those break-it-and-it's-yours deals."

"Yeah? Well, you're lucky I didn't burn the damned thing."

She leaned back, trying to get a grip on the situation. "Do you mind telling me what your problem is?"

"Certainly. My problem is today's luncheon theme. Let's just say it clashed with the topic of my speech—as you knew it would."

"Clashed? I spent half the night basting patches on the puppets' clothes, turning them into little bums. How could they clash with your speech?" Elizabeth dug through the files on her desk and came up with his list of scheduled topics. " 'Basic Bootstraps: Rising from the Bottom by Pulling Your Own Strings.' It was a perfect match."

The harsh line of his lips twitched. "I changed the topic last week."

"Oh? You didn't mention it to me."

His scowl faltered as his gaze darted away from her. "I didn't?"

"Not a peep. So, what did you change it to?"

Quint rubbed the back of his neck and shifted uncomfortably. Finally he mumbled, " 'The Value of Self-Image.' "

Elizabeth glanced at the goofy-faced puppet with patches on his elbows and knees. "Well, yes. I can see your point. I'll bet the poor-boy sandwiches didn't go over so well, either."

"As a matter of fact, everyone thought they were hilarious."

*Everyone but Quint.*

"Well, yes. I can see . . ." She was having trouble keeping a straight face. And it was clear Quint did not like being laughed at. "Anyway, I'm sure you got control of your audience once everyone settled down."

He barked a humorless laugh. "Oh, no. We kept them in stitches the whole time, we did, Elizabeth. Especially when I got to the part about dressing for success. They damn near laughed me off the dais over that one."

Quint dug into his pocket and produced a fistful of wadded bills and loose coins. He slapped them onto the desk blotter in front of her.

Elizabeth corralled a couple of quarters before they rolled off onto the floor. "What's this?"

"Call it a gratuity. Forty-six bucks and change. They took up a collection for me—even the waiters chipped in. Since the damned derelict dummies were your idea, I figure the proceeds belong to you."

Elizabeth dug her fingernails into her palms under the desk, trying to kill a smirk with pain. Quinton Lawrence locked in a roomful of out-of-control people for nearly an hour. And she had missed it.

"You witch. You're trying not to smile."

She glanced up sheepishly. "How am I doing?"

He narrowed his eyes threateningly. But some of the tension had left his body. When her grin finally broke free, he sighed and shook his head, looking deflated.

"At least, everyone—almost everyone—had a good time," he said. "Who knows? Maybe they thought the joke was intentional."

She pointed a finger at him. "Maybe it should have been."

Quint considered that for a moment. Then he nodded and almost smiled. "Maybe you're right. An occasional change of pace keeps the mind sharp. But I still think you ought to stick with catering and deep-six this puppet mania of yours."

Elizabeth sidestepped his suggestion, no longer sure that the choice was hers. Certainly it never had been his. "So, you aren't going to lynch me at sunset?"

From the way his gaze locked briefly with hers before sliding down over her body, she sensed that he was thinking of far less violent things to do with her. A flash of heat sizzled through her.

"Speaking of sunset, Elizabeth, what are you doing after work?"

"Visiting Jake."

"Ah, yes. Jake."

He shoved his hands into his pockets and stared down at the floor for a moment. Was he recalling his own disquieting visit with her grandfather? Elizabeth wasn't sure.

"Tell you what," he said. "I'll go to the nursing home with you this evening if you'll go out with me tomorrow night."

Elizabeth couldn't conceal her surprise. She hadn't invited him to go along, and part of her wasn't certain she wanted him to. What was the use of keeping up the pretense that they could mean something to each other when Quint would be flying out of her life in a few weeks? But a greater part of her leapt at the chance to steal every moment in his company that she could, while she could.

"Sounds like a winner to me," she said.

His smile momentarily dispelled Elizabeth's fear that she had made a foolish decision. When she was again alone in her office a few minutes later, however, she had a sick feeling she'd just taken a giant step toward disaster.

That evening, Elizabeth hurriedly showered and slipped into sleek wool stirrup pants, a ski sweater, and supple leather boots. She was running late, thanks to a last-minute meeting of catering staff Marge Holt had called.

Elizabeth also still harbored doubts as to the wisdom of continuing to see Quint socially. She kept having frightening visions of herself being swept toward the brink of a powerful thundering waterfall. Even so, she paused to dab on an expensive new perfume that she had purchased at one of the hotel shops before heading home.

She fingered the cut-glass perfume atomizer. She still hadn't grown accustomed to such extravagances. In a way, she hoped she never did. Wealth was like love—it was the thrill that made it worthwhile.

And the security, she thought. Wealth provided material security. Love provided security for the heart. Unless you were in love with a man who wouldn't stay.

"Your life is turning into one big contradiction," she muttered.

Quinton Lawrence could make her blood boil in ways she had never dreamed possible. But he wasn't all-powerful. He had his soft underbelly, just like everyone else. In that respect, at least, they were equals. On the other side of the coin, Elizabeth was becoming increasingly aware of her own inner strengths. She couldn't stand idly by and permit Quint or anyone else to manipulate her like a puppet.

She grabbed her belted cape from the closet, and was hurrying toward the door, when she noticed the blinking green light on her telephone message machine. With a groan, she went around the bed and rewound the tape. As she pushed the play button, she mentally crossed her fingers, hoping it wasn't Marge Holt.

The tape hissed. For a few seconds, she thought the caller had decided not to leave a message.

"Hello, Elizabeth."

She leaned closer, straining to hear the oddly high-pitched, muffled voice.

"In case you're wondering about Kasper . . . the dummy is safe."

Elizabeth sucked in her breath and nearly knocked the machine off the bedside table in her haste to turn up the volume.

"I'll call again later to let you know how you can get it back."

*Ransom,* she thought, feeling as if the wind had been forcibly driven from her lungs.

"If you don't believe I have Kasper, I'll be glad to send you one of his ears."

She clapped a hand over her mouth, her eyes wide with horror at the gruesome offer. She had a hideous, albeit ludicrous, image of unwrapping a blood-soaked handkerchief to reveal Kasper's detached ear.

The line clicked. Seconds later, the machine beeped and shut itself off. Elizabeth stared at it as if it were a venomous snake. Her joy at learning that she might recover Kasper after all had come and gone in the blink of an eye. In its place, a terrible thought nearly drove her to her knees. Because, to get Kasper back, she might have to sell the other puppets and thereby forfeit Jake's security—and that she could not do.

"Elizabeth, you've informed the police of the thief's message. That's all you can do for now. It won't help matters if you give yourself a nervous breakdown before they've had a chance to check out the tape."

"I'm not giving myself anything." Elizabeth stepped out into the icy wind and slammed the car door.

Quint got out the other side and looked at her across the low roof of the sports car. She looked back at him. Then she opened the door and closed it again, gently this time.

"Is that better?"

"Not really." He pulled his collar up around his ears and came around to her side. "You're better off letting those hostile emotions out."

She lifted her eyes to the star-studded winter sky and trudged off across the parking lot toward the nursing-home entrance. Quint got there half a stride ahead of her and pulled open the heavy glass door. She had already opened her belted cape by the time they entered the heated vestibule.

Quint whistled softly through his teeth as she

shrugged out of the cape. His gaze slid down over her ski sweater and thigh-hugging stirrup pants. She flushed lightly, suddenly feeling naked. The thought of standing nude in front of Quint drove the blush still deeper.

*Don't be such a giddy little twit, Elizabeth,* she thought. *After what you shelled out for the outfit, you'd have been disappointed if it hadn't gotten his attention!*

"Did you say the voice on your recorder sounded disguised?" he asked, still fondling her with his gaze.

"That's right. It could have been a woman."

"Or a boy?"

Elizabeth had been temporarily distracted by the pleasurably flattering strokes of his gaze. Now her ragged nerves flared anew. "Aren't you jumping to conclusions, pointing the finger at Nicky?" Her voice rasped with badly suppressed anger.

"I'm not pointing the finger at anyone, Elizabeth. But he must be on your mind, or you wouldn't have been so quick to infer that I had."

Elizabeth suddenly felt as if a rug had been jerked from under her. Quint was right. He hadn't mentioned Nicky, so why had she so readily assumed he had? She'd already concluded that the voice on the tape couldn't have been the boy's. He would never have called Kasper a "dummy."

She shook her head, tears of remorse stinging

her eyes. This seemed to be her day for suffering the exquisite tortures of guilt.

"Oh, hell, Elizabeth. I didn't mean to make you cry."

Quint swept her into his arms and kissed her. Elizabeth's lips parted in surprise. The kiss deepened and warmed. The anguish flowed out of her mind, replaced by a kaleidoscope of bright swirling colors. When he finally released her, Elizabeth wobbled unsteadily on rubbery knees.

"Quint . . . you caught me by surprise."

He smiled and took a ragged breath. "Me, too. Should I apologize?"

"I'm not sure." She half closed her eyes, her mind still drifting in a sensual fog. "Maybe you should do it again, so I can make up my mind."

He hesitated. "You have no idea how much I want to. But in case you haven't noticed, we're being watched."

"What!"

Quint moved so she could see past him through the inner glass door of the vestibule. Several elderly residents of the nursing home sat in plastic chairs in front of the lobby television set. But they weren't watching the screen. Instead, their bespectacled eyes were all focused on the little scene in the vestibule. Elizabeth winced in embarrassment as a frail old woman in fuzzy slippers waved, then gave her a thumbs-up.

* * *

Whistling under his breath, a burly attendant in white pants and T-shirt took one last careful swipe at Jake's bony jaw before dropping the safety razor into a pan of water. Elizabeth waited at the doorway until he had toweled her grandfather's face and gathered up the shaving equipment.

"I'm running a tad late," the man chuckled as she came into the room, trailed by Quint. "But we're all spiffed up for company now. Right, Jake?"

Jake stared unresponsively at the ceiling. When the attendant was gone, Elizabeth moved closer and took her grandfather's hand. Quint wandered around the room for a moment, idly humming snatches of the blues tune the attendant had been whistling. He eventually stopped at the foot of the bed, drumming his fingers on the metal bed frame.

Elizabeth gasped as Jake's dull eyes shifted in Quint's direction. She didn't have the nerve to tell Quint that finger-drumming had been a habit of her father's. He seemed to figure that out for himself, however. The drumming halted abruptly, and he crammed both hands into his pockets.

Jake's spindly legs stirred beneath the blanket. He made a harsh croaking sound in his throat. Then, "Is Kasper okay?"

Quint's hands shot out of his pockets as Elizabeth sat down sharply in a chair next to the bed. She gaped at her grandfather, then at Quint.

That was the first coherent sentence she had heard Jake utter since his stroke, and he had said it to Quint.

"Sure, Jake." Quint nodded, barely missing a beat. "Kasper's just dandy."

Elizabeth hung on to Jake's hand, too astonished to speak. Quint glanced at her as he moved around to the opposite side of the bed. Jake's eyes seemed to clear as they followed him. For just a moment, the two men gazed into each other's faces. At last, Jake sighed. He murmured something incoherent, and his parchmentlike eyelids fluttered closed.

Elizabeth peered intently at her grandfather, studying each craggy line and contour. Had his fleeting venture into awareness been a fluke? Or had Quint—and Kasper—really triggered something?

"Too bad you can't bring the puppet in to show him." Quint said softly, voicing her own thoughts. "Seeing Kasper might jumpstart his mental faculties. He needs something."

Quint was right—Kasper might be just the trick to bring Jake back to her. But there was a big catch. She might not be able to ransom Kasper without forsaking Jake's security, and that, of course, was out of the question.

Elizabeth swallowed convulsively. She felt as if she were balanced on a shaky rope bridge over a mile-deep crevasse.

* * *

The next morning, Quint awoke with Kasper on his mind — and couldn't shake it. Trying to switch his thoughts to Elizabeth or even to his work only made the crazy "possession" worse. The blasted dummy spoiled his concentration during his regular prebreakfast workout, then survived a blistering shower. By that time, he was in no mood to eat. Skipping breakfast altogether, he went straight to the hotel.

Unfortunately so did Kasper. Halfway through the morning seminar, Quint looked down at Nicky Elledge seated attentively on the front row and finally figured out what he had to do to exorcise the damned wooden demon. The opportunity came shortly after the session ended, as he cornered Nicky at the bubble-gum machine down the hallway from the Royal Ballroom.

"Hi, sport." Quint reached casually over the boy's shoulder and poked a coin into the slot. Nicky twisted the handle and handed him a green jawbreaker. Quint popped it into his mouth. "Got a minute?"

"Sure, Mr. Lawrence." Nicky looked up eagerly.

Quint motioned for him to follow. Seconds later, they were in a quiet side corridor across from a row of plush telephone booths with etched-glass doors, velvet-cushioned seats and miniature crystal chandeliers. Quint leaned back against the wall and folded his arms across his chest, wishing he had a clue as to how to begin.

"You're a smart kid, Nick." *To get the truth, you should first speak the truth.* "I like you."

Nicky beamed. "Thank you, sir."

"It's also been brought to my attention that you don't exactly have a sterling reputation when it comes to honesty." Quint watched the kid's head duck as if he had been punched. The reaction disturbed him. "I like to think I have a good eye for reading people. And the way I read you, I figure you're taking a bum rap. If you're a thief, I'm Michael Jordan."

"Huh?" Nicky looked up and blinked.

"I'm being straight with you, Nick. Are you man enough to be straight with me?"

"Yes, sir!"

"Good." Quint uncrossed his arms and placed his hands on Nicky's narrow shoulders. "Someone took Kasper. Correct?"

Nicky nodded, wincing slightly when the subject of the stolen puppet arose.

Quint looked hard into his eyes. "Well, someone left a message on Elizabeth's answering machine, claiming to know where Kasper is. Do you know who did that?"

"I didn't steal Kasper, Mr. Lawrence."

"That wasn't my question."

Someone came down the corridor and entered one of the phone booths. Quint didn't shift his gaze from Nicky's pale eyes. *You know who took the dummy,* he thought. *Sure as I'm stand-*

*ing here, you know. I can see it in your eyes.*

"I don't know anything about a message, Mr. Lawrence. I swear."

"I believe you, son," Quint said truthfully.

"Please, Mr. Lawrence, don't mention this to my mom or to Mr. Thompson! It'll just mess things up."

Quint was taken aback by Nicky's obvious anguish. "Sure, Nick. This is just between you and me." He paused, then added, "Is there anything you'd like to tell me?"

For a moment, the poor kid looked as if he were being torn in half. He took a couple of deep breaths, his face bunching from a violent inner conflict. When he finally let out the last breath in a whoosh and shook his head, Quint couldn't bring himself to hold it against him. He just wished the kid would open up so someone could help him.

He patted Nicky's shoulder. "Okay, sport. We'll let it go for now."

"Yes, sir." Nicky looked immensely relieved.

"Come on. We can't keep the luncheon crowd waiting."

The boy grinned suddenly. "What's the topic?"

"Don't hold your breath, pal. I'm not going to stand up there and make a damned fool of myself today. The topic is 'Word Power.' Elizabeth has planned a back-to-school theme with an upscale lunch-box menu. No surprises, this time. I checked."

* * *

Late that evening, Elizabeth whirled lightly on her toes as she slipped out of her cloak in the foyer of Quint's condo. He applauded, grinning, then draped their outerwear over a chair near the door.

"As a child, I dreamed of being a figure skater, Quint." She executed another graceful maneuver, still caught up in the ice show they had seen after dinner.

"What stopped you? You certainly have the figure for it."

Elizabeth smiled, her skin warmed by the ravenous look he gave her. "I don't know. Maybe I was afraid to reach for a star that high."

Quint's smile died. He suddenly looked serious.

She plucked at the soft fabric of her dress, dismayed that her statement had apparently struck such a sour note with him. "Anyway, I suspect it was the cute little outfits the skaters wore that really grabbed my imagination. I have a deep dark confession to make—I've been a closet clothes freak all my life."

"Well, I'm glad you've come out of the closet at last." Quint gazed into her eyes as he traced a finger along the neckline of her short, clinging jersey dress, from the shoulder to her cleavage to the other shoulder. Elizabeth shivered. He noticed, and repeated the action in the opposite direction.

Her mouth went dry. If he had pulled her into his arms right then, she would have melted. Instead, he took her hand and led her down the hallway past the living room. Elizabeth tensed. She had agreed to come up to his place for a nightcap. The possibility that a drink could lead to something else added to the electricity that had been building between them all evening. But surely Quint wouldn't be so insensitive as to try to march her straight to his bed, would he? A sudden chill of disappointment shot through her.

Elizabeth was trying to decide how to extricate herself from the situation without repeating the painfully awkward scene in her apartment when, just short of the pool room, he steered her through a doorway and switched on the light. Instead of being confronted by Quint's bed, however, she found herself in a paneled room filled with an impressive array of conventional and high-tech exercise equipment.

"I have something to show you before we have that drink." He sounded serious.

Elizabeth paused at a bench press. A bar with enormous lead weights on each end rested on a rack above one end of the bench. "You actually lift that?"

Quint glanced at the weights and nodded distractedly, as if they were of no significance. He continued on to the far wall, bare except for a box frame containing a chrome-plated whistle mounted on red velvet. They stood there for a while just staring at the whistle. Judging by Quint's taut jaw, she suspected that the whistle was some sort of icon. But why?

"I, uh, keep it to remind me . . ." He spoke hesitantly, straining for the words.

Her curiosity sat up and took notice. But she remained silent, sensing that he was moving out onto unstable ground. He gripped her hand tightly.

"It belonged to my high-school football coach—the first man I ever trusted." Quint tilted his head, frowning, as if listening to his own past. "I thought Coach hung the moon. Right up until he betrayed me."

Elizabeth surveyed Quint's expression. "And now you hate him?"

"Hate?" He looked startled. "No, not at all. In a way, I guess you could say, by selling me down the river, he shaped the rest of my life. Instead of hanging around scratching the bottom of some barrel for a living, like a lot of other ex-jocks, I grabbed for the gold ring. Coach lit one hell of a fire under my tail, and I guess it's still burning."

"How did he do that?" Quint was beating around the bush. Now that her curiosity was aroused, Elizabeth was anxious to hear the rest of it.

"I was dumb as a brick back then." He raised a silencing hand when she started to speak. "No—not that kind of dumb. I got good grades

213

in school. But my old man was an alcoholic, the sort who sits around in his skivvies all day and knocks the stuffing out of his family when the Bears get beaten by a cellar team. My mother got fed up and left us when I was about Nicky's age. After that, I spent so much time trying to hide the drunk from the other kids that I didn't have much social life. So I didn't develop a lot of street smarts. I was naive."

Elizabeth stood transfixed by the magnitude of her misconceptions, aware of how difficult it was for him to reveal them to her. Quint seemed so at ease with the trappings of wealth. She had taken it for granted that he had come from the kind of background that gave a person a leg up on the competition. Discovering that he was a self-made man in every sense of the word made her question her sense of perspective.

"I was a good ball player in high school," he went on. "Not great, but good enough to be scouted by a top university. The recruiter offered me a cash bonus if I signed. Nothing spectacular, but I was hungry enough to grab at anything. Coach knew about the bonus—he even gave his tacit approval. And he sure as hell didn't say anything about it being illegal."

"But he must have known."

"Sure, he did. But I didn't find out until the university athletic program got caught up in an NCAA investigation during my sophomore year. By then, Coach had gone on to become head knocker at the state university—which just happened to be our major rival. His testimony at the hearings caused my team to be put on probation. I lost eligibility and had to transfer to a smaller school."

"But that didn't scuttle your future in pro football."

Quint smiled crookedly. "Being nominated for the Heisman Trophy my senior year didn't hurt."

"I didn't know about that."

"Join the rest of the world population. I placed a solid last in the balloting. But I was happy as a pup in a bed of daisies, because the Kansas City Chiefs picked me up as a last-round draft choice." He laughed dryly. "And as they say, the rest is history."

"From humble beginnings . . ."

"True." He put his arm around her shoulders and pulled her close. "I just wanted you to see that stars are never too high, never too far away. And you don't always have to place first in order to win. Not if you're in for the long haul."

Elizabeth slipped her arm around his waist, still adjusting to her new vision of Quinton Lawrence. With it came a new understanding of his reluctance to risk a personal relationship.

She grinned ruefully. "Do you think it's too late for me to check into skating lessons?"

"That's the spirit." Quint gave her a squeeze, then glanced at his watch. "Before we have that drink, I have to field a fifteen-minute phone interview from a radio talk show in San Francisco. Do you mind?"

In the living room, Quint settled her on a deep-cushioned couch and disappeared into the adjoining study. Elizabeth sat eyeing the plush peach-and-white oriental rug and the tasteful paintings on the dark-paneled walls. The room bore the too-perfect mark of a professional decorator.

Elizabeth had an urge to kick off her shoes and toss the meticulously arranged accent pillows off the couch onto the floor. When she imagined stretching out there on the plush rug to await Quint's return, the spacious room suddenly felt close and overheated. She got up, crossed to the doors opening onto the broad covered balcony, and let herself outside.

An icy wind buffeted the twelfth-floor balcony. She stood at the waist-high concrete railing, hugging herself and breathing in the cold night air. A crescent of moon hung against the velvet black of the sky. Below, the city lay before her in a glittering field of lights that spread all the way to the river and beyond. *As far as you care to reach*, she thought. Her teeth chattered from the cold. Or, possibly, from the dream.

Some time later—long enough for the cold to have chilled her more than she'd realized—the door opened and closed behind her. A suit coat slid around her shoulders, one that smelled of Quint and held his warmth. Elizabeth pulled it snugly against her, still gazing out at the city.

"You have an incredible view, Quint."

He murmured agreement and handed her a snifter of brandy. "See that white building on the other side of the plaza?" Quint pointed to her apartment house. "That's where my girl lives."

Elizabeth nearly dropped her glass. *My girl.* She raised the snifter to her lips and took a slow sip of the cognac to steady her nerves. The liquid coursed down her throat and formed a warm puddle in her stomach. But when he stepped up close behind and wrapped his arms around her, pulling her back against his broad chest, she knew the brandy wouldn't be enough.

She slipped a hand from the cozy depths of his coat and touched his sleeve. The muscles in his arm twitched. He would be chilled clear through soon, as she had been. She worried about that, but still couldn't bring herself to suggest they go inside. She wanted to stay there in his arms forever, with the city at her feet.

*My girl.*

# Chapter Twelve

"We shouldn't have stayed out there so long." Quint led Elizabeth over to the recessed bar in the living room. "You're shivering."

She stood close to him as he picked up a crystal decanter and poured more dark cognac into their snifters. She couldn't quite bring herself to tell him that her shivering wasn't entirely from the cold. She watched him replace the stopper in the decanter, every movement seemingly in slow motion. Since the moment he'd put his arms around her out on the balcony, time seemed to have slipped into a different dimension.

He left the glasses on the marble-topped bar and curled his arms around her again. Elizabeth nestled against him, closing her eyes as he stroked her windblown hair. With her cheek pressed to his chest, she felt his heartbeat quicken. His coat fell to the floor. Quint's big hands roamed her bare shoulders, driving the chill from her flesh.

Elizabeth drew back slightly from his chest, and his lips settled warmly over hers. She lost herself in the gentle, lingering kiss. When he finally held her away from him to gaze down into her eyes, she felt dizzy.

"My sweet Elizabeth," he whispered, slowly tracing the contours of her face with his fingertips. "I love you so much."

Her eyes suddenly widened. He saw the shock on her face and cocked his head. "Didn't you know that?"

She couldn't move. She couldn't speak. She could barely breathe.

"I guess not," Quint answered himself. "My fault, precious. I haven't had a lot of practice at falling in love."

"Or staying," she managed.

He considered that for a moment, then nodded. "As I said before, it's what I do."

His words brought her back to earth with a jolt. *He's stolen your heart — and still won't stay.* Knowing it was coming, she had prepared herself. The hard reality hurt, but Elizabeth told herself she could stand it. She had made it through worse devastation in her life, had suffered greater losses. And after all, she and Quint had never actually committed themselves to each other.

"I'm in love with you, too, Quint." Elizabeth started to add that love alone was not enough. That she couldn't possibly consider a long-term relationship on a no-strings-attached basis. That she would rather wound herself now, rather than risk being wounded more deeply if she cast her heart brashly into a frightening void with no boundaries or limitations. But he pulled her into a fierce embrace that squeezed the air from her lungs.

"Who said it isn't a perfect world?" He laughed exultantly.

The joy in his voice was contagious. She could rationalize the situation until she was blue in the face, but still wouldn't be able to deny her feelings for Quint. Not tonight, at this moment, with his powerful heartbeat racing to keep pace with her own. Elizabeth offered her lips to him again. This time, the kiss was intense, demanding. She pressed herself against him, and he groaned hoarsely.

Their lips parted abruptly. Quint took a half step back, swallowing audibly, the frenetic roving of his hand suddenly stilled. He took a ragged breath. Elizabeth realized he was forcibly reining himself in—and she knew why. He had wanted to make love to her once before, that night at her place, but she had slammed the door on their passion.

Not this time, she thought, crossing an invisible threshold as she gazed into his dark eyes. Tonight, this one glorious night, she would not deny him—or herself—anything.

Elizabeth slid a hand up his broad chest and unfastened a shirt button. Just one. The heat flared in his eyes, streaming like molten lava into her own. Quint took another ragged breath, then reached over and scooped up their brandy snifters with one hand. He held her close against his side as they moved slowly across the living room. In the hallway they paused to kiss again—a dream-like interlude of blurred images and broken whispers.

He didn't turn on the light when they entered his bedroom. Glowing dimly through the window, the lights of the city provided illumination enough. In the soft shadows beside the bed, he helped Elizabeth undress, ritually removing each item. She returned the favor. Quint threw back the spread. A tiny night-light in the big headboard shone down on one corner of a deep blue pillowcase. He laid her back slowly, smiling as his hands moved down over her.

"You're like a nymph in a fairy wood," he murmured. "I feel as if I've stepped into a fantasy."

She touched his muscular arms, his quivering chest, his flat hard abdomen. He growled with pleasure and pulled her against him. She thought she should be nervous, but she wasn't. When his lips moved to her shoulder and then down her body, leaving a path of fire in their wake, she surrendered to a soaring passion such as she'd never before known.

"Oh, sweet Elizabeth," he breathed. "You're too rich for my blood."

They both continued tasting, exploring, touching skin that had become hypersensitive with desire. Their tender rite of discovery grew feverish, quickening the urgency of their impassioned journey.

"Elizabeth, I need . . ."

"I want . . ."

Quint torched her lips with a fiery kiss as their bodies joined. Elizabeth cried out softly and, for an eternal moment, time stood still.

They dozed. Awoke to make love again—languidly this time, adrift in a sensual euphoria. Dozed once more. Sometime after midnight, Elizabeth opened her eyes to the darkness, aware that she had been smiling in her sleep.

Her legs were entwined with Quint's, his arms curled possessively around her. She lay perfectly still, listening to the slow steady rhythm of his breathing, unwilling to disturb his sleep. After a while, she placed a hand gently on his chest and traced a finger lightly down the valley between his pectorals.

"Keep that up, and I'll ravish that gorgeous body of yours. Again."

Elizabeth was surprised he was awake. "Is that a promise?" She rolled Quint onto his back and stretched out atop him, her head on his chest.

"On second thought," he said, "I might just let you ravish me this time."

"Huh-uh. It's your turn."

She stroked a fingertip lazily down his side. Quint squirmed and brought her hand to his lips, nibbling at her fingers. His other hand glided down her back and shaped itself to the contour of her hip. The silence of the night closed in around them again. Quint was the first to break it.

"A penny," he said, squeezing her hip.

"You're overpricing my thoughts." Elizabeth touched her lips to his chest. "Besides anticipating what you're going to do with that hand, I was just thinking about Kasper."

He seemed to stop breathing. Suddenly she felt as if she were lying on a pile of hardwood lumber.

"I have to say, Elizabeth, it's a tad demoralizing for a man to hear his bedroom technique mentioned in the same breath with a *dummy*."

She couldn't quite tell if he meant that as seriously as it sounded. If he did, she decided, he was definitely overreacting.

"I didn't mean to offend your male sensibilities, Quint. But Kasper does mean a lot to me. Enough so that I've made up my mind to ransom him if I can."

"What?" Quint slid her off his body and rose onto one elbow. "Do you know what you're saying? If you spend a fortune getting Kasper back, where's the gain?"

Elizabeth sat up, pulling the edge of sheet around her. "You don't understand, Quint. Getting Kasper back isn't a matter of gain or loss. To me, he's beyond value. If I'm lucky enough to get him back, I have no intention of ever selling him."

"Oh, great." Quint threw up a hand. "You won't sell the thing, so you're willing to shell out a fortune for no gain at all."

"I don't see it that way. And frankly, I don't care much for your tone of voice."

They stared at each other for a long moment, two stonelike shapes in the darkness. A hard knot filled Elizabeth's throat as the silence dragged on.

Then Quint reached out and gripped her arm, stroking her skin with his thumb.

"I have no right to judge how you handle your inheritance, sweetheart." His tone was conciliatory. "It's just that you're doing so well with your work at the hotel. You're right on track to win Marge Holt's job and the experience it'll bring. After all that effort, I'd really hate to see you get your team tangled up and kiss goodbye the money you'll need to start your own catering business. And to look after Jake."

Her skin tingled. Elizabeth wanted to sink back into his arms and erase their tense words with the heady warmth of his kiss. She might have let herself take that easy route, if he hadn't mentioned Jake.

"I've been thinking a lot about my grandfather since Kasper was stolen, Quint. I want to see that he gets the best care possible, and the sale of the first two puppets has pretty much insured that."

"For the short term. But nursing-home care costs an arm and a leg. If Jake doesn't get better, you'll end up right back where you started—flat broke and desperate."

"That's a bridge I might not have to cross if I can get Kasper back," she said. "Kasper might help Jake get better."

Quint's thumb kept up its incessant stroking. Elizabeth closed her eyes and bit her lip, willing herself to be strong.

"It's a mistake to split your forces, Elizabeth. Believe me, if you keep yourself focused on your objective, the catering directorship is well within your reach."

"I am keeping myself focused." Her voice quavered slightly. She forged ahead. "But not on the hotel. I've come to realize that the Parkway Arms can't take me where I want to go, so I plan to leave my job."

His hand jerked away from her as if scalded. "You can't do that!"

"I beg your pardon?"

Quint sat up. "You heard me. You can't quit your job. Not after all that work."

Elizabeth drew back toward the edge of the bed, confused. "It's *my* job, Quint. I can do what I want with it." She could walk out of the hotel tomorrow and never look back if it suited her. Uncle Uri's crate of puppets had given her that choice.

His tone became brittle. "I thought you had better sense than this, Elizabeth."

Hurt by his attitude, she didn't know what to say. Quint was acting as if she had betrayed him. What difference did it make to him whether she kept her job at the Parkway Arms or became a missionary on the dark side of the moon? Once his seminars were over, he wouldn't be in town long enough to notice.

*His ego is bruised. He doesn't want you to stray one step from the Quinton Lawrence Path to Success. He has to control everything he touches—even you."*

"Quint, it truly pains me to say this. But I think

you're taking your own seminar lectures way too much to heart."

Elizabeth slid off the bed and began groping around in the dark for her clothes, hurriedly dressing as she went. He moved to the edge of the mattress and started to get up.

"Don't bother." She slipped her dress over her head and swept a foot over the plush carpet, searching for her other shoe. "I'll get a cab home."

"The hell you will. I'll take—"

She whirled, anger overtaking pain. "I will take a cab home." Elizabeth pronounced each word carefully, the frigid edge in her voice freezing Quint in place.

A moment later, she found the errant shoe and fled the luxurious condo, making it to the elevator before desolation hit her like a fist. She leaned against the mirrored wall, clutching her stomach, and let the hot, choking tears come.

Sunday afternoon, Elizabeth sat with her elbows propped on her desk, her forehead resting on her fingertips. The other offices were deserted, most of the lights switched off, making the catering-services area as good a place as any to nurse her headache.

She hadn't slept a wink after returning home from Quint's last night. After pacing her tiny apartment until past noon, waiting for him to call—and waiting for Kasper's kidnapper to call with a ransom message—she had given up and gone to the hotel. There was no point in torturing herself over two people who were currently beyond her reach.

*Two people. You just thought of Kasper as a person. Wouldn't Quint have a field day with that?*

She stared down at the note from Vivian Elledge, detailing minor menu changes for next Friday's prenup. Changes. Always changes. Why were they so easy for other people and so blasted painful for her? She was rich—Grant reminded her of that at least every other day. For once in her life, she was standing on the side of the fence with the lush green grass. It was just her rotten luck to discover that the real value of wealth lay not so much in what it could buy, but in the choices it opened up.

The headache crept around from the base of her skull to pinch her temples. Quint, Kasper, and Jake. Her own loony Three Musketeers, swash-buckling through her life, slashing her dreams to shreds. She couldn't choose one without losing one or both of the others. Was she being greedy in wanting all three?

"Elizabeth?"

Her head snapped up. Quint stood just outside her door as if he didn't quite dare to cross the threshold. He was impeccably attired in a gray pin-striped suit and blue tie. Almost the exact shade of blue as the sheets on his bed. For a sear-ing moment, the memory stole her breath and she couldn't find her voice. It was truly amazing, she thought, how much trouble she had breathing when she was around Quint.

"I've been looking all over for you." He spoke hesitantly, his usual self-confidence oddly lacking.

Elizabeth watched him move into her office. As he approached her desk, she noticed the shadows under his dark eyes, accentuated by the fluorescent lights. She apparently wasn't the only one who had spent a sleepless night. She was still trying to assimilate that when Quint leaned over and placed a single yellow rose on the blotter in front of her.

"I meant it when I said I love you, Elizabeth." He straightened slowly and moved back to the doorway. "I was hoping we could go get a cup of coffee and talk about, you know, last night."

She couldn't take her eyes off the perfect rose. Everything she felt for Quint, every tremulous desire of her body and soul, seemed embodied in the half-opened blossom. She thought she had cried herself out in the elevator last night. But only the anger had been dissipated. Her eyes brimmed afresh as pain clamped a steely band around her throat.

"I have work . . ."

Without looking up, Elizabeth motioned at the files scattered over her desk. If she looked at him, Quint would see how much she still wanted him. She couldn't bring herself to put them both through that again. He loved her — but he wouldn't stay. Even worse, there wasn't room in his life for her dreams. At least he'd been honest with her.

"I understand." He sounded subdued, resigned.

She waited for him to say more. The silence grew thick and oppressive, like the air before a summer storm. When she finally could stand it no longer, Elizabeth shifted her gaze longingly—to the empty doorway.

A handful of customers sat at the copper-topped tables in the Penthouse Lounge atop the Parkway Arms on Sunday evening. Grant Holbrook was alone at the horseshoe-shaped bar, nursing a Manhattan and watching two men talking quietly in a booth across the room. He recognized both, although he'd met only one—the portly hotel magnate. George Keen appeared to be his usual ebullient self, stoking down pretzels as fast as the bartender could replenish the bowls. But Quint Lawrence, even in the muted lighting, looked some the worse for wear. In a grudging sort of way, Grant felt sorry for him.

He had spoken briefly on the phone with Elizabeth an hour ago. Although she had said nothing specific, he knew her well enough to read between the lines—something had gone seriously wrong in Love Land. She and Lawrence were now among the wounded. Grant knew the feeling. He had been there. But he wasn't sure that Lawrence didn't deserve the condition.

Grant was pacing his second Manhattan, trying to insure that his sobriety survived the wait, when Keen finally got up to leave. Lawrence was making moves to follow when Grant slid away from the bar and, drink in hand, cornered the big ex-jock.

"Mr. Lawrence?" Grant held out his hand. "Mind if I barge in on you for a few minutes?"

"I was just leaving." Lawrence gave his hand a firm but perfunctory shake and started to rise from the leather seat.

Grant held his ground. "My name's Grant Holbrook. I'm a friend of Lizzy's. Make that Elizabeth's."

Lawrence locked his gaze with the smaller man's for several long seconds. Then he settled back onto the seat and motioned for Grant to join him. As Grant slid into the booth, Lawrence signaled the bartender for another drink. They sat quietly studying each other until he was served.

"I guess Lizzy told you about me," Grant said.

"Not really. just that you're helping her sell the puppets." Lawrence toyed with his glass without drinking. "But I figure it's more than that."

"Was, not is. We were engaged."

Lawrence glanced up.

"Ancient history," Grant added. "We're just good friends now."

"Oh." Lawrence looked relieved, but not totally.

Grant wished he had decided ahead of time just how to broach the subject that was bugging him. But he hadn't, so he simply waded in.

"Being a longtime friend of Lizzy's, I've gotten to know a good many of the hotel staff, including her boss. Which means I'm plugged in solidly to the grapevine. Frankly, Lawrence, there's a rumor afloat concerning Lizzy that

230

bothers the hell out of me."

Lawrence looked him straight in the eye, unblinking, waiting for the rest. Grant couldn't quite read him, couldn't quite make up his mind what he thought of the man who was probably Lizzie's lover.

"I hear you've made a wager with George Keen." Grant watched him closely. "Scuttlebutt has it that you're out to win the hotel-chain account, and you're using Lizzy as a pawn."

Lawrence dropped his gaze to the table. He took a slow drink from his glass and grimaced. "It sounds like a crate of rotten apples the way you put it."

Grant shrugged. "Pretty it up—if you can."

After making a series of wet rings on the tabletop with the bottom of his sweating glass, Lawrence finally shrugged. "I do have a bet with Keen."

"Which Lizzy knows nothing about, I take it."

"That was a mistake." Lawrence rubbed both hands down his face. "I should have told her at the outset, because the wager was in her best interest. In order for me to win, *she* had to win Marge Holt's job. And that's what Elizabeth wants. Wanted."

"So, why don't you tell her now?"

"Can't." Lawrence shook his head emphatically. "She'd blow sky-high. I'm already on her blacklist. We had a little, uh, dispute last night."

"So I gathered." Grant didn't expect Lawrence to give him a blow-by-blow account, or even as much as a thumbnail sketch. So he was somewhat surprised when the guy bounced a fist off the table and riveted him with his penetrating black eyes.

"Holbrook, I don't give a flaming fig about winning the hotel-chain account—not if it causes Elizabeth one second of concern. But I'm worried crazy about this damned obsession of hers with puppets. I can't help feeling she's using them as an excuse to hide from the risks of her own potential. Last night, she told me she plans to quit her job here at the hotel. But she *can't* have suddenly lost interest in a goal she's had for years—starting her own catering business. That doesn't make sense."

Grant smiled bemusedly at the other man's frustration. He was even beginning to feel a certain kinship with Lawrence. Lizzy did have a way of getting under a man's skin without even trying.

"I wasn't aware I'd said anything funny," Lawrence muttered tightly.

"You didn't. I was just remembering how she sometimes made me want to pull my hair out."

"I'm not interested in hearing about it, pal." Lawrence made another series of wet rings on the table, his jaw muscles working as if he were chewing a piece of leather.

"I suppose not." Grant liked the fact that Lawrence didn't jump all over him with questions about his past relationship with Lizzy. He hadn't expected to find that kind of decency lurking behind all the hype and notoriety that surrounded the complex man seated across the table. "Would I be way out of line asking where Lizzy's decision to quit her job at the hotel leaves you two?"

Lawrence stared off across the dimly lit lounge. After several minutes, he shook his head. "She's going off into a fantasy world, with this puppet mania. I wouldn't even begin to know how to live there."

Grant planted his elbows on the table and rested his chin on steepled fingers. He stared into the middle distance for a long time, his eyes squinted pensively. Finally he straightened, folding both hands into the shape of a pistol—aimed at Lawrence.

"Tell me, friend, do you love Lizzy?" Grant already knew the answer. He just wanted to hear it from the horse's mouth, as it were.

Lawrence shifted uncomfortably and looked very close to telling Grant it was none of his business. If he did, Grant was prepared to walk away and let him stew in his own juices.

Instead, Lawrence nodded. "Very much."

"Good. Because I think I have an idea . . ."

Vivian Elledge closed the door quietly and leaned her head against the smooth panel, listening to the sound of Byron's footsteps recede down the corridor. His parting kiss, still warm on her lips, had left her feeling as giddy as a young girl. She squelched a giggle and turned her back to the door, staring dreamily into the sitting room of the hotel suite.

Byron wasn't the most handsome man in the

world. His front teeth were slightly crooked, and his dark wavy hair had receded considerably. But he had all the qualities that mattered to her in a man — honesty, intelligence, a sense of humor. The list went on and on, and Byron matched it as if he had been custom-designed just for her.

Best of all, she found she no longer compared him with Todd. Byron stood on his own, without the dubious distinction of being better or worse than someone Vivian had loved before. She took that as the best possible sign.

The door to Nicky's room stood slightly ajar. Vivian tiptoed across the sitting room and pushed it open, automatically checking to make sure the door to Nadine's adjoining room was closed. It was well past midnight. Her sister-in-law would be under the influence of one of her sleeping pills by now.

Vivian crept into the room, which was dimly illuminated by the light from the sitting room. Nicky lay curled in a ball on the edge of his bed, one fist wedged under his cheek. He looked so young and vulnerable, she thought, watching him lovingly.

She felt a sudden pang of guilt that she had somehow let Nicky down. Ordinarily a loving, trustworthy child, his occasional aberrant behavior baffled her. Vivian had experienced a terrible sense of dread when the Mason woman's puppet was stolen. But she had finally gotten over that when no one appeared to suggest that Nicky might be involved.

She gently tucked the covers around his narrow shoulders and smoothed a wisp of hair from his forehead. It was going to be all right this time. Nothing was going to spoil her upcoming wedding. She would have a soulmate with whom to spend the rest of her life, and her son would have the loving father he so desperately needed.

Vivian kissed Nicky lightly on the cheek, picked up a comic book from the floor beside the bed, and turned to steal silently out of the room. She made a slight detour to deposit the comic book on the dresser—and then dropped it on the floor again in shock.

Her wide-eyed gaze fixed on the cluttered top of the dresser. On the corner, next to a jumble of new comic books, a man-size train conductor's cap, and an orange glow-in-the-dark yo-yo, lay a dark shape. She reached out and touched it with a trembling fingertip. A piece of dried-up leather, curled at the edges.

Vivian clamped a hand to her throat, strangling a sob. She forced herself to pick up the chunk of leather and carry it to the doorway. Even in the brighter light from the sitting room, she wouldn't have known what it was if Nicky hadn't insisted that she troop down to the hotel jewelry store with him last month to view Elizabeth Mason's antique puppet on display in the window.

Nausea rose from her stomach. Vivian leaned heavily against the doorjamb for support, staring at Kasper's ear through a blear of tears.

# Chapter Thirteen

A cold lump of fear filled Vivian's chest. She eased down onto Nicky's bed, staring at the curled shred of old leather in her trembling hand. *Please, God, not again,* she prayed. *Not this time.*

She reached out and gently shook her son, feeling strangely wary, as if she were awakening a sleeping dragon. Nicky stirred. She shook him again, harder, impatient now. If she didn't hurry and get this over with, she might lose her nerve and flee the room—and the terrible truth. He opened his eyes and looked up at her, blinking groggily in the dim light from the sitting room.

"Mom . . . ?"

"Wake up, Nicky. This is important." Vivian held the leather scrap in front of his face. "Where did you get this?"

Nicky squinted at the object, his face scrunched up in concentration. "What is it?"

"That puppet Kasper's ear."

His head jerked slightly and his eyes widened, as if he had been slapped awake by an invisible hand. He drew away from the damning evidence in his mother's hand. Vivian wanted to cry.

"Where'd you find it, Mom?"

"On your dresser." Even in the dim light, she could see a sheen suddenly appear on his face. He was sweating. "How did it get there, Nicky?"

He shook his head. "I swear, I don't know!"

His voice had risen. Vivian shushed him, glancing toward the door to Nadine's room. Her sister-in-law had been sending up warning flags almost since the night Elizabeth Mason's puppet was stolen. But she didn't want Nadine to be a part of the painful confrontation. Not yet. For the moment, this was between Vivian and her son.

"What do you know about this, Nicky?" She strained to keep fear and accusation from her tone.

Nicky turned his face toward the shadows. Through the sheet and thin blanket separating them, Vivian felt a shudder that made her heart sink.

"I didn't put it there," he whispered.

Vivian knew her son well enough to tell at once that he was lying. She curled her fingers around the leather ear, willing herself not to break down. Tears wouldn't help. But what would? She tried to pull Nicky into her arms, but he resisted her and squirmed to the far side of the bed.

"Please, tell me," she pleaded softly.

"I can't. I don't know!"

*Yes, you do!* Vivian wanted to scream the words, but didn't dare utter them at all. She couldn't call her son a liar. Not to his face. Not even now.

Minutes ago, she had been the happiest woman in the world. But sometimes there was a thin line between joy and misery, and she had just stumbled across it. Byron was kind, generous, and understanding. But there was one area in which he was totally inflexible. When it came to integrity and honor, he held himself and those around him to the rigidly high standards of a medieval knight. She had once heard him say that if honor wasn't pure, it didn't exist at all. Coming from Byron, it hadn't sounded at all pompous.

The fact was, Vivian agreed with her fiancé. But didn't that leave Nicky standing outside the castle walls? She stared across the bed at her precious son, feeling trapped between two powerful loyalties.


Late Monday morning, tension had Elizabeth's nerves wound close to the point of snapping. The number five loomed hugely in the back of her mind. Only five more days remained of Quint's seminar series. And it was just five days until the Elledge-Thompson prenup bash. By next weekend, she consoled herself, it would all be over. Then she could submit her resignation to the Parkway Arms Hotel without feeling she was leaving anyone in the lurch.

The problem was, in spite of the lure of her puppets, she wasn't sure she could walk away from her catering work as easily as Quint was going to walk away from her. Her inheritance had given her the courage to make the move. But it provided no reassurance that the move was sensible, or even sane.

She mentally shelved the dilemma as she hurried to the Tea Room for a noon meeting with Vivian Elledge. She found the woman seated at a small table under a high mullioned window, tracing patterns on the white tablecloth with her manicured fingernail. As Elizabeth pulled out a heavy brocade chair and sat down, she was alarmed by her client's pale drawn appearance.

"Are you feeling all right, Vivian?"

"Sure." Vivian smiled wanly and glanced at her with haunted eyes.

Elizabeth toyed with a file folder she had brought along, pondering how to frame her next question without being unnecessarily indelicate. If Vivian and her fiancé had quarreled over the weekend, they wouldn't be unique. Elizabeth's catering experience had opened her eyes to at least one rule of thumb: the more elaborate the ceremonial plans, the greater the prenuptial jitters. The last week before a wedding could be downright volatile.

"I guess Mr. Thompson is getting pretty antsy, now that your big day is approaching." Elizabeth tried to make her comment sound offhand.

"If he is, he doesn't show it." Vivian's smile turned wistful. "When it comes to grace under pressure, Byron wrote the book."

Strike two, Elizabeth thought. But something was definitely amiss and, with the prenup arrangements hanging in the balance, she couldn't afford to pretend otherwise. At the risk of sounding like an interrogator, Elizabeth worked her way on down her list of possibilities.

"How is Nicky handling all this?"

Vivian blanched. She drew both hands into her lap, suddenly looking bereft. Concerned, Elizabeth set aside the folder and leaned toward her.

"What is it, Vivian?"

Vivian raised her chin and squared her shoulders, but wouldn't meet Elizabeth's searching gaze. "There is something you should know . . ."

Moved by her client's obvious distress, Elizabeth instinctively reached out to her. Vivian drew back stiffly, as if afraid she could not get through what she had to say if they so much as touched.

"I was in Nicky's room last night." Vivian dragged her designer purse onto her lap and unfastened the magnetic clasp. Then she glanced around the room as if having second thoughts. "Oh, what could I have been thinking of, Elizabeth? Not *here*." Vivian quickly snapped the clasp shut.

"Do you want to go someplace quieter?" Turning to glance at the neighboring tables, Elizabeth spotted Quint watching them from the entrance across the room. Her heart lurched almost painfully. As he started wending his way toward them through the mostly occupied tables, Elizabeth felt a rush of warmth, combined with an icy stab of dread. How could she face Quint right here, in a roomful of people?

"Yes . . . please." Vivian's voice was strained. "It really is something important."

"What?" Elizabeth distractedly returned her attention to her client.

Vivian shoved back her chair, entangling herself in the tablecloth in her haste to rise. A moment ago, she appeared to be on the verge of revealing something disturbing about Nicky. Elizabeth wasn't about to lose that opportunity. Besides her concern for the boy, there was an outside chance that the revelation might have something to do with Kasper. Elizabeth grabbed her folder and hopped to her feet.

Quint halted midway across the room, confounded by their rush for the exit. Flushing hotly at the look he gave her, Elizabeth murmured a polite greeting in passing, grateful for the excuse to avoid an encounter with Quint. But it was an agonizing breed of gratitude. As she caught up with Vivian and followed her out into the corridor, Elizabeth felt as if she were being torn in two.

By Thursday, Quint had learned the hard way how it felt to be shunned. Every time he tried to approach Elizabeth in the hotel, she zipped off in the opposite direction. She didn't answer her phone at her apartment. When he left trumped-up questions on her answering machine, she deposited polite written responses in his slot at the hotel's front desk.

Quint paced the lobby at the end of the day, muttering to himself, oblivious to the sidelong stares of hotel guests. He had never been so frustrated in his life. The gloriously magical hours he and Elizabeth had spent making love on Saturday night had only whetted his appetite. But the attraction went far beyond the merely physical—not that there had been anything *mere* about that part.

He didn't just want Elizabeth. He wanted to *be* with her. He wanted to hold her close and tell her things, deep important things he had never told another living soul, not even himself. He wanted to sit and look at her, and let the sound of her voice wash over him like warm spring rain. He wanted to laugh at her jokes. He wanted to give her daisies in winter and take her to the remote Himalayas to make snow angels in July.

"Dammit, I want to breathe!"

A shopping bag thudded to the floor at his feet. Quint stopped pacing and glanced at it in confusion. A small elderly woman stood next to the bag, peering up at him as if he had just turned plaid.

"Young man, have you been drinking?" She sniffed the air suspiciously.

"No, ma'am." He picked up the bag and handed it to her. "But I'm open to suggestions."

She sniffed again, this time in disdain, and turned away. Quint was about to resume his pacing, when the door to the service corridor leading to the staff offices swung open. Elizabeth emerged, wearing her belted cape and carrying a heavy briefcase. He stood transfixed as she threaded her way across the crowded lobby to the main entrance. She was already outside before he got his head together and chased after her.

Elizabeth skipped up onto the curb on the north side of the parkway and kept walking fast. She was aware from the sound of jogging footsteps behind her that someone was hurrying to catch up. She had an idea it was Quint, having glimpsed him in the hotel lobby moments ago. She'd hoped he hadn't seen her. As miserable as she had been these past few days, avoiding his company was easier to handle than being near him—wanting what she could never have.

Quint slowed to a walk beside her, his frozen breath ripped from his parted lips by the light early-evening breeze. Neither spoke as they continued up Broadway through Country Club Plaza toward her apartment. But the ache in Elizabeth's chest grew steadily as the distance to her apartment shrank. Finally, unable to stand it any longer, she veered desperately onto a side street and led him into the neutral territory of a coffee shop.

They took a booth by the cold-fogged window, where they studied the menu in minute detail before choosing coffee and jelly rolls. When the waitress finally brought their order, Quint didn't even bother doctoring his brew before shoving the coffee and roll aside.

"Look at me, Elizabeth."

The harsh whisper brought her gaze up to his face. She registered his anger first, then the pain. His white-knuckled fists rested on the table between them. Before she realized what she was doing, Elizabeth had covered one with her hand. His fist opened instantly and their fingers entwined. She allowed herself that much, although his touch was devastating.

"Now, listen. You once told me that you don't believe in one-night stands," he said hoarsely. "In that case, how the hell can you walk away from what we shared Saturday night? How can you pretend we aren't crazy in love with each other?"

Elizabeth looked into his eyes and tried to swallow, but couldn't. Beneath the anger and pain, the glow of her own reflected yearnings was too bright. The sages were wrong, she thought—love didn't conquer all. When two people were as far apart as she and Quint, love became a merciless torture chamber.

"Come on, Elizabeth. I know you've been as cut up these past few days as I have. Otherwise, you wouldn't have worked so hard at avoiding me."

She looked away.

"Dammit, sweetheart, talk to me!"

"I can't!" she managed. "Talking about it will just make it worse."

Quint sighed and shook his head. "It doesn't have to work that way." He paused, then added, "I had a long talk with Grant Holbrook."

"You what?" Elizabeth tried to withdraw her

hand. He resisted briefly before releasing her. She pressed herself flat against the back of the seat. "What is this? Have you two been conspiring behind my back?"

"Conspiring to what?"

"Manipulate me."

He waved a hand in a gesture of dismissal. "Grant hardly impressed me as the conspirator type. But he does have a good head on his shoulders. He came up with an interesting strategy for you." Quint smiled. "Actually, for us."

Elizabeth relaxed slightly. Quint was right — Grant wasn't a behind-the-back sort of guy. She had never been suspicious of him in her life.

"The puppet theme you came up with for my luncheon was a huge success, even if it did blow up in my face," Quint went on. "Grant thinks it would be a good idea if you permanently combined the puppets with your own catering business. You could make a killing catering children's parties, conventions, and such."

She leaned forward, the suggestion captivating her imagination at once. "That approach never occurred to me, Quint. Do you really think it's a good idea?"

Some of the tension bled from his expression. "Why not? Enthusiasm is half of success, and the concept obviously got your adrenaline pumping right off the bat."

Elizabeth stared into space for a moment. She could see a lot of problems with the idea that would have to be worked out. For one thing, she would need a lot of different kinds of puppets, in order to adapt the concept to a variety of client needs. And she would have to find experienced puppeteers—or else train them herself. In spite of such obstacles, however, the approach seemed like a natural. All at once, she wanted to run outside and shout it from the rooftops. Only one thought reined in her elation.

"What is it?" Quint frowned, sensing her constraint.

"Kasper. He's more than just a puppet to me, Quint. He's . . ." Elizabeth searched for the right words, but couldn't find them. "I can't even think of starting up a business involving puppets until I get him back."

Quint began toying with the plate his jelly roll sat on, moving it around between his fingers in the middle of the table. "Don't you mean *unless* you get Kasper back?"

She sucked in her lips, watching the plate slide back and forth, back and forth. Finally she reached for her purse. "Vivian Elledge gave me this on Monday." She placed the scrap of curled leather on the table. "Kasper's ear."

The plate suddenly stopped. "Where the devil did she get it?"

Elizabeth began picking nervously at her own jelly roll. "She saw it on the dresser in Nicky's room. She learned the next day that the hotel housekeeper had found it on the floor while cleaning the suite."

Quint closed his eyes for a few seconds and

pressed a fist to his lips. He looked ill. Seeing how hard he took the news about Nicky made her feel even worse about it than she already did. Elizabeth hadn't realized Nicky had come to mean so much to him. She had a feeling that until now Quint hadn't realized it, either.

"Vivian searched the room later, but she didn't find anything else," Elizabeth said. "Just the ear."

"I don't want to believe this." He fingered the leather scrap. "Have you notified the police?"

"Not yet. I want to have a showdown with Nicky first — just the two of us, away from his mother and aunt. I want to know what he has to say about it, without all the hysteria that a group confrontation would create. I'm pretty sure he's been hiding from me all week. But I'm going to track him down tomorrow if I have to turn the entire hotel inside out."

Quint handed back the ear. She returned it to her purse, then sat playing with the jelly-roll crumbs. "I still can't figure out exactly how Nicky fits into Kasper's disappearance, Quint. He didn't put that message on my answering machine. I'm certain of that."

"He must have had an accomplice."

She nodded glumly. He placed his hands gently over hers and drew them away from the sticky jelly-roll crumbs. Elizabeth sat very still as he stroked the insides of her wrists with his fingertips for a moment. Then he placed his elbows on the table and brought her fingers to his lips. Gazing into her eyes, he slowly sucked the jelly from them, one at a time.

"Didn't anyone ever teach you not to lick your fingers?" Her voice caught in her throat as tiny shock waves charged up her arms.

"Sure," he said huskily. "But nobody said anything about yours." He finished with one hand and went to work on the other.

"I'd better be getting home now, Quint."

"It's dark out. I'll walk you the rest of the way. Wouldn't want you to get mugged."

His teeth lightly scraped the tip of her index finger. Elizabeth shuddered. "You'll get cold."

"Very."

"You'll have to come up to my apartment and get warm . . ."

"That might be the sensible thing to do."

". . . before you call a cab."

"Perhaps."

## Chapter Fourteen

"I dream of you every night, Elizabeth." Quint cradled her against his bare chest and nuzzled her hair.

"What kind of dreams?"

Elizabeth opened her eyes, still groggy with sleep. Peering across the room at the first hint of gray light beyond her tiny balcony, she snuggled deeper under the blanket, not ready for morning. She didn't want to ever have to leave the endless fascinations of the lusty male body she had spent almost an entire night rediscovering.

"Erotic dreams," Quint said after a while. He had curled a muscular leg around hers.

She nibbled playfully at his chest, smiling when his pectoral muscles jumped. "Tell me about them."

"I'd rather show you."

With a low growl, he rolled atop her. Bracing himself on his elbows, he fanned her silky hair across the pillow and kissed her. The kiss deepened, reigniting the passion that had smoldered and flared all night long.

The conflagration had begun at the coffee shop, last evening, as he slowly sucked the jelly from her fingertips. By the time they made it to her place, both of them knew he would stay the night. A trail of clothing stretched from the front door straight to the bed, beginning with Quint's necktie and Elizabeth's left shoe. She had removed his tie herself. Until last night, she wouldn't have believed it possible to want a man with such total abandon.

His lips slid from hers, traveling like a red-hot ember down her neck to her shoulder. She laughed aloud at the pleasure-shock. He touched, stroked, nibbled, until she thought she would go mad. The quickening rasp of his breathing told her she was not alone. And then he laughed, too, a deep, joyfully savage sound as the flames of desire consumed them.

"That was quite a dream," Elizabeth said some time later.

"I thought you might appreciate it." Quint raised his head from the rumpled pillow and squinted over his shoulder at the pale light of dawn. "Judas priest, it's sunup!"

"Friday the Terrible. Why don't we call in sick?"

He chuckled and crawled out of bed. Before she could protest, he scooped her into his arms and carried her into the bathroom. After adjusting the water tap, he deposited her in the shower stall and stepped in with her.

"Dear heart, I really do need to get to work no later than today," she said as he dribbled fragrant liquid soap over her from the pump bottle.

His lathered hand glided smoothly down her flank. "We have all the time in the world."

They nodded goodbye to each other in the hotel lobby. Very businesslike. After Quint strode off toward his final morning session, Elizabeth glanced at her watch. She was only ten minutes late for work—a minor miracle. Yesterday, and the lingering hurt she had felt toward Quint, seemed light-years away. She could not clearly recall what it had been like not to be painlessly, head-over-heels in love.

Marge Holt was hard at work at her desk when Elizabeth rapped lightly on the director's door frame, pleased that she wasn't the least bit nervous about confronting the woman.

Marge glanced up sharply. "What is it?"

"I need to talk to you about my employment here at the Parkway Arms."

"Oh?" Marge leaned back, stretching her thin lips into a condescending smile as she motioned Elizabeth to a chair. "That's right. This is the last day of Quint Lawrence's seminars, isn't it? I suppose it is time for me to make up my mind."

Elizabeth looked at her blankly for a moment, uncertain what Marge was referring to. "Since you've mentioned it, I've made up *my* mind."

Marge raised one heavily penciled eyebrow and looked down the harsh line of her nose at Elizabeth. "I do believe the decision is mine, Elizabeth. Not yours."

Thoroughly confused, Elizabeth strummed her fingers on the arm of the chair. Not only had Marge Holt ceased to intimidate her, she found that her patience with the older woman had worn tissue-thin.

"I don't know what decision *you* have in mind, Marge." Nor did Elizabeth care. "But I've come to officially give you one month's notice."

The director's face froze, then sagged. She stared at Elizabeth in disbelief. "You're quitting?"

"I don't care for the word 'quit.' Let's just say I plan to go on to better things."

"But you were up for my job!" Marge whopped her hand down on the desk, sending papers and pencils flying. "A great deal of work has gone into priming you for it."

Elizabeth bit her tongue to keep from cracking up. Marge hadn't lifted a finger to prime her for anything these past weeks. What was more, since going to work at the Parkway Arms, Elizabeth had seen the director fire other subordinates without a twitch of remorse. What drove Marge crazy now was that Elizabeth intended to leave on her own initiative. Marge liked to be the one who pushed all the buttons.

"On the other hand—" Marge smiled maliciously "—it'll be interesting to see how the esteemed Mr. Lawrence takes your desertion of his cause."

"What cause?" Elizabeth's self-assurance suddenly shuddered. The director's smile warned her that she didn't really want to hear Marge's explanation. At the same time, Elizabeth knew she must.

"What cause?" Marge echoed. "Why, his wager with George Keen, of course. Lawrence bet that he could turn you into catering-director material in six weeks flat."

Pain swelled in Elizabeth's chest. She dug her fingernails into the chair arms and somehow managed to keep her expression impassive. "Bet what?"

"If I approved of you as my replacement—" Marge glanced at the ceiling, as if to indicate the utter remoteness of that possibility "—Lawrence would be given a contract as human-resources consultant for the entire Parkway Arms chain."

The light in the room seemed to dim. A deafening roar filled Elizabeth's ears. She had a terrifying sensation of free-falling through space and, for one endless moment, was convinced she was in the process of dying.

*I dream of you every night.* Quint's words held a very different meaning now. A bubble of nausea filled Elizabeth's throat.

Marge was watching her with hooded eyes. Elizabeth rose shakily, conscious of a need to escape the catering director's ridiculing smile. The room tilted. It seemed to take forever to reach the doorway. But Elizabeth somehow managed to make her way out of the suffocating confines of Marge's office.

"He's been using you," Elizabeth whispered into her hands when she was at last slumped at her own desk. No wonder Quint was so upset when she told him last weekend that she planned to leave the hotel. He knew that would cost him his bet.

She pounded a fist into her lap again and again, refusing to surrender to soul-scouring tears of humiliation. How could she have loved Quint so much? How could she love him still? She couldn't breathe, or even reason. Eventually, a cold numbness seeped in. Little by little, it filled her up, squeezing out all emotion. When she at last felt as empty and dry as a vast meteor crater, she sat motionless for a long while, trying to erase last night from her memory.

An hour later, Elizabeth stalked resolutely out of the pastry kitchen, satisfied that preparations were well under way for Vivian Elledge's prenup festivities. By five o'clock that afternoon, Quinton Lawrence would be out of the Royal Ballroom for good—and out of her life forever. Transforming the decor from a seminar hall to a gala party room by eight o'clock would be a tight squeeze. But her little army of workers was ready and waiting.

Elizabeth kept moving, never slowing long enough to let herself experience the pain. With Quint soon to be gone, she had only Jake to think about. And Kasper—she hadn't forgotten about him. She reached into the pocket of her skirt and fingered the leather ear. As soon as she made a quick call to the florist to triple-check the final delivery of Vivian's flowers, she would begin seriously searching for Nicky.

Taking a shortcut behind the front desk, she hurried through the door into the corridor leading to the staff offices and ran smack into George Keen. He staggered back a step, loosing one of his basso-profundo chortles.

"Such energy!" Keen tugged his vest back down over his belt and winked. "If Marge Holt doesn't select you as her replacement, I do believe I'll call foul."

"That won't be necessary, Mr. Keen." Elizabeth hesitated. She liked the hotel owner. He and his wife had treated her like an equal that evening at Quint's place last month. She almost wished she didn't have to tell him the rest. "I've given Marge a month's notice."

"Indeed?" Keen looked flabbergasted. "Is there a problem with—"

"No." She suddenly stopped. Reminding herself that Keen was a part of Quint's underhanded conspiracy, Elizabeth reversed herself. "Yes. As a matter of fact, there's a big problem. I don't like being used as a pawn, Mr. Keen. Marge told me about your wager with Quinton Lawrence."

"She what?" Keen's face reddened. He cast a virulent glance back down the corridor toward the catering-services offices.

"I had already made up my mind to leave the Parkway Arms—for purely personal reasons—before she dropped that little bombshell." Elizabeth

255

swallowed back her anger and the sharp edge it had given her voice. "But it did bolster my conviction that I was making the right decision."

Keen's face had gone from red to purple, his jowls swelling. Even in this state of near-apoplexy, however, he reached out and patted Elizabeth's hand placatingly. "You have every right to feel as you do, my dear. I apologize for keeping you in the dark all this time about the wager. That was unnecessary—and entirely my decision. Would it serve any purpose, at this late date, if I were to beg you to reconsider?"

Elizabeth couldn't believe that George Keen himself had just begged her to stay. It so jarred her that she almost flirted with the idea. Almost. One thought stopped her cold: if she stayed, Quint just might win his bet.

"I won't stay under any circumstances, Mr. Keen."

*Won't stay.* The words reverberated in her head. In the course of a single morning, she had become like Quint. With that thought came a resurgence of pain, along with the hollow ache of loneliness.

"In that unfortunate case, please excuse me—I have an ax to sharpen." Keen did an impressively military about-face and stalked off toward the catering offices.


By noon, Elizabeth was too busy—and too nervous—to eat. Final preparations for Vivian Elledge's prenup bash were falling perfectly into place. Still, the closer that event approached, the more anxious Elizabeth became—over Nicky. After tomorrow's wedding, Vivian and Byron Thompson would leave on an extended honeymoon, while Nadine returned to Boston with Nicky and his secret. Elizabeth might never find out what had happened to Kasper.

On the way back to her office from the decorations staging area across the hall from the Royal Ballroom, she stopped by the pastry kitchen. Last-minute work on the prenup buffet was in high gear, and Chef Anjou was in his usual frenetic orbit, haranguing a platoon of assistants putting the final touches on sheet after sheet of petits fours.

Next door in the main kitchen, Chef Brady's assistants were busy stuffing mushrooms and filling tiny puff pastries with shrimp. At the end of a long stainless-steel work table, she spotted trays of elaborately-arranged fresh fruits, ready for dipping into pots of white and dark chocolate sauce. The sight of chocolate reminded her of Quint and sent her fleeing from the kitchen area.

Minutes later, she came to an abrupt halt in the doorway of her office. She stared in dismay at 272 individually-cellophane-wrapped, long-stemmed American Beauty roses. She didn't have to count them. That was the exact number she had ordered from the florist—one for each female guest at the Elledge-Thompson party.

"Oh, wonderful," she murmured in exasperation.

The florist had instructions to deliver all the

fresh flowers to the staging area, but instead, the roses filled every flat surface in her office, their heady fragrance nearly stifling in the small room. Elizabeth scooped up a large armload and turned back to the door.

"Hi, precious." Quint stood in the doorway, his gaze fastened on the bundle of perfect red roses in her arms. He leaned slightly to one side and looked past her at the piles of roses on the filing cabinet and chairs.

Elizabeth stared at the small bouquet of paper-wrapped daisies he held. Her vision blurred and, for a moment, she forgot all about the pain from which she had been running all morning.

Quint looked from the mountains of roses to his fistful of daisies and winced in embarrassment. "Talk about lousy timing."

She couldn't have agreed more. His timing was terrible, but not for the reason he imagined. She shifted the roses in her arms so she could reach for his small bouquet. Daisies in winter. The gesture touched her deeply, adding yet another layer of conflict to the war of emotions that had been going on inside her since her meeting with Marge Holt.

"You deserve roses, Elizabeth. Tons of them."

She didn't dare tell him that the handful of daisies seemed more real to her than all the roses on the planet. So, while common sense demanded that she toss the daisies and Quint right back out the door, her heart resisted.

Before she realized what was happening, he

bent and pressed his lips to hers. She sucked in her breath as her entire body seemed to go up in flames. For just an instant, she returned his kiss hungrily. Then the pain returned with dizzying force.

"Don't," she said, backing away.

"Don't?" He grinned. "Why not? You did."

"Just . . . don't." Looking at him was like driving a steel stake through her chest. So she kept her eyes downcast.

Something about him shifted. He stood quietly for a moment. When he spoke again, his voice had changed, deepened. She could tell without looking that his grin was gone.

"What is it, Elizabeth?"

She cleared her throat. Bracing herself against a corner of the desk, she raised her eyes. "I gave Marge a month's notice this morning."

"You quit?" He shook his head once, as if to clear it. "I can't believe you actually did that. You haven't even recovered Kasper yet. You said yourself that the plans for opening your own catering service hinged on getting the dummy back."

"Kasper isn't a *dummy*, Quint—he's a string puppet, a marionette. And I didn't *quit*. I resigned." She drew herself up.

"Sorry, but I fail to see the distinction."

Elizabeth chose to ignore his point. "You needn't be so upset. As the saying goes, you win some, you lose some."

He rubbed his neck furiously. "What in Sam

Hill does winning and losing have to do with this?"

Elizabeth couldn't keep the bitterness from her laugh. She wanted to throw something at him. But the roses didn't belong to her, and no force on earth could have made her let go of the daisies.

"Come now, Quint. Surely you haven't forgotten your little wager with Mr. Keen."

He flinched as if she had slapped him. "Oh, jeez."

"You didn't think I'd find out, did you?"

He took a step toward her. Elizabeth retreated to the far side of her desk. She had a crazy vision of Quint chasing her around and around the desk, like a scene from a slapstick movie. Instead, he reached back and clamped a hand to the door frame, leaning heavily on it.

"Oh, baby," he said. "Of course, I thought you'd find out. I was going to tell you myself."

"Is that so? Well, why is it that you didn't get around to doing that *before* you slept with me?"

Quint swore under his breath. The curse was intended for himself, not her, she was certain. Well, she thought, he had it coming.

"What about last night, Quint?" She bit her lip. She had almost said "my darling." "Did you think you could manipulate me more efficiently . . ."

"It wasn't like that."

". . . if I thought you loved me?"

"I do love you!" he said in a harsh whisper. "And you damn well love me."

Her chin quivered. She clenched her teeth to

keep the tremor from spreading. "Yes, I do love you, Quint. Isn't that sad? And isn't it sad you don't carry a whistle?"

"A whistle?"

"Yes. Then I would have something to hang on *my* wall, to remind me I was betrayed by someone I trusted."

His eyes seemed to glaze over. Or perhaps she was viewing them through the haze of her own heartache. He raked his hair off his forehead. A vein stood out at his temple. Another pulsed visibly along the taut muscles of his neck. He glanced at his watch and cursed again.

"Elizabeth, now isn't a good time to get into this."

"Isn't that what they say about all disasters?"

"I have a speech to give. We can talk later."

"I'm sorry, Quint. Apparently I haven't made myself clear. There isn't going to be a 'later' for us."

Quint looked at his watch again and banged a fist into the door frame. He started to leave, then changed his mind, then checked his watch once more. Finally, with an anguished glance at Elizabeth, he stormed out of the office.


Vivian tapped lightly on the half-open door to Nadine's room. Without waiting for a response, she went in and sat on the end of the bed. Her former sister-in-law wasn't there, but the doorway to Nicky's adjoining room was open. A moment later, Nadine marched through it carrying a stack of schoolbooks.

"That boy!" Nadine sniffed irritably and dropped the books onto a luggage rack under the window. "Always gallivanting off somewhere, ignoring his lessons. He hasn't even begun the geography report I assigned last week."

Vivian watched from the bed, listening to Nadine prattle on about the impact of overpopulation on the ecosystem of Madagascar. Nadine had a tendency to prattle when she was overwrought. Her mouth had been going a mile a minute ever since Vivian had shown her the puppet ear she'd found on Nicky's dresser.

"I gave the ear to Elizabeth Mason," Vivian said, cutting into Nadine's monologue.

Nadine abruptly stopped flipping through the books. She stood looking out the window, her back to Vivian. "What did she have to say?"

"Not what I expected. She said she wanted to have a talk with Nicky before she went to the police. She said she owed him that much."

"Owed him?" Nadine turned.

"Yes. She's been giving Nicky puppet lessons, you know. They've become good friends."

Nadine seemed to ponder that for a moment. "Has she spoken with him?"

"I don't know — I'm afraid to ask." Vivian pressed icy fingers to her lips. "I'm a coward, Nadie, and a terrible mother."

"You most certainly are not!"

"Yes, I am. I've failed him. When Todd was alive, Nicky never . . . took things."

Nadine sank onto the bed, shoulders drooping. Her hands twitched fitfully in her lap. Once again, Vivian was struck by how much Todd's older sister had aged recently. She seemed almost frail, in a way that Vivian couldn't quite put her finger on.

"I've put it off all week, Nadie." Vivian took her hand and found it as cold as her own. "I hoped and prayed it wouldn't come to this. But you know what I have to do. I have to tell Byron about the ear."

"No!" Nadine shook her head vigorously. A wisp of gray hair came loose, falling over one eye. She made no move to brush it back.

Vivian released her hand, startled. "No? But, Nadie, I couldn't possibly keep Byron in the dark about this. If Nicky has taken Elizabeth Mason's puppet, Byron must know about it today."

"But he'll call off the wedding, Vivian. It happened before, with that banker."

"You don't have to remind me." Vivian pressed her hands to her stomach to quell a ripple of nausea. "But that was different. *Byron* is different. He's too good a man to let something like this destroy what we have. The one thing he could never forgive is deception."

She rose and went to the door. Nadine remained seated on the bed, her hair askew, her hands twitching in her lap. Vivian glanced back at her with a twinge of regret. After all these years, she thought Nadine was getting too old to handle crises.

With a sigh, Vivian crossed the sitting room to her own room. As she prepared herself for the call to Byron, she suddenly felt old, too.

Quint stepped back from the dais, acknowledging the spirited round of applause with a nod. He couldn't imagine what had brought on the enthusiastic response to his luncheon speech titled "Bouncing Back with Style." Still rocked by the falling-out with Elizabeth, he had felt flat from the word go, merely delivering a series of inane homilies by rote.

Near the back of the room, he glimpsed a flash of gold and heard a muted *pock*. Off to the left, a flash of silver. *Pock*. Suddenly, the room erupted with a flurry of gold and silver paddles, sending up a shower of plastic Ping-Pong balls. Of course, he thought, with a bleak smile. He should have realized that Elizabeth's sometimes wacky, always imaginative catering themes would add pizazz even to his most uninspired speech. The woman was absolutely priceless.

He left the luncheon and headed back to the Royal Ballroom for the afternoon seminar session, taking with him a provocative sense of having tasted a rare harmony of shared experience. He rolled it around in his mind and found to his profound surprise that he savored the feeling of not being alone. No—"savored" was not the word. He *craved* it, knowing that there was only one person in the world who could satisfy that thirst.

"Elizabeth." Quint whispered the name aloud as he strode into the Royal Ballroom.

A crowd was already gathering. He scanned the faces quickly, hoping against hope that Elizabeth had put aside her newly sullied opinion of him and decided to sit in on this final session. He stepped up on the low stage, trying to get a look at the back row.

And spotted Nicky.

The kid was hunkered down, obviously trying to be inconspicuous. Quint hadn't seen him at the seminar all week—not since the puppet ear was found in his room. Now, the moment he caught sight of Nicky, the boy bolted for the door. He was already gone before Quint responded to gut instinct and bounded off the stage to give chase.

Nicky was fast and quick. His small size gave him a decided advantage in the hallway and lobby crowds. With a flashy swivel-hipped move that reminded Quint of the skinny little running back he had been in junior high school, the boy cut around an elderly couple. Still, Quint almost caught him at the elevators. But a bellhop pushed a loaded cart across his path at a most inopportune moment, and Quint went sprawling over a matched set of Oscar de la Renta luggage. He looked up just in time to see Nicky plastered against the back wall of the elevator car, his eyes as round as saucers, as the brass door glided shut.

Before Quint could budge, the neighboring elevator door opened. Elizabeth stepped out, looking tired and frayed around the eyes. When she saw him lying on the floor, she stopped and stared at him, along with a dozen or so other people.

"Quint, what are you doing?"

"Making a spectacle of myself."

"Well, you do it very well."

He grinned up at her, already as embarrassed as he could get. Almost nose to toe with the stylish suede pumps Elizabeth had slipped on her delightful little feet after their night of lovemaking, he decided to make the most of his position.

"I was about to execute a classic flying tackle when I was shamelessly interfered with." Quint jabbed a thumb over his shoulder at the jumbled pile of luggage the bellhop was reassembling on the cart. "But since I'm down here, I don't suppose it would do any good to grovel at your elegantly-shod feet and beg your forgiveness."

A titter of puzzled laughter swept through the gawking spectators. Flushing deep red, Elizabeth stepped over him and stalked off toward the banquet rooms.

"I guess not," Quint murmured.

He sprang to his feet, brushed off the front of his suit, and again gave chase. Elizabeth was easier to catch. He herded her over next to the corridor wall, shielding her from passersby with his back.

"Actually, I was chasing Nicky," he said.

That got her attention. "You saw him?"

"I saw his shirttail." Quint shook his head, with

a grudging smile of admiration. "The kid runs like a thief." She winced, and he added quickly, "Just a figure of speech."

"Nicky ran away from you?"

He nodded. "Greased lightning."

Elizabeth sagged back against the wall and pressed a finger between her eyes. "Poor Nicky."

"Poor Nicky? I'm the one who got clipped."

"This isn't funny, Quint. Don't you see? Nicky thinks you hung the moon. If he's running away from you, he must be frightened half out of his mind."

Quint rubbed his neck. He had been thinking the same thing from the moment he took off after the boy. He liked Nicky. Quint kept catching little glimpses of himself in him. The kid obviously needed help, and were it not for a certain rogue luggage cart, Quint might have found out why.

"Elizabeth, let's not overlook the fact that the puppet's ear was found in Nicky's room. He might be running because of guilt."

She squeezed her eyes shut and sighed. "I don't care. He's a child, Quint. And he's in trouble."

He reached out to touch her cheek, but she turned her face away. "You'll make someone a terrific mother someday, Elizabeth."

She stiffened. So did Quint as he stumbled onto an extraordinarily sublime new thought — he wanted this woman to be the mother of *his* children. He felt a sudden overwhelming desire to build a nest somewhere far away from the madding crowd, and hold Elizabeth close to his heart for the rest of his life. But he had blown that possibility sky-high by arrogantly believing he had a right to reshape her life for her own good.

"Let me go, Quint. I don't have time to stand around talking right now."

"How about later?"

"I'm swamped today."

"Tomorrow?"

"Quint."

"Next week?"

*"Please!"*

Elizabeth pushed past him, a pained look in her soft hazel eyes. She almost broke into a run as she fled down the hallway. A desolate heavy feeling settled into his chest as Quint watched her turn a corner out of sight.

## Chapter Fifteen

Pale winter sunlight filtered through the slats of the venetian blinds. Elizabeth dropped her coat and purse onto a chair near the door and crept past Jake's bed to place her bouquet of daisies in an empty vase on the window ledge. The jaunty white blossoms cheered the room, lifting her own spirits a notch above the cellar in which they had dwelt since morning.

She fingered the delicate petals, remembering the way Quint had looked when he handed them to her. The image wobbled, then came back in the way he'd looked a couple of hours ago, when he had cornered her after his final luncheon speech. Elizabeth was still angry and hurt, but Quint was hurting just as much. She took no satisfaction in knowing that.

Turning away from the window, Elizabeth leaned over the bed railing and touched her lips to Jake's bony forehead. His closed eyelids fluttered briefly, his thin lips moving in and out slightly with each breath.

"I can't stay long, Grandpa." She kept her voice low, so as not to awaken him. "It's a madhouse at the hotel this afternoon. I just had to come out and sit with you for a few minutes, to sort of get my head together."

She quietly lowered the railing and eased onto the edge of the bed to hold his hand. She gasped, almost hopping right back off again when his gnarled fingers curled around hers. She stared down at their clasped hands, barely breathing. He hadn't held her hand since his stroke.

"Grandpa, are you awake?"

The thin figure beneath the blanket remained motionless. She sighed. Common sense told her that his grasp of her hand had been caused by a simple muscle spasm. He had those all the time.

Then she noticed the blanket. It was rumpled, as if Jake had been moving around on the bed. But that couldn't be. Jake had lain virtually immobile for more than a year. *Except for the night he mistook Quint for your father.* Her eyes burned. Elizabeth turned her face from the window light. Her gaze settled on a box on the tray table a few feet away.

"Candy?" Without letting go of Jake's hand, she slipped off the bed and stretched over to wheel the table closer. "Grandpa Jake, where on earth did you get this?"

She eased back onto the bed and pulled the two-pound box onto her lap. The ribboned lid came off easily, revealing an assortment of cream chocolates in individual paper cups. Several cups were empty. She chose a piece and sunk her teeth into incredibly rich chocolate.

*Chocolate.* Suddenly her throat constricted. She stared wide-eyed at the box. Surely not, she thought in confusion. The sinfully delicious morsel seemed to swell monstrously in her mouth.

The door opened. A day attendant entered with a fresh hospital gown. When he saw Elizabeth, he hung the gown on a hook behind the door.

"I'll change him later," he said cheerfully, and started to leave.

"Wait!" Elizabeth pointed at the box as she struggled to swallow the humongous ball of chocolate. "Do you know who sent that?"

The attendant grinned. "No one sent it, miss. A gentleman brought it in personally."

She gulped. Perhaps Grant had dropped by again, she thought, grasping at straws. "Was he sandy-haired, sort of stocky?"

"Well, no. This one was a tall drink of water. Lots of muscle, from the look of him. Wore a black leather trench coat over a suit." He rubbed his jaw. "Come to think of it, I believe it was the same fellow who came visiting with you a while back."

Quint! Elizabeth scooted the box back onto the tray table. "When did he bring the candy?"

"Why, just about an hour ago, miss. He didn't stay long. After he left, I opened the box for Mr. Mason. But don't you worry. We're keeping an eye on him to make sure he doesn't pig out on the sweet stuff before dinner."

She started to protest that Quint couldn't have been there that afternoon—he had been conducting a packed seminar since one o'clock. But the attendant left abruptly, in answer to a soft bell chime in the corridor. Elizabeth sat unmoving for several minutes, her gaze fixed on the empty paper cups in the candy box. *After he left, I opened the box for Mr. Mason.* She replayed the words over and over in her mind, trying to get past the sense of unreality they created. Four chocolates were missing, not counting the one she had eaten. And Quint apparently hadn't touched them.

"Grandpa Jake?" On closer inspection, she noticed a tiny smudge of chocolate on her grandfather's lower lip. Elizabeth checked his fingers and found still more evidence that he had, indeed, raided the box of chocolates.

Her skin prickled as if she'd seen a ghost. She glanced at the rumpled blanket covering his motionless matchstick legs. Her head began to throb, a sharp ache that started somewhere in the vicinity of her heart and twanged into the base of her skull.

"Grandpa Jake?" She said his name louder this time. He slept on undisturbed, although he was snoring slightly now. Her eyes narrowed suspiciously. Could he possibly be faking?

The thought seemed outrageous. He wasn't aware enough to fake anything. And even if that were not the case, why would he hide from her behind those shuttered eyelids?

In a way, she realized, there was a cruel kind of

logic to the idea that Jake would hide if he could. After all, Quint was lost to her. If she couldn't reach the man she loved, why should she be able to reach the man she treasured?

Elizabeth sat with Jake for a few minutes longer, alternately stroking and kissing his hand, hoping to gently coax him into wakefulness. When his snoring only grew more raucous, she reluctantly slid off the bed and headed back to the hotel.


"Exactly one hour, Philippe." Elizabeth tapped her watch.

Chef Anjou lifted his chin and glared down his long nose at her. "You are 'overing, *ma chérie*. I do not permit 'overing in my kitchen."

She smiled contritely and scurried toward the door. The pastry chef was as territorial as a badger.

As soon as she cleared the door, Elizabeth sagged against the wall. The Elledge-Thompson prenuptial party was barely an hour away, and Chef Anjou had chosen this moment to play the sensitive culinary artiste. She dug her fingers into her stomach, wondering if it was possible to develop an ulcer in the course of a single evening.

Her decorating crew had charged into the Royal Ballroom like a commando assault force as soon as the last of Quint's seminar participants cleared out. By the time she made it back to the ballroom, they had the long, cloth-draped banquet tables in place and were attaching floral arrangements to the walls.

While she called instructions up to a workman on a ladder, a service door swung open and four men rolled in a gigantic pink ice flamingo atop a dolly.

"Incredible!"

Elizabeth whirled at the familiar voice. Quint stood inches away, marveling at the sculpture. He looked pretty incredible, himself, in his tailor-made tuxedo. Her heart leapt at the sight of him, then plummeted like a wounded duck.

His look of wonder didn't change when he shifted his gaze from the magnificent pink flamingo to Elizabeth. But his eyes warmed, again sending her emotions on a roller-coaster ride. His lips parted as he took in her white satin evening dress and the way she'd piled her glossy hair atop her head, leaving feathery wisps of cinnamon-colored curls at her slender neck.

"Quint." It was the only thing she could think of to say. The buzz of frenetic activity that surrounded them seemed to fade into the distance. She cleared her throat and tried again. "Where are you off to?"

He glanced down at his tux. "Nowhere. I mean, I'm here to attend Byron's party."

"But it's by invitation only!" she blurted.

Quint reached into a pocket and produced a folded sheet of engraved hotel stationery on which Byron Thompson had scrawled a makeshift invitation. Elizabeth stared at it in disbelief.

"I'll bet a hundred different people have tried to wheedle their way onto the guest list," she said. "How did you manage?"

He lowered his voice. "Simple. I moseyed over to Byron's hotel and reminded him where he and I had met. That's basic procedure when scrounging favors. First, establish a connection. Then, take it down to an emotional level. I told him I was hopelessly in love with the caterer of tonight's affair. At that point, he offered me a fine Havana cigar—I suppose he could sense something coming at that point and was trying to buy me off cheaply. But I took that as a sure sign he was about to cave in, and so I kept up the pressure, explaining how I had stupidly steered our courtship onto the rocks. When he understood how important it was for me to be near you this evening, he came through like a prince."

Elizabeth was appalled. "I can't believe you told Byron Thompson about our private . . . situation."

Quint leaned closer, his smile tightening into an expression of fierce determination. "My dear sweet Elizabeth, believe this—if it would do even one ounce of good, I would run a full-page ad in the *Wall Street Journal* declaring that kissing you is like being carried to paradise on the wings of a thousand angels. And that making love to you leaves me feeling like some kind of mythical god. And that just standing here beside you, wanting to touch you so badly I ache, is the most perfect state of celestial, mind-shattering peace I have ever known."

Elizabeth stared at him, captivated by the intensely sensuous images his words evoked. Then she glanced around in a sudden panic to see if anyone had overheard him. To her relief, she found her small army of workers far too busy to eavesdrop.

The decorations were rapidly taking shape. On the low stage at the other end of the ballroom, band members in white dinner jackets had appeared and were unpacking instruments. A second giant flamingo glided gracefully in through the service entrance. Noticing that the first one was being placed too close to the center of the primary buffet table, she used that as an excuse to put distance between herself and Quint.

Nevertheless, Quint continued to shadow her around the room, occasionally kibitzing, but mostly just watching and smiling tenaciously. Feeling stalked, Elizabeth could barely think with him so near.

"I paid Jake a quick visit this afternoon, Quint." She moved him out of the way as busboys carried in big stainless-steel bins of chipped ice to place at designated locations on the tables.

"Me, too." When Elizabeth glanced up at him, he added, "I gave the seminar class a sticky problem to solve so I could be away for about forty-five minutes."

"Why? I mean, why did you go?"

Quint shrugged. "I needed to have a talk with

your grandfather. He seems like a pretty okay guy."

Not for the first time that afternoon, Elizabeth struggled with a sense of unreality. To hear Quint talk, you'd think he'd sat and chewed the fat with Grandpa Jake. But that wasn't possible. Jake didn't talk. He didn't do anything anymore.

*Take a second look, kiddo. Jake sure enough stoked down a handful of cream chocolates when nobody was looking.*

She was about to yield to temptation and demand that Quint tell her precisely what he had supposedly discussed with her grandfather when a line of kitchen assistants began rolling in cartloads of buffet delicacies. She watched attentively as they settled big rectangular trays atop the bins of chipped ice.

"No, No!" She rushed forward, raising her voice above the band tuning up on the stage. "The stuffed crab goes on the end!"

"So, who's going to notice?" Quint asked from behind, bending so close his breath warmed her ear.

Elizabeth persisted, unwilling to settle for less than perfection in even the smallest detail. As if concurring, Quint let her finish supervising the arrangement before ushering her toward an empty room just to the right of the stage.

"Quint, the party begins in less than fifteen minutes," she said as he closed the door. "I don't have time to play games."

"Then I'll cut to the chase." He swept her into

his arms as an alto saxophone swung into a slow romantic tune, and the other band members gradually joined in on the haunting melody. "May I have this dance?"

She was already pressed against him, held fast by his hand flattened firmly against the small of her back. Their bodies moved together in perfect harmony from the very first step. He bent his head toward hers, nuzzling the fragrant softness of her hair.

Elizabeth closed her eyes and hardened her heart, straining to hold herself mentally apart from him. She couldn't, simply couldn't let herself get sucked into an emotional vortex from which there was no escape. She had become a stronger person in the weeks since Uncle Uri's wonderful gift arrived. Taking the title from Quint's best-selling book, she told herself this was *her* time to be. She neither needed nor wanted anyone to pull her strings—not even Quint. Maybe especially not Quint.

He whirled her dizzily around a Queen Anne table and performed a neat little dip. "Quint, this is ridiculous."

"No. This is heaven."

"I have to go."

"We all do. Each to our own destiny, at our own pace."

Her eyes blinked open. "What does that mean?"

Quint locked his hands behind her shoulders and looked down at her as they danced in place. "I had no intention of using you when I made that wager with George Keen, sweetheart. That isn't my style. In fact, I wanted you to use *me* as a stepping stone to . . . well, to race forward to your full potential. Pretty arrogant, huh?"

He didn't wait for her comment. "That remark you made about my coach's whistle hit me where it hurts. I didn't realize how easy it is for someone to feel betrayed by those they care about when they're not in a position to see things from that other person's perspective."

The band segued into another dreamy tune. Elizabeth barely noticed. Their feet had stopped moving. They swayed to the rhythm, like slender reeds bending in a gentle breeze. She scraped her thoughts together, still in control of her feelings in spite of his strong encircling arms.

"It isn't just the wager, Quint. Though maybe if anyone but Marge Holt had told me about that, I wouldn't have taken it so hard."

He caressed her bare back with the knuckles of one hand. She swallowed dryly, shaken by the repeated rushes of warmth that fired through her body. She didn't know how to tell him to stop without letting him know how much his touch affected her.

"So, what's the rest?" he asked.

"The puppets, mostly. You don't understand what they mean to me, Quint. You never will."

"I've been a jackass, sweetheart. But I'm not an idiot. You're willing to go to any lengths to get Kasper back. Obviously puppets are in your blood. I just wish I meant one-tenth as much to you."

She couldn't make up her mind whether to laugh or cry. "Quint, you mean every bit as much to me as the puppets. That's the problem."

He stopped swaying and held her at arm's length. "What's the problem?"

"You won't stay. It seems as if everything in my life has been taken away this past year and a half. My folks. Jake. Kasper. I need a relationship I know I can depend on. Forever."

He smiled. "Jake hasn't been taken away from you. I had a nice little chat with him this afternoon."

"You what?"

"Well, I have to admit, he needs work. His vocal cords are pretty rusty, and he started out thinking I was your father again. But his mind seemed to get clearer the longer we talked." Quint frowned. "Didn't you notice when you visited?"

"No. I think he was playing possum, pretending he was asleep."

His frown collapsed into a chuckle. "Oh. I told him not to mention I'd been to see him. I thought it might upset you. But he's still a little foggy-headed, so I guess he went a touch over-board."

Elizabeth felt the same dizzy sense of unreality she had experienced when she discovered that Jake had helped himself to the candies. "What did you talk about?"

"You. How concerned you were about his long-term care. How much better it would be for you if he quit lying around like a turnip."

"Quint!"

"It's called tough love, Elizabeth. Sometimes it works, sometimes it doesn't. That's why I went alone. I didn't have the nerve to try it with you watching." He grimaced at the thought. "I never would have forgiven myself if it had backfired."

"I'm not sure how I feel about your talking to Jake that way."

"You don't like it—I didn't expect you to. But it did seem to crank up his mental faculties. He even asked about Kasper again. And . . . Juniper?"

"He asked?" Elizabeth waited to awaken from the dream. Her grandfather had talked to Quint, had actually asked him questions. Little bubbles of heady excitement rose in her like freshly-uncorked champagne.

"When the conversation turned to you, he got all weepy." Quint grinned crookedly. "I have to tell you, sweetheart, I came close to it myself. You're a damned frustrating woman."

Elizabeth gave him a gentle punch in the chest, her eyes brimming. The day had changed pace too many times for her to keep up, and her emotions were hanging by a fragile thread. But she stubbornly refused to let herself go and trust that Quint would catch her.

"If Jake really does come back to me," she said, "I'll be more determined than ever to embrace puppetry. It's always meant so much to him."

"What if you don't get Kasper back?"

She shuddered. "Don't say that."

"You see, that's what worries me about this puppet business, Elizabeth. I sometimes get the feeling you're using it to avoid reality. For instance, the way you keep putting off telling the police about Kasper's ear being found in Nicky's room."

"I can't—not yet." She tried to back away, but his arms held her close.

"Sure, you can. What you really mean is that you *won't*." He spoke in a flat voice, like a teacher correcting a student's grammar. Then he smiled. "You don't like to make waves. But waves can shake up the still waters of a pond and keep it from going stagnant. They can also rock the boat. In Nicky's case, that might be just the ticket."

"Tough love?"

"Something like that."

Elizabeth sighed. He could be right. Quint had risked rocking Jake's boat that afternoon, apparently resulting in a major breakthrough. Maybe it was her turn now. But time was running short. Nicky would probably be in bed long before tonight's party wound down. Tomorrow morning, the Elledge family would be caught up in a maelstrom of activity in the hours before Vivian tied the knot with Byron Thompson.

She was trying to figure out how to fit a final confrontation with Nicky into that crowded agenda when Quint tightened his grip on her. Elizabeth pressed her hands against his chest, trying to maintain an illusion of distance as he bent to kiss her. But the moment his lips touched hers, the last thread of her willpower snapped. Her lips parted, and she sighed into his embrace.

The kiss seemed to go on for a long time, the heat of it smoldering between them like a carefully banked fire. When they finally parted, neither was trembling with the feverish urgency of desire that had seized them last night. In its place, the ache of a far deeper yearning burned in Quint's dark eyes, and she felt herself reaching out to it longingly.

"The party guests will be arriving soon," she heard herself say. "I have to get back to work."

Quint closed his eyes and pressed his freshly-shaven cheek to hers for a moment. Then he made it easier for her by leaving the room first.

Elizabeth waited for a moment, collecting herself before joining him in the Royal Ballroom. That was the moment the nagging thought stole in, slicing through the mellow afterglow of their kiss. Was Quint still manipulating her?

# Chapter Sixteen

The band shifted to a livelier number as the gaily festooned ballroom began filling with the cream of Kansas City society. Elizabeth scanned the guests once more, this time spotting the mayor chatting with a member of the powerful greeting-card family that owned a sizable chunk of the city. Their elegantly accoutred wives each held a long-stemmed rose, handed out at the door.

While Elizabeth watched, Quint emerged from a knot of foragers at one of the buffet tables. From the looks of his sample plate, he had made serious inroads on the seafood. He began circulating, drifting easily from one cluster of guests to the next, sharing his hors d'oeuvres as he went.

A natural-born party animal, Elizabeth thought with a smile.

Quint was also hands-down the most handsome man in the room. Individually and in groups, women's gazes gravitated toward him. Men, too, followed his progress through the growing crowd with the kind of admiring glances usually reserved for sports legends and war heroes. He seemed remarkably oblivious to the attention.

Elizabeth experienced a surge of almost personal pride when both the mayor and the greeting-card tycoon appeared eager to draw him into their exclusive little foursome. While their wives scrutinized him openly over their champagne glasses, Quint swept the room with his gaze and found Elizabeth standing alone near the service entrance. He bowed slightly in Elizabeth's direction and very distinctly mouthed, "I love you."

Elizabeth blushed against the mint-white satin of her evening dress, caught completely off-balance by his semipublic declaration.

Guests continued to pour in, the babble of voices and laughter competing with the unfailingly romantic music drifting from the stage. She checked the time. Vivian Elledge and Byron Thompson didn't plan to make their grand entrance until the party had been under way for an hour. Elizabeth still had twenty minutes or so to touch base one more time with the catering staff in the kitchen before the big moment.

She turned toward the door leading to the service corridor, trying not to let herself think about how tired her feet already were. The door burst open just as she reached for it.

"Vivian!" Elizabeth stared at her client's elaborately-coiffed hair, ornamented with a thin diamond tiara. Instead of the breathtaking designer gown that Vivian had bought for the occasion, however, she wore wrinkled slacks and a baggy sweatshirt. "Why aren't you dressed?"

Vivian grabbed her arm and hurried her out into the corridor. Glancing back, Elizabeth just had time to register that Vivian's fleeting appearance at the doorway seemed to have gone unnoticed by the party guests—all except Quint. Then the door thumped shut.

"Elizabeth, I've been looking all over for you. I need your help."

In the unflattering fluorescent lighting of the corridor, Vivian appeared pale and drawn. Her eyes were red-rimmed, as if she'd been crying. Elizabeth had an uneasy certainty that the woman's problem involved far more than simple pre-wedding jitters.

"Calm down, Vivian." Elizabeth gently but firmly pried Vivian's fingers off her arm before they could leave a bruise.

"I can't. It's Nicky. He's disappeared."

"Nonsense. It's a big hotel. You can't have looked everywhere." While trying to track him down that week, Elizabeth had sometimes wondered if Nicky knew the place better than she did. "He's probably down in the video arcade."

"No, you don't understand." Vivian took a deep breath that calmed her not at all. "After I returned from the hairdresser this afternoon, I told Byron about finding your puppet's ear in Nicky's room. Byron insisted on having a talk with him on the spot—alone. He didn't want Nicky to feel we were ganging up on him."

"That sounds like a sensible—and sensitive—approach." It was, in fact, the precise course that Elizabeth had intended to follow, if she had succeeded in finding the boy.

"Oh, yes. Byron's that way. I thought he would have a fit when I told him about the ear. But he just hugged me and said—"

"What about Nicky?" Elizabeth asked impatiently.

"When Byron went to talk to him, Nicky ran out of the room, crying." Vivian wrung her trembling hands, shaking her head. "We've been trying to find him ever since. It's been hours."

The door swung open and closed behind Elizabeth. Vivian looked startled as Quint joined them, still carrying his picked-over buffet plate. Elizabeth was relieved to see him.

"What is it?" Quint slid an arm easily around Elizabeth's shoulders as he took in Vivian's anxious expression, coupled with her casual attire.

Elizabeth filled him in quickly.

He made a soft growling sound through his teeth. "Here we go again."

"Nicky thinks so much of you, Quint." Elizabeth touched his hand on her shoulder. "If you went looking for him, at least he might not run from you."

Quint gave her an exaggerated sardonic look. "You seem to have developed a short memory." He scowled, apparently recalling the merry chase Nicky had led him on that afternoon. Then he shrugged and handed her his plate. "What the heck—it won't kill me to give it a shot."

As he walked off down the corridor with Vivian, Elizabeth had to restrain herself from following. But the party was in full swing, and like it or not, that was still her primary responsibility. She tried hard to force everything else onto the back burner as she hurried on toward the kitchen. But she couldn't get Nicky Elledge off her mind. Because whenever she thought of the boy these days, she felt an almost eerie nearness to Kasper.

"Have a heart, kid. I'm too old to be playing hide-and-seek." Quint strode quickly down another deserted hallway, chagrined that he had been reduced to talking to himself.

His evening had turned seriously sour. Quint had planned to spend it within sight of Elizabeth — perhaps even within occasional touching distance — in the process of trying to work his way back into her good graces. Instead, he was traipsing through endless hotel corridors in search of a needle in a haystack.

At the elevator, he jammed a knuckle into the call button and stared down at his mirror-shined shoes while he waited. The whole idea of finding a scrawny little eleven-year-old in a place the size of the Parkway Arms was ridiculous. Face it — the kid didn't even have to hide. If Nicky just kept moving, chances were virtually nil that he would ever cross paths with Quint.

The brass door glided open, and he stepped into the chandeliered elevator. His fingers waggled over the control panel as he tried to make up his mind. It didn't really matter which floor he chose.

Or did it?

Quint pursed his lips. He wasn't one of those people who had perfect recall of their childhood. But he could see back far enough to know that a kid Nicky's age wasn't likely to play the odds. The boy was scared enough to run, which meant he had something pretty damned serious to hide. In the mind of a kid, Quint figured, the first order of business would be to hide himself as quickly as possible.

He squinted one eye, narrowing down the premise one step further. Spur-of-the-moment hideouts weren't necessarily the best. But once a kid went to ground, he wasn't likely to have the nerve to venture back out in search of a better refuge.

"Let's just give that a spin." Quint punched the five button and rode up to the floor on which the Elledge suite was located.

Seconds later, he was standing outside the suite where he had left Vivian twenty minutes ago. He slid his hands into his pockets as he glanced up and down the empty corridor. Mentally flipping a coin, he strolled on up the thick carpet runner toward where the corridor angled to the right.

A dozen feet past the corner, the hallway ended at a heavy metal door marked Fire Exit Only. The door could be opened by pushing a horizontal red bar. Nicky couldn't have gone past that point without setting off the alarm system.

Quint retraced his steps, walking faster now, his

eyes alert. He passed the Elledge suite again and kept going. Near the opposite end of the corridor, he suddenly stopped. His pulse quickened. He drew his hands from his pockets. Then he moved forward slowly, one silent step at a time, the sound of his footfalls muted by the carpet.

When he reached the doorway to the fifth-floor refreshment alcove, he paused, listening. Hearing nothing, he took one last step forward and looked inside. A soft-drink machine stood in the corner to his right. Next to it was a snack machine, followed by one containing toothbrushes, razors, and other toiletry items. A hulking stainless-steel ice dispenser extended the line to within a foot of the left wall.

The alcove appeared empty, except for the vending machines. But as the saying goes, appearance could be deceiving. Quint dropped to the floor, peered under the ice dispenser—and smiled triumphantly. The machine had four sturdy steel legs and one pair of high-top sneakers.

He sprang to his feet and leaned casually against the door frame. Now that he had found Nicky, he didn't quite know how to proceed. Being dragged out by the scruff of his neck would be humiliating for the kid. Quint rejected that idea out of hand. After some thought, he decided to let Nicky make his own choices.

"You must be feeling pretty rotten right now, Nick." He spoke softly, his voice barely carrying above the collective hum of the vending machines. "I can't make that go away—not by myself. You have to help. You can start by coming out of your hidey-hole."

Quint waited a couple of minutes, then added, "I won't come after you, son. But if your mom comes out of your suite and sees me standing here, you can bet she will."

Half a minute later, a thin arm appeared from behind the ice dispenser. Nicky sidled out slowly, tight-lipped, his pale face bunched. He hadn't been crying—at least, not recently—if his eyes were any indication. Quint was surprised. The kid didn't look scared at all. He looked trapped, to be sure. But most of all, he just seemed . . . locked in.

"Nick, your mom is coming unglued with worry. But I guess you're smart enough to have figured that out for yourself."

Nicky bounced his gaze off Quint, then seemed to clench his jaw tighter shut. *He's getting a death grip on that secret of his,* Quint thought. He took a step back out into the corridor to give the boy a little breathing space.

"I can be a pretty good listener, Nicky, if you give me the chance." So far, Quint had done all the talking, giving the boy time. If he pushed too fast, Nicky would only retreat deeper into silence. On the other hand, Quint couldn't allow this to develop into a permanent stalemate. He dug into his pocket for three quarters. "How about a Mello Yello?"

Nicky glanced at the pop machine and nodded. A nod was a start, Quint thought, and moved over to the machine. As soon as he took his eyes off Nicky, however, the boy was off like a flash. Quint cursed under his breath, spilling the coins on the tile floor, and bolted after him.

"This isn't happening." Elizabeth stared at Nadine Elledge's drab gray traveling suit and said it again. "This isn't happening."

"I'm sorry, Miss Mason. My mind is made up." Nadine tugged at the front of her tailored suit jacket. She wore a bleak expression, her face drained of all color. "I'll be leaving for Boston this evening."

"But what about your sister-in-law's wedding tomorrow?" Her mind reeling, Elizabeth walked a few paces down the service corridor, turned, and marched back to confront Nadine. "And this evening's party. Surely, you intend to stay for that."

Nadine shook her head adamantly. "Vivian is no longer my sister-in-law. My dear brother, Toddy, is gone."

Tears suddenly sprang to the woman's eyes. Elizabeth wondered if they were for Vivian or her late brother. *Or for herself.* She wanted to tell Nadine she was being selfish if not outright childish. But the raw pain in the woman's eyes was too evident. Elizabeth couldn't help responding to that, in spite of her own frustration.

"Can you at least tell me what brought this on?" She put a hand on Nadine's padded shoulder. Nadine drew away, as if she couldn't bear to be touched.

"It's this trouble over Nicky. I just can't . . ." Nadine faltered. She gave another harsh tug at her jacket front, as if slamming the door on a weakness. "It's best if I go now, don't you know."

Nadine's eyes held an oddly panicked look as she whirled and stalked off down the corridor. Watching her rigid back and her hands fisted stiffly at her sides, Elizabeth felt a ripping headache coming on.

She stepped back and cracked open the door to the Royal Ballroom, quickly surveying the party. The band was outdoing itself, drawing more and more guests onto the dance floor. Everyone seemed to be having a high old time, unaware that their festive mood was about to be kicked in the teeth.

With a sigh, Elizabeth closed the door and headed for the kitchen. She was a catering manager, not a family counselor. As weeks of careful planning and hard work careered toward disaster, however, she couldn't get her mind off Nicky. She had a sickening feeling that his secret had become an enormous anchor around his family's neck.

*Kasper is missing. Now, so is Nicky.* She still couldn't see the connection between the two. But she could feel it—an invisible spiderweb in the hazy shadows. She took a deep breath, trying to wrench her mind back to the work at hand as she pushed through the double swinging doors into the pastry kitchen.

Elizabeth almost ran into Chef Anjou. He stood just inside the door with a house phone pressed against one ear, one stubby finger stuck in the other. The din of clattering pans and jabbering chef's assistants was deafening. When he saw Elizabeth, the portly chef thrust the phone at her.

"For you, *ma chérie,*" he bellowed. "A breathless maniac."

"A what?" She took the phone as he rejoined the frenzy of activity surrounding the long worktables. Copying the chef's pose, she clamped the receiver to one ear and pressed her thumb into the other, just in time to catch an earful of remarkably creative language unleashed in a familiar voice. "Quint?"

The voice shut off abruptly, then resumed at a noticeably reduced decibel level. "Elizabeth, that overinflated windbag threatened to hang up on me."

"Really? And what did *you* threaten?"

Another brief silence, accompanied by the sound of heavy breathing, as if he had been sprinting. "I have a carpet burn on the elbow of my tux and a sneaker-sole print on the front of my shirt. I didn't think it was too much to ask that egotistical jerk to pass along a simple message to you."

"What message?" He seemed to be talking through clenched teeth now. She could barely understand him, although his anger was coming through loud and clear.

"I have Nick."

Elizabeth gave a little hop of excitement and almost dropped the phone. "Where are you?"

He paused. "I'm not sure. I think we passed through three time zones before I caught him. But I'm pretty sure we can find our way back to the Elledge suite if you care to meet us there."

"I'm on my way." Elizabeth banged the receiver down and flew out the door.

Quint was leaning against the wall in the corridor outside the Elledge suite when Elizabeth arrived. His tie was unknotted and his shirt collar open. He looked hot and tired. At first, she thought he was alone.

As she drew near, however, she spotted Nicky. He stood pressed against the wall next to Quint, one thin wrist firmly handcuffed by Quint's big fist, his face pale as a sheet.

"Nicky, where have you been? Your mother was frantic." Elizabeth cupped his face in her hands, but he wouldn't look at her. She glanced up at Quint, who shook his head.

"He isn't talking." Quint jiggled the boy's arm, which moved limply. "What do you say we get this over with, pal?" He reached past the boy and rapped sharply on the door.

While they waited, Nicky's eyes darted from side to side. If he hadn't been held fast, Elizabeth had no doubt he would have taken off like a scared rabbit.

The door opened. Vivian Elledge stepped into

the doorway, still clad in rumpled slacks, looking more frayed than ever. Byron Thompson appeared behind her, placing supportive hands on her shoulders. He seemed surprised to see Quint.

When she saw her son standing next to Quint, Vivian choked back a sob of relief and pulled Nicky into her arms. Nicky hugged her back fiercely. But when she released him, his glum expression remained unchanged.

"Come on inside." Byron motioned everyone into the sitting room.

Nicky scuffed over to the couch and slumped onto a cushion between his mother and Byron. Elizabeth took one of two armchairs, and Quint perched on the chair arm beside her. For a moment, they all sat staring at Nicky. Quint was the first to break the strained silence.

"Nick, remember what I told you about getting stuff off your chest?" He waited for the boy's barely perceptible nod. "Well, why don't we begin with the subject of Kasper?"

Nicky lowered his chin a notch and seemed to grow a shade paler. Vivian combed her fingers through his hair, murmuring encouragement.

"Go ahead, son." Byron placed a hand on Nicky's quivering knee. "We can work out anything if you'll just talk to us."

Nicky lifted his eyes and peeked across the low coffee table at Elizabeth. She knew shame when she saw it, and was confused. She still couldn't believe that he had actually stolen Kasper, that she had misjudged him that much. But what else would cause Nicky to look so shame-faced?

She leaned forward and peered straight into his eyes. "It's okay, Nicky. We'll love you no matter what. I promise."

His shoulders twitched. He sighed and gave an almost imperceptible shake of his head. Elizabeth could have screamed in frustration.

A sharp knock sounded on the sitting-room door. She got up to answer it and found a bellhop standing in the corridor.

"Miss Elledge called for a luggage cart, ma'am." He pushed a metal cart into the sitting room, then looked expectantly at each of them in turn.

Vivian stared back at him, baffled, as Elizabeth suppressed a groan of despair. Her headache pounded more fiercely.

Across the sitting room, a door swung open and Nadine Elledge appeared. She had a coat and purse over one arm and held a tapestry carry-on case. Her eyes were red-rimmed and puffy. She nodded to the bellhop and indicated with a tilt of her head that her bags were inside her room.

As the young man ducked in and out of Nadine's room, loading piece after piece of matching tapestry luggage onto the cart, Vivian slowly rose from the couch. "Nadie, you can't be leaving. Not now." Vivian took an uncertain step toward her, then stopped.

"It's for the best." The rigid coolness in Nadine's tone was at odds with the pain in her expression. A slight tic began at her left eye, spreading quickly to her cheek.

The bellhop emerged with the final piece of luggage—a small, round-topped trunk not much larger than the carry-on case Nadine had held. Elizabeth heard a gasp as he placed the trunk on the top of the stack. She looked at Nicky. The boy's gaze darted frantically between Nadine and the trunk on the luggage cart. His entire body trembled, his narrow chest rising and falling sharply. Every eye in the room gravitated toward him, drawn by the noise and intensity of his labored breathing.

*"No!"* Nicky suddenly sprang from the couch and dashed over to the luggage cart. Grabbing the round-topped trunk, he lowered it gently to the floor and began fumbling with the straps and latches that held it closed.

"Nicky, what . . . ?"

Vivian's startled reprimand died on her lips. Like everyone else, she watched him throw the double straps back, then claw at the small swivel latch. The latch popped open. Nicky carefully raised the lid and reached inside.

"Good Lord!"

"Judas priest!"

Byron and Quint's exclamations overlapped as Nicky lifted out the contents of the trunk for all to see. Elizabeth stood paralyzed for a moment, then sank to her knees in front of Nicky.

"Kasper." She breathed the name, hardly daring to believe her own eyes.

Nicky held the antique marionette by its strings, making the puppet eye level with Elizabeth. She had forgotten how perfectly, wonderfully ugly Kasper was, with his rakish grin and mocking eyes. She traced a finger over his bulbous nose and straightened the jaunty cap on his head. Then she spread her arms to enfold both Kasper and Nicky in a tight embrace.

"I'm sorry, Elizabeth," Nicky whispered, still trembling.

She squeezed him harder, careful not to mash Kasper between them. "Thank you for giving him back to me." Her throat constricted. She kissed Nicky on the cheek and, grinning through tears, smooched Kasper loudly on the nose.

Someone sobbed. At first, Elizabeth thought it had come from her, and she almost laughed at herself. Then she heard it again, a strangled sound. She turned in time to see Byron rushing across the room toward Nadine.

# Chapter Seventeen

The bellhop had gone, leaving the loaded luggage cart parked in the sitting room. Still feeling dazed, Elizabeth had returned to the easy chair, where she held Kasper on her lap. Quint was back on the chair arm, absently toying with Kasper's wooden hand.

"Feeling better now, Nadie?" Vivian turned the damp washcloth over and pressed the cool side to Nadine's forehead.

Nadine nodded, eyes closed, her head resting on the back of the couch. She took another sip of the ice water Nicky had fetched from the compact refrigerator. This time, her hand didn't shake. Her wracking sobs had given way to a kind of dull lethargy, as if something inside her had collapsed.

Byron took the glass from her and placed it on the coffee table. After helping Nadine to the couch, he had stood back and watched Vivian and Nicky trying to calm the woman's astonishing bout of hysteria.

All the while, Elizabeth had been watching Byron, wondering what he was making of all this. She still couldn't quite put the pieces together, either.

Nicky stood at the end of the couch, gnawing his fingernails as he eyed his aunt gravely, looking as if he needed a hug in the worst way. Elizabeth held out a hand. He came to her at once, but kept a sharp eye on his aunt.

Elizabeth was getting tired of waiting for someone to speak. Of all the people who deserved answers, she reasoned, she about headed the list. At last she asked softly, "Nicky, how did you know where to find Kasper?"

He looked down at the floor, his face splotched red. He was still having trouble talking about it. Finally he said in an undertone, "I saw her hide him in the trunk."

Four sets of eyes stared at him, then shifted to his aunt. Nadine uttered a faint moan and seemed to shrivel into herself. Taking the washcloth from Vivian's hands, she sat wringing it in her lap.

Byron wandered over and sat on the corner of the coffee table near Nicky. "Can you tell me something, son?" he asked.

Nicky hesitated, then nodded.

"Why didn't you tell anyone about this before?"

Nicky swallowed dryly, making a clicking sound in his throat. "Aunt Nadie loves us a lot. It didn't seem right to snitch on her." He glanced at Elizabeth. "I'm really, really sorry."

"You don't have to keep apologizing, sweetheart," she said. "I understand."

And she did. Would she have been able to snitch if the thief had been Jake? The very idea was as incomprehensible to Elizabeth as the realization that his aunt was a thief must have been to Nicky.

"Nick, this doesn't make sense." Byron tilted his head, frowning. "How can you believe your aunt loves you—how could you protect her like that—when she tried so hard to make everyone believe you were a thief?"

"She was afraid," Nicky said simply.

"Of what?"

The boy took a deep breath and seemed to give Byron's question some thought. Nobody hurried him. "I guess Aunt Nadie was scared that when you married my mom, there wouldn't be room for her in our family anymore. That, and some other stuff."

Byron wiped a hand across his mouth. "What stuff, son?"

Nicky lowered his voice, as if that would keep his aunt from overhearing. "Well, you know how Aunt Nadie is about my dad."

Every head in the room, save one, nodded.

"I don't think she feels right about Mom getting married to anyone." Nicky poked at the carpet with his toe, casting a sideways glance at his mother. "I think that's why she took that banker guy's watch."

302

Vivian left her former sister-in-law and moved to the edge of the table beside her fiancé. Nicky fell into her arms, and she held him in a long rocking embrace as tears streamed down her cheeks.

"Oh, my poor precious baby," she murmured. "All those times I doubted and wondered. Can you ever forgive me?"

"Mom, I love you." Nicky's voice broke.

After a while, Byron put a hand on the boy's head. Nicky turned and looked at him.

"Son, this is very important to me," Byron said softly. "How do you feel about me?"

Nicky turned toward him, keeping an arm around his mother's neck, and looked Byron straight in the eye. "I guess if my mom likes you, sir, you must be okay."

Byron reached out and squeezed Nicky's arm, his lips clenched in a tight grin. Elizabeth glanced up at Quint. He was smiling, his eyes shining with pride. Then he shifted his gaze to Nadine, and the smile changed to an odd troubled expression. *It's as if he's seeing a ghost,* Elizabeth thought, puzzled.

Vivian sniffled, embracing the two men in her life. As they released each other, she turned and jabbed an accusing finger at Nadine. "How could you?" she demanded. "How could you blame those thefts on a child? *My* child?"

Nadine bowed her head for a long time. When she finally spoke, the words came in a rush.

"Don't you see? I couldn't bear the thought of Toddy's son being raised by another man, Vivian. If you remarried, I would lose both of you."

Her voice caught. She shook her head fiercely, as if she couldn't believe her own duplicity, and went on. "When you got engaged to that banker, the idea just came to me. He was such a pompous twit. I made it appear that Nicky had taken something—and it worked. So, when Byron came along, I tried it again. Only Byron isn't a twit, so it didn't work."

She pressed the twisted washcloth to her eyes. "I've made such an evil, evil mistake. Now, I've lost you forever. I don't deserve to be part of a decent family."

There was no self-pity in her voice, only dreadful resignation. For a while after she finished, Elizabeth could hear the faint whisper of air through the suite's ventilating system. Then Nicky pulled away from his mother's embrace and edged around the coffee table to stand next to Nadine.

After a moment, she seemed to sense him there, and she lowered the washcloth. She gazed at him almost longingly with red swollen eyes. "Do you hate me, Nicky?"

Nicky thought about it for a moment. Elizabeth couldn't see his face, but there was something undefinable about his stance that made her sense pity.

"No, I guess not," he said finally. "I'm just real mad at you."

Byron made a noise in his throat that was half grunt, half chuckle. Vivian burst into a fresh siege of hiccuping tears and leaned into his shoulder. Quint shifted suddenly on the arm of the chair, and Elizabeth glanced up to see his eyes cloud over. She took his hand.

"I have to tell you, Nick," Byron said, "I sure wouldn't mind having you in my corner if I ever needed a friend."

Nicky grinned. "No fooling?"

For the first time in weeks, Elizabeth thought, the boy didn't look old for his age. Without thinking, she pressed the back of Quint's hand to her cheek.

"Absolutely," Byron said. "It took a lot of guts for you to take the heat for something you didn't do. Twice. You're quite a guy."

Byron offered the boy his hand. Nicky looked surprised, then pleased. Elizabeth felt a lump rise in her throat as he slipped his smaller hand into Byron's and allowed his stepfather-to-be to give him a hug.

"What about Aunt Nadie?" Nicky asked in the awkward silence that followed.

Vivian looked at the broken woman on the couch, a last trace of rage flickering in her eyes. When it had passed, her shoulders sagged, and she sat looking deeply troubled. Byron got up and paced the room for several minutes, occasionally casting sidelong glances toward the couch. At last, he nodded to himself and propped a foot on the luggage rack.

"I have a proposition for you, Nadine." His tone was purely take-it-or-leave-it. "My mother lives in Malibu — a really nice place right on the beach. Close enough to my place for occasional visits, but not too close, if you know what I mean.

"Mom's getting on in years, and her vision isn't what it used to be. She shouldn't be driving, but she's a strong-willed woman. Likes to do things her way. She won't let me hire a driver for her. And the last time I suggested she get a live-in companion, she wouldn't speak to me for a month. Get the picture?"

Elizabeth, who had been listening as attentively as Nadine, nodded in unison with her.

"What I have in mind requires someone with a certain amount of acting ability," Byron went on. "Mom is stubborn as an ox, but she isn't stupid. She just wants to call her own shots. If she came upon a decent reliable woman who was in need — and who could also drive, play gin rummy, and take trips with her — I have a hunch Mom would have her moved into the spare room in a New York minute."

Byron dropped his foot from the luggage rack and planted his fists on his waist. "How about it, Nadine? Could you see yourself playing the role of a poor relation in need of a helping hand — in order to give a helping hand?"

Nadine's gaze fixed on the middle distance between them. Elizabeth could almost see the wheels turning as she examined the possibilities.

"I don't happen to believe in boarding schools," Byron added casually. "I think it's important for a boy to get plenty of fresh air and sunshine. So there's a possibility we might bring Nicky for a visit now and then—if he wants to."

Nadine glanced at Nicky. He stared back at her evenly, making no commitment. Whatever relationship the two had in the future, Elizabeth thought, would be based on how much respect Nadine Elledge could rebuild. Nadine seemed to recognize that, too. She returned her attention to Byron, and her expression held a new look of determination.

"I see." The dullness began to leave her eyes. She smoothed a hand over the fabric of her expensive wool suit. "A poor relation, you say?"

"Destitute. Mom is a corker—she loves to lord it over people. Living under the same roof with her would be a humbling experience, I assure you."

She drummed her fingers on her lap and glanced around the room. Her gaze eventually settled on Elizabeth. Nadine considered her for some time, lips twitching. Then she nodded to herself and said, "After all the trouble I've caused you, my dear, do you suppose you could be so kind as to help me locate a good thrift shop?"

"A what?" Elizabeth raised her eyebrows.

"A thrift shop." Nadine gestured at her suit. "It wouldn't do for me to show up on the dear lady's doorstep dressed fit to kill, would it?" She shot

Byron a sidelong glance. "Not if I'm supposed to be a poor relation."

Some of the tension seemed to go out of the air. Vivian gave Byron a relieved loving smile. He looked at Nicky for a moment, then extended his hand, palm up. Nicky hesitated, then slapped it with a low five, and grinned.

"Now, then." Byron glanced at his watch as he helped Vivian to her feet. "If I'm not mistaken, we're nearly an hour late for an important party, and you ladies aren't even dressed." He gave Vivian a resounding kiss and sent her off to change. "Hop to it, Nadine. This family-to-be is going to present a united front even if it kills you. I'll go help Nick choose a tie."

Seconds later, Elizabeth sat cradling Kasper, surprised at the speed with which the sitting room had cleared. Even Quint had slipped quietly away, gone before she realized he was missing. She could hear Vivian humming softly to herself in the next room. Behind another door, the sound of Byron's voice, punctuated by a sharp giggle. A luggage zipper sang open in Nadine's room. The Elledges were joyously digging themselves out of the rubble.

There was still the party to tend to, Elizabeth reminded herself. She forced herself up out of the chair, suddenly feeling heavy-limbed. Everything had worked out for everyone—everyone, that is, but her.

Quint had stolen away without so much as a

goodbye. She cuddled Kasper against her breast, but not even the cherished puppet was enough. There was no substitute for human warmth. And she had a miserable premonition that there would never be a substitute for Quint. As she let herself out of the sitting room, Elizabeth had never felt more alone.

The party in the Royal Ballroom ended with a flurry of exploding confetti-filled balloons at eleven o'clock. Half an hour later, Elizabeth stepped outside under the hotel portico and breathed in the cold night air. She was tired—and depressed. The party had gone well, in spite of the delayed appearance of its host and hostess. Even though she had been surrounded by party revelers all evening, however, Elizabeth hadn't been able to shake a pervasive feeling of impending loneliness.

Readjusting her grip on Kasper's strings, she headed across the lot to where she had parked her car—she'd brought it this morning because she knew she'd be leaving the hotel quite late. A breeze caught the puppet like a wind sock, sending its loose limbs into a clattering frenzy of motion. Preoccupied with keeping the strings untangled, she didn't notice a low sports car backed into the slot next to hers until the driver's door swung open. A shadowy figure emerged.

Elizabeth started. "Quint! You're always popping up where I least expect you."

"It confuses the enemy."

"Am I your enemy?"

Quint closed the door and moved toward her. "I sincerely hope not."

He stroked her cheek with the back of his hand, sending rivulets of fire down her neck. The musky scent of his cologne wafted to her, doing everything to Elizabeth's libido that the television ad claimed it would. She was glad he didn't seem to know that. If he kissed her now the way she wanted to be kissed, that would only make it harder to say goodbye.

"Let me drive you home," he said.

She shook her head. "I'm taking Kasper out to show Jake."

"Now? It's nearly midnight."

"Jake's sleep patterns are all messed up. The night attendants bend the visiting hours and let me go in and sit with him whenever I can." Elizabeth fussed with the puppet strings to give her hands something to do. "You didn't come back to the party this evening."

He jammed his hands into his pockets. "After this business with Kasper worked itself out the way it did, well, I had some thinking to do."

She waited for him to explain. Instead, he said, "Mind if I ride along to the nursing home with you?"

The suggestion caught her off guard. "It's late."

"I think I already said that."

Elizabeth smiled, wondering why she suddenly

felt so awkward around Quint. She sensed he felt the same way. It was as if some kind of fundamental change had taken place between them. And then it struck her like a cold wet towel—the seminars had ended, and he was about to go. Since leaving the Elledge suite earlier that evening, he had spent hours figuring out how to tie up a loose end named Elizabeth Mason.

She told herself she could handle it. She closed her mind to the pain, turned her back on the hollow thunder of a tidal wave gathering in the vast emptiness that had been her heart.

"Sure, you can ride along," she said.

"Here, I'll carry the ugly little dude."

Instead of taking Kasper by the strings, Quint gripped him under the arms. The puppet's head lolled sideways. Elizabeth cringed inside, but let go of the control strings. He edged around to the passenger side of her car, holding Kasper away from him the way a confirmed bachelor might hold a baby with a dirty diaper. But after he had worked himself onto the seat, he settled the puppet onto one knee.

Elizabeth kept an eye on both of them during the drive to the nursing home. She had a silly feeling that Kasper ought to be wearing a seat belt. At least, it seemed silly until she noticed Quint unconsciously bouncing his knee.

The nursing-home parking lot contained only the cars belonging to the staff. Elizabeth pulled in near the entrance. Quint followed her up the sidewalk to the door. By the time an attendant answered the buzzer and let them inside, Quint had untangled Kasper's strings. Elizabeth led the way down the tiled corridor.

"These things are complicated," he whispered, lagging behind as he fiddled with the strings.

"Not once you get the hang of it." Elizabeth paused to reposition his hands on the crossbars.

"Oh, I see. They're sort of like chopsticks."

She looked at him askance. "You must be fun to watch at a Chinese restaurant."

Quint scowled, following her into Jake's room.

The night-light was on over the bed, the head of which had been raised slightly. The first thing Elizabeth noticed as she approached was that the lid was off the box of chocolates on the tray table, and half the top layer of paper cups were empty. Her grandfather appeared to be asleep. She leaned over and kissed his temple, slipping her hand into his. Something stuck to her fingers. She turned his hand over, uncovering a creamy chocolate morsel with a bite missing.

Elizabeth spun around and looked at Quint, her expression one of "See? I told you so!" He had come up behind her, still tugging at the puppet strings. Kasper went into a series of spastic contortions, as if someone had dropped an ice cube down his back.

When Quint finally noticed Elizabeth's expression and the candy morsel in Jake's hand, he said, "Ah."

That wasn't good enough. Not good enough at all. Elizabeth thought Quint ought at least to look a little surprised. Didn't he care that her grandfather—nearly catatonic for more than a year— had apparently spent the evening pigging out on chocolates? Didn't he think that was wonderful or exciting? Or even strange?

Apparently not. Quint helped himself to a piece of chocolate. Then he went back to the door and flipped on the light switch. Jake's eyes popped open.

"Grandpa Jake, did we wake you?" asked Elizabeth.

He turned his head and looked straight at his granddaughter for the first time in a year and a half. He didn't make a sound. She couldn't even tell if he recognized her. Still, she thought she might faint with joy.

"It's the chocolates," Quint said matter-of-factly.

"What?" Elizabeth couldn't take her eyes off her grandfather.

"The chocolates are loaded with sugar. It's stimulating his brain. Isn't that right, Jake?"

Elizabeth waved a hand at Quint dismissingly. "That's nutty."

"Then again," Quint said, as if she hadn't spoken, "maybe it's the company he's keeping."

He raised both hands over his head. Kasper sprang onto the foot of the bed. Tugging at the control strings, Quint walked the puppet up Jake's right leg, one clumsy, spastic step at a time. Jake's gaze shifted from Elizabeth to Kasper. As he focused on the mischievous face of the antique marionette, his gnarled fingers clawed the blanket.

"Juniper." The name rattled out of Jake's throat.

"No, Grandpa Jake." Elizabeth stroked his white hair with a trembling hand. "This is Kasper, the puppet Uncle Uri sent. He was stolen, but we got him back this evening. I'm sorry—I don't know where Juniper is."

"Juniper." Jake said it more clearly this time, followed by a word she didn't quite catch. When Elizabeth asked him to repeat it, he looked at her irritably. "Attic!"

She clapped a hand over her mouth. His old puppet was in the attic? The bottom dropped from her stomach as she realized how close she had come to committing an unforgivable error. Were it not for Uncle Uri's magnificent gift, she would have had to sell her grandfather's house to help cover the soaring nursing-home expenses. She had put most of Jake's furniture and personal possessions into storage when she put the house on the market. But with everything else she had on her mind, it had never occurred to her to lower the rickety old ladder and check the attic. She had a horrible vision of new owners cleaning out the attic and tossing a dusty old string puppet into the trash. The thought of Juniper buried forever in a landfill site made her nauseous.

"We'll bring Juniper on Sunday, Grandpa Jake. I promise."

"We?" Quint paused with one of Kasper's feet raised.

"I," Elizabeth quickly corrected herself. "I'll bring Juniper."

"It sounded better the first time."

She looked at Quint sharply. "You'll be leaving on your book tour next week."

"Monday afternoon. That gives me two and a half days and nights to promote my program."

"What program?"

He lowered his arms about a foot, and Kasper sat down on Jake's chest, facing Elizabeth. Jake immediately raised a hand to the puppet's back, as if rediscovering his sense of touch—a movement that did not go unnoticed by his two visitors.

As Elizabeth watched, Kasper crossed his right leg over his left, casually dangling his foot. For someone who had equated puppet controls with chopsticks only a few minutes ago, Quint was catching on fast.

"It's a three-point program actually." He bobbed the marionette's head slightly, as if it were doing the talking. "First, in light of your incredible success with the motivational-luncheon themes, I hope to recruit you to continue providing that service for all my future seminars."

Kasper froze, leaning forward slightly. Waiting, Elizabeth stared at his leering face, her mind suddenly turning to slush. For a long moment, it was not in her power to utter a word.

"Okay—on to point two." Kasper uncrossed his legs. "Since I'll be out of town for twenty-eight straight days, I would also like to recruit you to go shopping for a house. I'm sick of living so far off the ground. I want something with grass and trees and flowers. Maybe a big old-fashioned porch to sit on in the summertime. Swimming pool is optional. In short, I'm looking for a nesting site. Someplace to *stay.*"

"Quint—"

"Please don't interrupt till I'm finished."

Elizabeth sat perfectly still, listening. Kasper crossed his left leg over his right. The dangling foot quivered as a tremor transmitted itself down the control string.

"Last, but light-years from least, point three. I somehow have to persuade you to make me the happiest man in the world by letting me marry you."

Her vision blurred for just an instant. Then her gaze drifted up from Kasper's impish mug to Quint's anxiety-blanched face. He lowered his arms. Thanks to Jake's supporting hand, Kasper remained upright, seated on his chest.

"I don't want to be alone anymore, sweetheart," Quint said in a hoarse whisper. "Chasing success can be a lonely way of life. I never realized that until I met you and got to know what it could be like to have roots—a family connection. Sitting there watching Nadine Elledge, this evening . . ."

316

He shook his head. "It scared the hell out of me, thinking I could end up that desperate for a sense of home. I want deep binding roots." He grinned tensely. "I want little Lawrence seedlings popping up right and left. I want you."

Elizabeth stared across the bed into Quint's dark eyes, her pulse hammering in her ears. "I know of a house with a big front porch," she said with a scratchy voice. "It has a huge rolling lawn, and old oak and maple trees."

His Adam's apple jumped. "Good climbing trees?"

"The best. No swimming pool, but there's a great swimming hole practically within walking distance."

Quint looked at her hard, his hands clenching and unclenching at his sides. "This house—it wouldn't come with a built-in grandfather, would it?"

She wasn't sure she could get out the next word. "Maybe. If that's what you really want. And if you don't mind the sound of his lathe in the basement. Because when he gets better, he might be building puppets again. I'll be needing them for a catering-business idea I have."

He spared Jake the most fleeting of glances. "Sounds good to me. So, what do you say to my three-point proposal?"

"Well, let's see . . ." She nodded slowly.

"Yes? To which one?" Quint edged around the bed until he was next to her, his eyes searching hers. "Which do you agree to?"

"All of the above."

He threw his arms around her, lifting her off the floor and swinging her around and around until they were both dizzy. Then he sat her down and, with her arms coiled tightly around his neck, kissed her until she thought she'd melt.

They remembered Jake at the same moment. Their lips parted, and they turned to look at him without loosening their embrace. The old man lay asleep, Kasper nestled against his chest. And the pair of them were smiling.